A PLAIN SCANDAL

Praise for *A Plain Death*, book 1 in An Applewood Creek Mystery series

"As it turns out, Amanda Flower may have just written the first Amish romance-comedy. And all I can say is . . . bring on the next one!"

—*USA TODAY*

"This new series has mystery, some romance, and several amazing characters. These people are smart, clever, and want only the best for others. Amanda Flower is a talented author who gives readers what they have come to expect, a good mystery with a few twists and turns along the way."

—RT Book Reviews, 4 stars

"A gentle and thoughtful Christian mystery, this series debut will appeal to readers wanting to learn more about the diversity within Amish communities."

—Library Journal

"Romance and intrigue make a delightful tangle in this entertaining story. With authentic small-town instincts, Flower populates her tale with quirky characters that bring her story to life."

— CBA Retailers

"Amanda Flower's novel, *A Plain Death*, has everything any fan of Amish fiction enjoys—an endearing heroine, a wonderful cast of Amish and English characters, and an intriguing mystery to solve. Amanda's smooth writing style and clever touches of humor instantly caught my attention. I read the book in one sitting and am already anxious to read the next Appleseed Creek Mystery."

—*USA Today* and *New York Times* best-selling author, Shelley Shepard Gray

"Just when you think you've got this mystery figured out, Flower throws in another plot twist. *A Plain Death* is a tasty first installment of what promises to be an exciting new series. Well done!"

—Mary Ellis, best-selling author of *An Amish Family Reunion*

A PLAIN SCANDAL

An
Appleseed Creek
Mystery

AMANDA FLOWER

B&H
PUBLISHING GROUP
NASHVILLE, TENNESSEE

Published by B&H Publishing Group,
Nashville, Tennessee

Dewey Decimal Classification: F
Subject Heading: AMISH—FICTION \ MYSTERY FICTION \
HOMICIDE—FICTION

1 2 3 4 5 6 7 8 • 17 16 15 14 13

For Delia Teodosiu Haidautu
I'm forever thankful we were assigned
the same study hall in tenth grade.

Acknowledgments

I am so grateful for my wonderful agent Nicole Resciniti. She's in the business of making dreams come true and is the very best at the job. I thank my editors: Julie Gwinn for her thoughtful comments, and Julie Carobini for her eagle eye while critiquing all of the Appleseed Creek Mysteries. Each novel is stronger because of them.

I send best wishes to my writing buddies Amanda Carlson, Marisa Cleveland, Jen J. Danna, Marianne Harden, Melissa Landers, and Cecy Robson. I foresee bright and beautiful futures for all.

I'm so thankful for my family and friends who have supported me over the years. Special thanks to my mom, Pamela Flower, who never tires of reading my work—even the roughest of first drafts.

And finally, I want to thank my heavenly Father for allowing wishes made by a shy eleven-year-old girl to come true.

Chapter One

In the church's cloakroom, I searched for my black peacoat among the sea of black fabric. A flickering dome fixture in the ceiling lighted the way as my fingers rifled through the tightly packed garments. Wooden hangers knocked together like Asian wooden chimes, and I was no closer to finding the peacoat.

I should invest in brighter colored outwear. Black was the go-to color of choice for the Mennonites of Appleseed Creek, Ohio. Perhaps I would buy a nice royal blue or purple coat as an early Christmas present to myself. Red was out of the question, because it would clash with my hair.

Two women in long skirts and sensible shoes stepped into the tiny room. "I'm telling you, I've never seen anything like it," one of the women told her companion. Her brown-gray hair fell in a long braid from the base of her head to the waistband of her skirt. "It's scandalous and makes everyone in the district look bad."

Her friend pulled a ski coat from a hanger and struggled into it. The puffy jacket accentuated her plump figure. "And to attack the bishop's daughter like that."

"It's terrible. She's such a sweet girl. Not particularly bright, but sweet. I always prefer she wait on me at the bakery," the woman with the braid confided. "The bishop's daughter may give me the wrong change, but she does it with a smile on her face. The other girl who works there acts like she's doing me a favor by selling me a loaf of bread." She patted her slender hip. "As you can see, I've had a few too many of those."

"Don't be silly. You look like you live on carrots and salad." The woman's coat ballooned up near her ears as she leaned closer to her friend. "I've been thinking about all of this."

I should have let the ladies know I was there, but instead, I backed further into the closet to better conceal myself.

Braid nodded encouragement. "Yes?"

"This has to be some kind of message to Bishop Hooley."

"Could be. He's only been bishop a few weeks, but I heard much has changed in the district since he took the post."

"My Amish neighbor told me Bishop Hooley is more rigid than Bishop Glick, God rest his soul. Hooley forbade a man from attending Sunday services because the man's beard was too short."

Braid searched the top shelf of the cloakroom and collected child-sized hats, mittens, and gloves. "I heard Hooley broke up a youth social meeting. Sent everyone home and caused quite a stir in the community."

Braid picked up a fedora she'd knocked to the floor. "Some Amish parties are wild."

Her friend wrinkled her nose. "Most aren't, and my neighbor insisted there wasn't any drinking or carrying on at the party."

"How would she know? Was she there?"

"No. Her son told her."

Braid rolled her eyes as she set the fedora back on the shelf. "You know teenagers. Of course, the son would say the party was completely innocent. I don't have enough fingers and toes to count the number of times my children have lied to my face."

Ski Coat began to gather her children's hats and mittens too. "I say if Bishop Hooley thinks the Amish district needs stronger control, there must be a reason."

I stepped deeper into the closet and knocked the back of my head on a row of empty hangers. They clattered together and swung wildly on their pole. Ski Coat glared at me and whispered something to her friend. Braid nodded, and the pair collected the remainder of their coats and left the cloakroom.

I bit my lip. If the bishop chastised an Amish man about the length of his beard, what did he have planned for the Troyer family? Who attacked Bishop Hooley's daughter? How was she attacked?

Becky Troyer, my nineteen-year-old roommate, popped her head into the cloakroom, the cheeks of her heart-shaped face slightly red from the cold wind. Her long, blonde braid fell over her shoulder. "Chloe, what's taking so long? Timothy's waiting to take us home."

I felt a smile form when she said Timothy's name. Timothy was Becky's twenty-seven-year-old brother and I had a monstrous crush on him. I suspected he felt the same way about me, but we'd yet to discuss it. Both Becky and Timothy grew up Amish and left their district to live as English. Despite leaving the Amish way, they were close to their family—their parents, grandfather, and three younger siblings. "I can't find my coat."

She scanned the black wall of fabric and plucked my peacoat from its hanger on the first try.

I blinked. "How did you do that?"

"I know what it looks like." She handed it to me. Her blue eyes sparkled with mischief.

Outside of the cloakroom, Timothy waited for us. It took all of my willpower not to gawk at him. He and Becky shared the same white-blond hair and blue eyes. All the Troyer children had those features in common. He was just shy of six feet tall and had the muscular build of a man accustomed to working with his hands.

When he saw me emerge from the cloakroom, his eyes crinkled at the corners. A silly grin formed on my lips but faded when I saw who stood next to him.

Hannah Hilty, a tall, slender brunette, prattled in Timothy's ear. "I'm so proud of you, Timothy. Daddy said that you will find great success as a contractor and your business will rival his."

Timothy tore his eyes away from mine and bent his head to meet Hannah's gaze. As he did, his blond hair reflected the hallway's ceiling lights. "That's nice of your dad to say, Hannah. If I do half as well as he has, I'll consider myself successful."

"You already are." She placed a small, white hand on his arm as if in reassurance. Her pink-polished fingernails were filed to a sharp point. "Daddy says the Young contract is the biggest one in the county right now. He's so pleased his protégé got it." She sighed. "I wish you and Daddy would team up somehow."

I clenched my jaw. I knew exactly how Hannah wanted her father, one of the most successful general contractors in Knox County, Ohio, and Timothy to team up: with a wedding.

"That's a great idea, Hannah," her friend Kim cooed. Tall and rail thin, Kim was one-half of Hannah's cheering squad. Emily, the other half, was MIA.

Becky rolled her eyes at me. "Timothy, I found Chloe."

I tried to plaster a pleasant expression on my face but a scowl formed instead.

"Chloe, there you are," Hannah trilled as if she had just noticed me. "I was telling Timothy that you might have gotten lost. The church building can seem so large and confusing to a visitor."

Kim covered her mouth.

I forced a smile. "In the last few months, I haven't gotten lost yet."

Hannah shrugged. "It takes time to find your way."

Becky skirted behind Hannah and crossed her eyes at me. I stifled a laugh.

"Ready to go?" Timothy asked.

I nodded and buttoned my coat.

Hannah squeezed Timothy's arm. "Before you go, have you heard the news?"

I had a bad feeling about this.

Timothy fished leather gloves out of his coat pocket. "What news?"

For a second, I wondered if Hannah would say something about the conversation I overheard in the cloakroom. What did she know about the new rules in the Amish district or the bishop's daughter?

"Isaac Glick and Esther Yoder are set to marry on Thanksgiving Day. I'm so happy for them. They're the perfect match. I see lots of little Amish children in their future."

Becky paled. Isaac was Bishop Glick's son and formally Becky's suitor. Their relationship died along with the beloved bishop during the summer. Esther had been waiting not-so-patiently to snatch up Isaac for some time.

Kim's mouth bent upward in a crooked smiled, this news bulletin had been carefully orchestrated.

Timothy cleared his throat. "I knew they were courting."

Hannah laughed. "It *is* Amish wedding season. There's been a wedding every Tuesday and Thursday this month."

Becky took a step back as if she knew what would come next.

Hannah's long, canvas skirt ballooned around her ankles as she spun around. She placed a hand on her cheek. "I'm sorry, Becky, I forgot about you and Isaac. This news must be upsetting, considering . . ."

Sure, you did.

Becky fingered her long, pale-blonde braid. "I'm happy for Isaac."

Hannah placed a hand to her chest and sighed deeply. "Good. I would hate to upset you."

I'll bet.

Kim turned around, her shoulders moving up and down in barely restrained laughter. A smirk played at the corners of Hannah's mouth. After saying good-byes, the pair strolled down the hallway arm-in-arm, their heads close together.

I stole a glance at Becky as we stepped through the church's front door. She concentrated on the top of her boots—Ugg knockoffs we'd found on a trip to the Polaris Mall. Along with the boots she wore a knee-length pencil skirt, black tights, and a teal winter coat with a faux fur-lined hood over an orange sweater. She'd come a long way from her Amish upbringing of plain clothes. As for her physical appearance, the last remnant from her Amish childhood was her uncut, blonde air. Even braided, it hung all the way to her tailbone.

I pulled a cotton scarf from my coat pocket and wrapped it around my neck. The late November wind bit into my exposed skin. A fine dusting of snow blanketed the church lawn, and an earlier-than-normal winter storm warning was in the forecast for later in the week. It seemed Knox County was due for a frosted Thanksgiving in addition to the standard white Christmas.

In silence, we followed the walk that wrapped around the outside of the white-washed Mennonite church building to the parking lot. As we rounded the corner, Timothy's blue pickup truck came into view.

Other parishioners leaving the church gawked and whispered

to each other. Appleseed Creek Chief of Police, Greta Rose, leaned against Timothy's truck like she didn't have a care in the world. Mabel, Timothy's shaggy black and brown dog, stood in the bed of the truck trying, unsuccessfully, to convince the chief to scratch her between the ears.

Becky pulled up short. "What is she doing here?"

A knot formed in the pit of my stomach. There were few people I was less eager to see than Hannah Hilty, but Chief Rose was one of them. "I don't know, but it can't be good."

Chapter Two

Mabel barked a greeting and her black plume of a tail wagged at a frantic pace. Despite the gloomy autumn skies heavy with the promise of snow, Chief Rose wore her aviator sunglasses. "Long time no see."

I linked arms with Becky. "That's a good thing." My young friend began to shiver, but I wasn't sure if it was from the cold.

The chief removed her sunglasses and appraised Becky with her peculiar peridot-colored eyes. Today, they were surrounded by purple eyeliner. The chief's penchant for eyeliner was her one glint of femininity. Aside from the eye makeup, she was all business. "How's it going with your probation officer?"

"Fine." Becky stepped closer to her brother, pulling me along with her. "Did he say something was wrong?"

"No. According to Fisher, you are a model ward. He wishes he had twelve of you instead of the typical yahoos he gets saddled with." She placed a hand on her gun belt. "How do you like your community service at the after-school arts program?"

"I'm enjoying it," Becky said. "The children are great, and several are very talented."

Becky was on probation and completing court-appointed community service for driving without a license and getting into an automobile accident with an Amish buggy during the summer. She totaled my car in the process. Although the accident wasn't her fault—the brake line had been cut—it resulted in the death of Isaac's father, the Amish district's Bishop Glick.

"I'm glad. You have a site visit Tuesday." Chief Rose said this not as a question but a statement of fact. Clearly, she had been checking up on Becky.

Becky squeezed my arm. "Yes. Officer Fisher will be visiting the school and observing my interaction with the children."

"Good, and you have plans for when you complete your community service?"

Becky licked her lips. "I think I would like to teach art. Working with the kids has been so much fun—even more fun than working on my own paintings."

"That's a good plan," the chief said. "However, when you have a record, being a teacher is easier said than done."

Becky's face fell, and I resisted the urge to kick the police chief in the shins for discouraging her. I almost had Becky convinced to take the GED so she could apply to college to get the certification she needed to teach art.

I chimed in. "Becky's making great progress on her hours."

Becky pulled mittens from her pockets and slipped them onto her small hands all the while keeping her arm linked through mine. "My service should be completed early next year."

"Glad to hear it."

Timothy shifted his feet. "You're here to talk to Becky about her PO?" His tone was doubtful.

"I like to check in with my citizens." The chief blew on her bare hands. "I'm glad you all finally came out. My toes feel like ice cubes.

Snow's in the forecast for Thanksgiving. Leave your turkey outside. It will stay frozen."

"Greta . . ." Timothy eyed her warily.

She set her sunglasses back on her nose. "Curt Fanning and Brock Buckley are back on the street."

My heart skipped a beat. Curt and Brock were the guys who harassed the Appleseed Creek Amish community last summer, which ultimately led to Becky's accident and Bishop Glick's death. "What? How is that possible?"

Becky grabbed my hand. The wool of her mitten felt rough against my palm.

"Turns out, Curt Fanning's uncle was up to more trouble than his shenanigans in Knox County. The FBI's been investigating his shady business dealings for years, and they cut a deal with Fanning and Buckley to testify against him. The end result is the uncle spends life in federal prison, and Fanning and Buckley walk."

I shivered. Curt Fanning's drawn face, dirty goatee, and tobacco-stained teeth came to mind, followed closely by Brock Buckley's deceptive baby face.

"Do you think they would come back here?" Becky asked.

The chief tucked a short, brown curl behind her ear. "Hard to tell, but I don't see them going anywhere else. My officers are on the lookout for any sign of them."

Timothy's jaw twitched. "How long have they been out?"

"Two weeks." She frowned. "I found out yesterday. Suddenly, it occurred to the county sheriff I might want to know about it."

"We haven't seen them." Becky let go of me and wrapped her long, thin arms about her waist. "That's a good sign, right?"

"Could be. But then again maybe they're getting their act together before they come looking for you. Remember you and Chloe are the reason they went to prison. They are not your biggest fans." Chief Rose clicked her teeth. "My advice would be to watch your backs."

I shivered. "Are they driving the same truck?" My mind conjured up the image of a rusted green pickup that stalked Becky and me during the summer.

Chief Rose's brow shot up. "You mean that beat-up green pickup? Yes, as far as I know. According to the BMV, it's the only vehicle registered in Curt's name."

Timothy scratched Mabel behind the ear, and the dog leaned into his caress. "They can't possibly be dumb enough to bother the girls."

The chief pushed away from the truck and stood up straight. "I've learned not to underestimate the stupidity of criminals, and Fanning and Buckley do not have a reputation for being the brightest." She met each of our eyes in turn. "You see them, you call me." With that, she sauntered to her black-and-white police cruiser.

Timothy scowled as he watched the cruiser turn out of the church's lot. "The court shouldn't have released them."

I silently agreed. "We'll all be on the lookout for them like Chief Rose said. Chances are they will leave us alone."

"Not if they want revenge," Becky whispered.

I shot Timothy a look, then nodded at his sister, who looked like she was about to be sick.

Timothy frowned. "Let's not talk about them anymore. I hope you two will come with me tonight to Young's. Ellie Young has planned a killer menu."

Young's Family Kitchen was a favorite. I cocked my head. "Aren't the flea market and restaurant closed on Sundays?"

"Normally, yes." Timothy wrapped his plaid scarf more tightly around his neck. "Tonight is a meal for the men working on the pavilions. Ellie asked us each to bring guests. You know she will have more than enough food for everyone."

A smile broke out on Becky's solemn face. "Will she have pie?"
"This is Ellie we're talking about." He tweaked her white-blonde braid. "Of course she will have pie." He arched an eyebrow at me. "Will you come?"

I smiled. "How can we turn down one of Ellie's meals?"

Becky and Timothy shared identical grins, the similarities between brother and sister almost startling.

"Great," Timothy said. "I'll drop you at home now and pick you up around four. I have some errands to run this afternoon."

As Timothy drove us home, I stared out the window, looking for Curt's green pickup.

Chapter Three

The doorbell chimed through our rented house on Grover Lane, a block from Appleseed Creek, Ohio's central square. Becky lay on her stomach in front of the television on the hardwood floor, legs bent, her feet stirring up the air. Her upper half lay across a huge pillow with the word *woof* embroidered on top. Her chin rested in her hands. She'd been so proud when she bought that pillow with one of her first paychecks from Young's, where she worked as a part-time waitress, that I didn't have the heart to tell her it was a dog pillow. The pillow reminded me that Becky may look like any other English teenager, but she still had a lot of Amish left in her.

My Siamese cat Gigabyte curled up on her back while a Paula Deen marathon played on Food Network. Becky wasn't going anywhere any time soon. "I'll get it." I shook my head. She didn't even move.

I tried to settle my nerves as I placed my hand on the doorknob. I peered through the peephole and was relieved not to see Curt and Brock on the other side—not that I thought they would ever politely knock on my front door.

Instead of the two newly freed criminals, a man in his early thirties stood there wearing bold plastic-rimmed glasses over green eyes. His hair was coal black and precisely parted on the side as if he created the part with a ruler. He held a pair of gray earmuffs in his bare hands, and behind him, snow fell in large dime-sized flakes. I opened the door. "Dr. Tanner?"

He blushed. "You can call me Dylan."

"Okay." My forehead wrinkled. *Why is the chair of the biology department on my doorstep?* "Is something wrong at the college? Is your computer down? I didn't get a call or a text." I served as the Director of Computer Services at Harshberger College in town, and it wasn't unusual for me to get a frantic call from a faculty member during the weekend about an uncooperative laptop or a corrupted flash drive. However, this was the first time any of them made a house call.

"No, no, everything there is fine. At least as far as I know." His eyes grew wide behind his glasses. "Is this a good time for the walkthrough?"

I blinked. "The walkthrough?"

He frowned. "The walkthrough of the house."

"House? What house?"

"This one." His Adam's apple bobbed up and down like an ocean buoy.

"This house? My house?" He spoke in riddles. Why did the chair of the biology department want to walk through my house?

Becky poked her head out of the door. "Chloe, what's going on?"

Dylan held out his hand to her. "You must be Becky. I'm your new landlord."

My mouth fell open. "You're what?"

Concern flashed across his pale face. "Didn't the previous landlord tell you? He was supposed to send you a letter."

"Letter? I didn't get a letter." My landlord was a faceless man who owned a Cincinnati-based realty company. The only confirmation of his existence was the cashing of my rent check each month.

Dylan twisted the earmuffs so tightly that the plastic headband threatened to snap. "I'm so sorry. He was supposed to do that. I take it you didn't know I was coming today either."

I shook my head and stepped back, knocking into Becky as I did. "Please come inside. It's cold out." I closed the door behind the professor.

Dylan removed his leather gloves and tucked them into the pocket of his dark wool coat. "It's freezing out there. I predict snow on Thanksgiving."

"That's what everyone's saying." I gestured to the sofa. "Would you like a seat?"

He shook his head. "No. Why don't you give me a tour? I'm eager to have a look at the house."

I hesitated. "I didn't even know the house was for sale."

Dylan ran his hand along the marble mantel. "I've been watching this house for a while and snatched it up the minute it was posted online."

"You bought the house before seeing it?" I asked.

"I drove by a few times. Your old landlord told me you were the tenant. I knew it would be an easy property to manage. It was going for a great price and I didn't want to chance losing it. When I called and inquired about the property, I made an offer to the seller. I think he was grateful to be rid of it."

You knew I was the tenant and didn't say anything to me about it? Our offices were in the same building. How hard would it have been for Dylan to call me or even drop by my office at Harshberger to talk about it?

He walked across the wooden floors and peered through the large picture windows. Several of the panes still had the original handblown glass. "It has charm. It's one of the centennial homes in town. I always wanted to restore an old house like this."

Becky picked up Gigabyte from the floor and perched on the sofa. "Have you restored a house before?"

He swallowed. "No."

Becky arched a white-blonde eyebrow at me. I cleared my throat. "It will be nice to have a landlord in town when problems come up."

Becky squinted at me. "Timothy has always fixed everything around the house." She hopped off the sofa. "My brother works on the house when he can. He's the best carpenter in town, and now, he's starting his own contracting business."

Dylan unbuttoned his coat. "I'll keep that in mind in case I need any help."

"I want to give the tour," Becky piped up. "That way I can show him all the good work Timothy's done. You may not have noticed, but Timothy completely rebuilt the front porch of the house. When we first moved in, the porch was a mess. The floorboards were warped and the support beams swung back and forth." She tugged on his sleeve. "Let's start in the kitchen."

Dylan allowed Becky to lead him into the kitchen. She opened the cabinet under the sink. "See here. Timothy replaced the garbage disposal and the pipes."

He bent at the waist for a closer look. When he straightened up, he voice was stiff. "How much does Timothy charge for all these improvement? The previous owner didn't tell me he authorized any home improvements."

Becky didn't give me a chance to answer. "He doesn't charge anything. He uses materials that he has left over from jobs and his labor is free. We're family."

Dylan's jaw twitched. "That might be all well and good for you, but did he research the historical accuracy of the pipe and latches he installed?"

"I doubt it." I tucked one of the kitchen chairs under the table. "We were more concerned with making the house livable than historically accurate."

He adjusted his glasses. "Becky, please show me the rest of the *improvements*."

Becky guided him through the rest of the downstairs and led him to the second floor. Inside my bedroom she said, "He replaced the latch on Chloe's window." She demonstrated how to use the brass latch, which was most definitely not historically accurate. Becky pointed her thumb at the other window. "The other one doesn't open yet. Someone painted it shut. Timothy's going to fix that next."

"Hmm." Dylan sounded wary.

"You girls ready to go?" Timothy called from downstairs.

Becky abandoned the window and headed for the door. "That's my brother now." Timothy stepped into the room just as she reached the doorway. The siblings nearly collided.

Timothy held her by the shoulders. "Where's the fire?" He pulled up short when he saw Dylan standing next to me. "Am I interrupting something?"

Becky wiggled out of her older brother's grasp. "This is Dylan. He's our new landlord, and he also works with Chloe at the college." She shot Dylan an apologetic smile. "I forgot what you teach."

"Biology," Dylan answered.

Timothy pursed his lips. "I thought your landlord lived in Cincinnati."

"He does—did. Dylan recently bought the house," I said.

Dylan held out his hand and Timothy shook it. "Dylan Tanner. I've heard a lot about you."

Becky continued. "I showed him all the great work you've done on the house."

"I noticed you didn't use appropriate fixtures during repairs." Dylan smiled stiffly.

"I used what was available," Timothy said.

"That's admirable," Dylan adjusted his glasses. "However, your Amish techniques aren't in keeping with the period of the house."

Timothy's eyebrows shot way up. "My *Amish* techniques?"

"You are Amish, aren't you? That's what I've been told."

Timothy's lip curled. "By who?"

Becky jumped in. "Timothy and I grew up Amish but we have both left the church."

Dylan nodded as if that confirmed something for him. "From here on out, please don't make any more changes to the house without my authorization."

Timothy crossed his arms. "Your authorization?"

"I'm planning to restore this house to its original grandeur, using only historically accurate materials. A charming centennial home like this can sell for three times what I paid for it after restoration."

"You're going to flip it," Timothy said.

Dylan fiddled with a button on his coat. "I prefer the term *restore*."

Becky looked from the biology professor to her brother. "But we live here."

"I'm not asking you to move," Dylan assured her. "Your lease is still valid. However when I do sell the home, you will have to move."

"How long will this take?" I asked. "How extensive will the restoration be?"

He waved away my questions. "We will settle all of that in time."

I didn't like the sound of that.

Timothy shook his head. "I've worked on Appleseed Creek houses for years. Most people in town don't have the kind of money you want for this house, and you will price it right out of the neighborhood."

Irritation flashed across Dylan's face. "All I need is one buyer." He brushed his hands on his jeans. "I'd better get going. I'll see you at work tomorrow, Chloe."

"If you have time, I can show you the rest of the rooms on this floor," Becky said.

Dylan paused, then nodded. "I have a few more minutes." He followed her out of the room.

Timothy pushed my bedroom door nearly closed. He spoke quietly, as if half-listening to the tour going on down the hall. "How well do you know that guy?"

"He's the chair of the biology department at Harshberger. Our offices are in the same academic building, so I've run into him on campus. I don't know him more than to say hello."

"Isn't he too young to be working at Harshberger?"

"I'm younger than he is. What is he . . . thirty?"

"You're different. You're super smart."

I hid a smile. "Timothy, most of the folks working at Harshberger are super smart. It's a college after all." I locked the latch on the window Becky had opened.

"Did you know he was your landlord?"

"No, it was a surprise when he dropped by today. The previous owner was supposed to send a letter notifying me of the change. You know how great communication is with him."

"How do you know if it's true?"

"What do you mean?"

"How do you know this guy really bought the house? Did he show proof of the sale?"

I frowned. "I didn't think to ask him. Why would he lie about it?"

Timothy paused, as if considering his answer.

Becky called up the stairs. "Chloe, Dylan's leaving. Do you want to come down and say goodbye?"

I poked my head out of my bedroom door. "I'm coming." To Timothy, I said, "You have a point. I'll ask him now."

Downstairs, Dylan buttoned his coat. "Thanks for showing me around. Becky, you were a superb tour guide."

My face grew hot. "Dylan, I should have asked you this when you first arrived, but do you have a document that proves you're the owner of the house?"

Dylan's eyes cut over to Timothy as if he suspected where this question originated.

Timothy held his gaze.

"I do." He reached into his coat pocket and removed a folded piece of paper. "Here's the promissory note with my bank."

I read the note over. It looked legit to me. Timothy leaned over my shoulder in order to read it, his warm breath brushing the top of my head.

"When will you begin restoration?" Timothy asked as I refolded the paper and handed it to Dylan.

Dylan replaced the paper in his pocket. "I want to start right away." He nodded to Becky and me. "I'll be in touch, ladies."

Becky walked him to his car.

Timothy gripped the back of the armchair. "I don't like that guy working on the house while you two are here."

"Don't worry," I said. "It will be nice to have a landlord in town, and with the expansion of your business, you can't be wasting your time on this creaky old house."

"I don't consider it a waste of time." He sighed. "Even more, I don't like the way he looks at you."

My brow shot up. "How does he look at me?"

"The way I do."

If I didn't know better, I would say Timothy Troyer was jealous.

Chapter Four

Timothy turned into the entrance of Young's Flea Market. In front of the market was a large Amish restaurant called Young's Family Kitchen. It was the domain of Ellie Young, an Amish widow in her late sixties. Ellie had run the restaurant and flea market with the help of her sons since her husband died more than twenty years ago. Young's was a main tourist draw to Knox County, attracting visitors from all over Ohio who were interested in a great deal and a slice of Ellie's famous pie.

Normally, dozens of automobiles and Amish buggies crowded Young's massive parking lot, but today, there were only two cars in the lot and a handful of Amish buggies. The snow stopped for the time being, but the temperature steadily dropped as dusk fell over the county. The horses stood sentinel at the hitching posts with dark-colored blankets on their backs to protect them from the worst of the cold.

Timothy parked, and I placed my hand on the door handle. "It seems late in the year to be doing construction."

Timothy pulled a green stocking cap down over his ears. "The outdoor market closed for the season at the end of October. We have to finish the project while the market is closed. I want to get all the walls up before the weather gets worse. Unfortunately, winter's early this year." He opened his door. "We're here a little early, so let's go over to the job site, and I can show you around."

We climbed out of the truck. Becky shivered. She wore jeans, her faux Ugg boots, and teal ski jacket. "It's too cold to be outside. I'm going inside the warm restaurant."

Timothy shrugged. "Suit yourself." His eyes twinkled when his gaze met mine. My stomach did a little flip. I wasn't sure what Timothy and I were to each other, but I knew we cared for one another. I knew there wasn't anyone I'd rather spend time with and suspected he felt the same. Not knowing for certain, however, made me edgy.

There was one complication: I wasn't Amish. Neither was Timothy anymore, but I doubted his austere father would want his son to marry an English woman who was so far from their roots. Like me. I was a computer geek, a city girl, and the product of a broken family. In his father's eye, if Timothy wouldn't marry an Amish girl, a Mennonite would be a much better choice. Hannah Hilty came to mind.

Becky ran toward the restaurant and disappeared through the "Staff Only" kitchen door. Timothy skirted the truck and took my hand, leading me away from the restaurant to the three pavilions behind it. Our fingers intertwined.

Business could not be better for the Young family. To take advantage of their success, they decided to enclose the three pavilions that house the outdoor flea market. This way, the market could be open all year long. Timothy was the main contractor on the project. Although he had been a skilled and sought-after carpenter in Knox and its surrounding counties for years, this would be the first time he tried his hand at running the entire operation. If he

was successful, the Young job would catapult him to a whole new
level in his career. I knew he was nervous about managing all the
subcontractors, plumbers, drywallers, foundation workers, and
carpenters, who were both Amish and English.

Timothy subcontracted electricians too. Even though the restaurant and flea market were run by an Old Order Amish family,
electricity was allowed because it was a place of business. Home
was different for the members of the district. All the lights and
appliances in community members' houses ran on natural gas or
propane.

Timothy led me to the second pavilion. He pushed away the
plastic sheet that covered the entrance. The door hadn't been put
into place yet. "Watch where you step," he warned. "Most of the
guys are careful, but there may be a stray nail on the ground."

The floor was slab cement. Orange electric cords and clear air
hoses snaked across the floor. The seams in the drywall were still
visible. Clear tarps protected us from wind where doors and windows would be. The pavilion stretched the length and width of a
basketball court.

Timothy released my hand. "For the most part, this is going to
be an empty space with large windows to let the natural light in.
The Young family will rent it to any number of vendors as they did
before when it was open air, but now it will be open year-round.
They will be able to extend rental leases for space and increase their
prices. I don't think they plan to increase the rental price too much,
but whatever it is, vendors will be willing to pay. In this county,
there aren't other places like this where Amish can reach so many
tourists. *Englischers* love to spend their money here."

I knew that. When I first moved to Appleseed Creek, I bought
most of the furniture for my new house at Young's.

He smiled. "For the most part, vendors will bring their own
wares to sell and their own tables and booths to display them. If

they don't have the tables or booths, the Youngs will rent those to them along with the space. The pavilions will have central heating but no air-conditioning. It's too expensive, and the bishop put his foot down on that one."

"The restaurant is air-conditioned, and all of the downtown Amish shops are too. What's the difference?"

Timothy shrugged.

"What have you been working on in here?"

"I've been crafting the permanent booths for the produce and farmer stands. These Amish farmers will have a prime spot in the market." He stepped onto a raised platform and stood beside a wooden structure that came up to his chest. "We're going to stick a refrigerator unit in here to sell cheese and meats. I'm building the frame."

A huge contraption the shape and size of a lawn mower sat on the platform. "What's that?"

"An air-compressed nail gun. The carpenters helping me on the project are Amish and won't use an electric-powered one. This one is powered by diesel." He flipped on the switch, and the machine came to life. It sounded like an ill air-conditioning unit. He waved me up on the platform.

Since my legs were shorter than his, he gave me a hand up. "We're going to add some steps," he assured me. "You should make your mark on the pavilion too. You were the one to convince me to take this project after all." He picked up the nail gun and pointed it inches from the last nail. "I can show you how to use it."

"When am I ever going to need to know how to use a nail gun?" I teased.

The corners of his eyes crinkled. "You never know when a lesson like this will come in handy. We can finish this row of nails."

He held the gun out to me. Tentatively, I took it. It was much heavier than I'd thought it would be, roughly the weight of a dictionary, and my hand dipped under the unexpected heaviness. Timothy covered my hands with his and steadied my wrist. He guided the gun to the wood. In my ear, over the gun's air compressor, he said, "We'll hammer in five more nails, four inches apart."

I nodded, trying to concentrate on the nail gun instead of how close he was to me.

Bang! Bang! Bang! Bang! Bang! The air compression drove the nails into the wood.

"Perfect," Timothy said as he removed the gun from my hand and turned off the air compressor.

My hand ached from squeezing the trigger, and I suddenly felt a chill without him next to me. I ran my hand over the new nail heads in the plywood. "Computers are overrated," I said, feeling unreasonably proud of my work. "Maybe I should consider carpentry."

He laughed. "Maybe so."

I closed my eyes, imagining Timothy's vision for the place. In my mind, I saw the sunlight coming in through the windows and the English visitors from the city buying fresh produce and quilts from Amish men and women. "It's going to be great when it's done." I opened my eyes and found Timothy watching me with a particular expression on his face. Was that the expression he thought Dylan wore when looking at me earlier that afternoon?

I shivered.

Timothy hopped onto the platform. "Are you cold?"

I pulled my cotton gloves from my pocket. "I think it's colder in here than it is outside."

Timothy placed my small hands between his two larger ones. He rubbed his palms back and forth over my hands, his rough calluses scratching my skin. Warmth flowed into the small muscles of my knuckles and fingers.

His blue eyes were soft. "Better?"

I couldn't speak.

A gruff voice disrupted the moment. "Who's in here?"

Timothy dropped my hands, and suddenly my fingers were freezing again.

Near the door a portion of the plastic tarp moved and a large Amish man stepped into the work area. "Timothy? What are you doing in here? The site is closed on Sunday." He was at least six feet tall and had a long, brown, wiry beard that fell to the second button of his black wool overcoat. He wore a black stocking cap and wire-rimmed glasses instead of a broad-brimmed felt hat. As the weather got colder, more of the Amish men in town were trading their felt hats for stocking caps.

A fleeting look of irritation passed across Timothy's typically mild face as he helped me down from the platform.

The man eyed me. "Who are you?"

"I'm Chloe Humphrey." I held out my hand to him, but he didn't take it. I let it drop to my side.

"What are you doing on my job site? This isn't a playground," the man barked. He eyed me. "Or a courting buggy."

My face flushed. I knew it was the same shade of red as my hair.

"Relax, Ezekiel." Timothy stepped between us. "I was showing Chloe around. We're here for the workmen's dinner."

Ezekiel glared at him, his dark brown eyes magnified by his glasses. "That meal is meant for the workmen and their families. Is she a member of your family?"

"She's a close family friend."

Ezekiel's eyes narrowed. "No one is allowed on the job site after work hours—especially a close family friend."

A muscle in Timothy's jaw twitched. "It's my mistake."

"Don't let it happen again. My mother might like you and have convinced me to give you a chance, but there are plenty of other contractors in this county who can do your job. I don't want to have to find a third contractor for this job." Ezekiel disappeared through the plastic sheeting.

I gawked at Timothy. "Who was that?"

Timothy steadied himself. "Ezekiel Young."

"Young?"

He nodded. "He's Ellie's son."

"What did he mean by a third contractor?"

Timothy shook his head, clearly not wanting to talk about it. "Come on, let's go to the restaurant."

As I followed him out of the pavilion, disappointment washed over me. The moment we'd had, or I'd thought we'd had, was gone.

Chapter Five

E llie stood by the front door of the restaurant and looked every inch the Amish matron of the house. She wore a long, simple navy dress, a black apron with YOUNG'S FAMILY KITCHEN embroidered in white on the right pocket, and a white prayer cap over her gray, coiled hair. She placed her hands on her hips. "Where have the two of you been? Becky walked in here over twenty minutes ago." She examined each of us in turn. "I hope there's nothing going on I should know about."

Timothy removed his coat and scarf. "Nothing at all."

"Humph," Ellie said in return. Behind her, the gift and pie shops, which took up the front third of the building, were dark. Beyond the shops, the lights glowed in the dining room, and workmen and their families sat in sturdy oak chairs around white cloth-covered tables. "You shouldn't have taken so long, Timothy. As the general contractor you are the man of the hour."

Timothy mumbled an apology.

Ellie grunted acceptance. "The meal will be buffet style, so I hope that suits everyone. Being it's Sunday, my servers are off for the Sabbath."

I removed my gloves and stuck them into my coat pocket. Timothy took my coat and carried it over with his to the pegs on the wall.

"Good to see you again, Chloe. Staying out of trouble?"

"Yes, ma'am."

Ellie lowered one of her thick, gray eyebrows. "My son stormed through here a few minutes ago complaining Timothy had a girl in one of the pavilions. I figured it was you."

I ran a hand through my hair, trying to tame the static electricity my winter hat created. "Timothy showed me around the pavilions. He's so proud of the project and that your family gave him this opportunity to begin his contracting business."

The minuscule dimple on Ellie's left cheek appeared. "There's been a lot of talk in the district lately about you and Timothy."

"What about?" I gave up trying to fix my hair.

"Some folks say that you're courting. Are you?"

Were we? It wasn't a question I had the answer to.

I didn't know what to say. Ellie must have recognized my deer-in-the-headlights look because she changed the subject. "You should ignore Ezekiel. He can be," she paused as if searching for the right word, "testy."

Becky headed our way from the dining room. She reached us in time to hear Ellie's last comment. "Why's that?"

Ellie pursed her lips. "I don't rightly know, but the boy has been behaving strangely."

Becky's eyes widened. "He seems to be the same as always to me. Grumpy as an old raccoon."

Ellie shook her head as if Ezekiel's grumpiness wasn't the issue.

"Do you want me to help with anything?" Becky asked. "I can go around and refill water glasses. I feel kind of silly standing around not doing anything when I'm usually one of the girls waiting tables."

"No, it's Sunday. I won't ask any of my staff to work on the

Lord's Day. This is a special thank-you to the workers. You're a guest of your *bruder's* tonight."

Until she completed her one thousand hours of community service, Becky's work as a waitress at Young's Family Kitchen was on a part-time basis. I knew she'd like to work full-time to earn more money for English clothes, art supplies, and celebrity cookbooks, so the sooner she finished her hours the better. Becky enjoyed working at Young's and was comfortable there, having known Ellie and her family all her life. The biggest challenge was getting to and from work each day.

Becky wasn't able to drive nor was she allowed to learn—a stipulation set down by the court after the accident. Young's was four miles from Appleseed Creek, so Becky rode her bike to work most days. Occasionally, she talked Timothy or me into giving her a ride, and I imagined when the roads were icy during the winter, one or both of us would have to chauffer. Perhaps she'd find a job in town by then.

Timothy returned. "I'm starved."

This made Ellie smile. There was nothing she loved more than feeding people. "*Gut.* I saved your family's usual table by the window overlooking the crop fields. Not much to look at outside the window this time of year." She frowned. "I'd hoped you would bring your *grossdaddi* today."

Becky hid a smile. The Troyer children suspected Ellie had a crush on Grandfather Zook. Considering Ellie's comment, they might be right.

Timothy kept a straight face. "*Grossdaddi* hasn't been feeling well. This time of year his post-polio syndrome acts up. The colder weather bothers his legs and joints."

"I'm sorry to hear that. I'll make him some of my famous chicken and dumpling soup and stop by the farm this week." She removed a scrap of paper and a stub of pencil from her apron pocket and made a note on it.

Becky had to turn away so that Ellie didn't see her face. Ellie gave her a beady glare. "I saw that smirk. Now, get in there before I have a mind to give your seats away to a more appreciative group of *kinner*." She marched in the direction of the kitchen.

Becky grinned from ear to ear. "I can't wait to tell *Grossdaddi* Ellie Young asked about him."

Timothy tugged on her braid. "You shouldn't tease your *grossdaddi*."

Becky rolled her eyes. "It's not like he doesn't tease us."

Inside the dining room I was relieved the meal was buffet style, so I could control my portions. Since moving to Appleseed Creek, I'd gained eight pounds and was on a diet, not an easy task going into the holidays in Amish Country. I finally begged Becky to stop cooking for me. If she had her way, I would eat four-course meals three times a day. A diet like that might work fine for her since she was on her feet waitressing most of the day, but I work ten-hour days at a desk behind a computer screen. The extra treats Becky snuck into my lunch began to add up.

Becky and her brother piled their plates high with roast beef, fried chicken, and sliced ham. I sighed and stuck to the salad bar. What I wouldn't give for their metabolism.

Even at the salad bar, I pondered every calorie and steered clear of the Amish potato salad and coleslaw. Both had enough sugar in them to set me back a week. By the time I got to the table, Becky and Timothy were already seated and eating along with Hannah Hilty's parents. As I approached the table, conversation ceased, and my appetite disappeared. Seeing the Hiltys was one way to stick to my diet. Beth Hilty was an older version of her daughter. Her husband John had deep-set eyes and was perpetually tanned from a lifetime of working outside. John was Timothy's mentor. He was the person who gave Timothy a job and asked him to attend the Mennonite church after Timothy decided to leave the Amish.

I slipped into the empty bent paddle chair at the round table. "Hello," I murmured.

Beth nodded at me but said nothing.

A confused look passed over Timothy's face. "You both know Chloe from church, don't you?"

Beth Hilty patted a napkin to her mouth. "Yes. Hannah has mentioned her."

My heart sank. I could only guess what Hannah had said to her parents about me.

"Is Hannah here?" I hoped that my reluctance to see Hannah didn't show in my voice.

"No, she is not." Hannah's mother cut her ham slice into tiny pieces. "She's volunteering at the church this evening, heading up the Thanksgiving can drive. Hannah does a lot of volunteer work for the church."

So she looks more attractive to Timothy. The snarky thought flashed across my mind, but I didn't regret it. My interaction with Hannah had been minimal, but I doubted the brunette beauty did anything without an ulterior motive.

John cleared his throat. "I'm glad to see you on this job, Timothy. To be the lead contractor on this project is a boost to your career. By the end of it, you will have more work than you know what to do with."

Timothy took a sip of water. "It's gone well."

"Ezekiel Young can be a tough man to work for," John said. "How has he been for you?"

A dark cloud passed over Timothy's face, but he didn't say anything.

John nodded as if Timothy's silence was answer enough. "Ezekiel and I have worked together before. His personality can be . . ." John paused. "Challenging."

Beth swallowed a delicate bite. "John was the one who built the original pavilions."

John laughed. "That was ages ago. I'm happy Timothy got this job."

"What are you doing on this project, Mr. Hilty?" Becky asked.

"Nothing too much. One of my subcontractors is installing the electrical. Even though I'm not doing the hands-on work, Ellie insisted on inviting Beth and me." The laugh lines around his eyes appeared. "I wasn't about to turn down a free piece of pie, and I think Beth was happy for a break from the kitchen."

Beth narrowed her eyes at her husband before turning to me. "Chloe, what is it that you do?"

A bit of carrot lodged in my throat. I took a gulp of water to push it down. "I'm the Director of Computer Services at Harshberger College."

"That's a good school. It does a lot for the town." John forked a bite of roast beef. "Do you like it?"

I nodded and reached for a piece of bread, hoping that would push the carrot down my throat. Carbohydrates didn't count when you risked choking to death.

Beth speared a potato with such force I felt bad for the potato and her fork. "Hannah is a classroom aid for the kindergarten class. She loves children. I'm sure she will make the perfect mother. She plans to homeschool her children." She took a sip of water, appraising me over the top of her glass. "I believe that's the best way to educate children. Do you have much experience with children?"

The carrot wouldn't budge. "No," I squeaked. "I mean not as much as Hannah. I have a younger brother and sister, but I don't see them often. They live in California."

Beth sniffed. "Will you homeschool?"

I nearly dropped my fork. "Homeschool what?"

"Your children."

Children? What children? I'm only twenty-four.

I drank more water and shot Becky a pleading look.

"I've been working with the after-school art program since September," Becky chimed in. "The kids have been great."

Beth tucked her napkin under the side of her plate. "The children who attend those extra programs aren't the troublemakers who worry me. Believe me, you should hear some of the stories Hannah tells. They will raise the hair on the back of your neck."

I'm sure anything that Hannah says to me will do that.

Beth wouldn't give up that easily. "How do you feel about homeschooling?"

"I never thought about it before. I guess it would depend on where I was in my career—"

"You think your career is more important than your children?"

You mean my *fictitious* children. I started to cough. The carrot wasn't going anywhere, and my water glass was empty.

John shook his head. "Beth, leave the poor girl alone."

Beth stabbed another potato so hard her fork scratched the porcelain dish. "It's something everyone should think about before they have children." She leveled her gaze at me. "Or before they even think about having children."

Who's thinking about having children? I started coughing again.

Becky pounded my back. "Chloe, are you okay?"

"I'm fine," I managed to croak, holding up my glass. "I need something more to drink."

Timothy half-rose from his seat, and I waved him back down. "No, no, I can get it." I hurried away from the table clutching my glass.

There was a beverage table beside the buffet. I filled my glass to the brim with water from the pitcher and guzzled it down.

"Thirsty?" A deep voice spoke into my ear as I refilled my second glass.

I spun around and splashed Ezekiel Young in the chest with water. "I'm so sorry!"

"No harm done." His dark brown eyes twinkled. His glasses were off, but there was no mistaking it was him.

He took my glass and refilled it from the pitcher before handing it back to me.

"Thank you." I blinked. "I'm sorry about earlier at the work-site. Timothy was only showing me around."

He raised one of his eyebrows. "Earlier at the worksite? Wasn't me. I think I would remember meeting you."

I blushed but wondered how he could have forgotten so quickly. *And why is he being so nice? He may even be flirting with me.*

An amused twinkle played in his eyes as he watched these thoughts move across my face.

Ellie stomped over to us, hands on hips. "Uriah, what are you doing standing out here? I need you to carry some more trays of food to the buffet."

I tilted my head and looked at him. "I thought your name was Ezekiel."

Uriah grinned.

Ellie rolled her eyes. "Ezekiel is his twin brother." She scanned the room. "I can't find him either. Lately, he keeps disappearing. Uri, do you know where your brother is?"

He shook his. "Nope."

"I wish you'd keep better track of him."

"Am I his keeper?"

"Yes." She swatted at him, and he ducked away laughing.

"The twins are both bent on giving me a headache, each in his own special way."

Twins!

"Do they work here?"

"They co-own the restaurant and flea market with me. Ezekiel runs most things. Uri, well, Uri doesn't have much of a mind for business."

"Do your other children work here too?"

She shook her head. "I have four daughters. All are married and have families of their own. Neither of my boys has found the right girl to marry yet."

The twins had to be in their early thirties. As far as marriage goes, that was late by Amish standards. If Timothy never left the Amish, he certainly would have been married by now at age twenty-seven. Maybe the same was true for the Mennonites, and that was why Beth Hilty was so adamant I decide the educational path of my nonexistent offspring. At twenty-four maybe she considered me an old maid. Hannah was only two years younger than me, and Beth seemed eager to marry her eldest daughter off. I suspected who the groom would be if it were up to her and Hannah.

Ellie narrowed her eyes. "Is something wrong?"

I refilled my water glass and smiled. "No. I'm fine."

"If you say so. I need to get back to the kitchen. Don't pay any mind to the twins."

I promised I wouldn't and returned to my table with my water glass in hand. Becky was in the middle of describing her art classes to the Hiltys.

As I took my seat, Timothy whispered in my ear. "I see you had a run-in with Uri Young."

I nodded. "Why didn't you tell me Ezekiel Young had an identical twin brother?"

He shrugged. "I didn't think of it. Ezekiel wears glasses and Uri doesn't. Besides, they're easy to tell apart by their personalities. The twins couldn't be more different."

I agreed that much was true.

Chapter Six

I woke up to screams. My heart pounded in my chest. It didn't matter how many times I heard those cries, they always shook me. The illuminated numbers of my bedside clock read 1:04 a.m. A scream came again, and I jumped out of bed. The icy hardwood floor sent a chill up my pajama-covered legs. I stumbled into my slippers and grabbed one of the blankets off of the bed. I wrapped it around my shoulders as another scream disturbed the quiet.

In the hallway, Gigabyte's sleek shadow moved back and forth in front of Becky's door. He hissed softly. He was no more used to these episodes, which were becoming alarmingly more frequent, than I was.

I opened Becky's bedroom door. In the streetlamp's light, which streamed through the window, she lay sprawled across the bed. Her sheets and blankets were twisted around her legs so tightly I feared they might cut off her circulation.

She thrashed back and forth, her eyes squeezed shut, and moaned to herself.

"Becky!"

"I'm sorry, Isaac!"

I crossed the room and touched her shoulder. "Becky! Becky! Wake up! You're having another nightmare."

She sat straight up in the bed, smacking me in the chin with her forehead. I bit down on my tongue. "Ow!" I stomped on Gig's tail, and he yowled so loudly the neighbors surely heard. The cat bolted out of the room. "Sorry, Gig," I called after him.

Becky held her forehead and panted. "I have a headache."

"I have a chin ache." I rubbed the sore spot.

She blew air in and out of her mouth, trying to control her breathing. "What happened?"

"You were screaming."

In the dim light given off by the night-light across the room, I saw tears glistening in her eyes. "I'm sorry."

"Becky? Did you have the nightmare again?"

She closed her eyes. "I saw the buggy at the bottom of the hill. I saw his face."

"It was a dream. It wasn't real." I wrapped my blanket more closely around my body.

She shook her head, her face ghostly white. "No, it was real. I hit him again."

"Try to forget."

"I can never forget it. Never."

I took her hand and sat on the edge of the bed. "Then let's pray you remember less often." I bowed my head. "Lord, please help Becky as she deals with this terrible memory. Make it possible that she may find peace in her dreams. In Jesus' name. Amen." I opened my eyes. "Did that help?"

"Nothing can help."

"Don't say that."

Becky lay back down and rolled on her side. "You don't know what it's like to live with guilt. It weighs me down every night. No matter what *gut* I accomplished during the day, it means nothing when I close my eyes."

"I do know what it is like, Becky. I know better than anyone. My father blamed me for my mother's death when I was only fourteen." She had been on her way to pick me up from a friend's sleepover on an icy night in January, lost control of her car on a patch of black ice, and crashed into a tree. What relationship my father and I had also died that night. I untwisted Becky's sheets and blankets away from her and covered her slender body.

She rolled over to face me. "This is different than your mother. That was a long time ago."

Her words stung, and I stepped back from the bed. Time had not healed the tension between my father and me since my mother's accident. I turned to go.

"Chloe?"

I closed my eyes for a brief moment before facing her again. I didn't want her to know how much her words hurt me. She was suffering. She didn't mean what she said.

"Do you think Chief Rose is right?" Chloe asked. "Do you think Curt and Brock will come looking for us?"

"No, not if they're smart. If anything happened to us, they would be the first people anyone would suspect. It would only land them back in prison, and I doubt they want to go back there."

"I'm afraid they aren't very smart, like the chief said."

I was afraid of the same thing but didn't say so.

AS I WALKED TO Harshberger early the next morning, I remembered the conversation I'd overhead between the two women in the church's cloakroom. I had meant to ask Timothy about it, but thoughts of Curt and Brock and the Hiltys pushed the memory aside.

Typically, because of the traffic, I avoided walking through the square on the way to work. When I say traffic, I mean Appleseed Creek traffic that consists of eight or nine cars and twelve Amish buggies. The memory of the Mennonite women's conversation in the cloakroom caused me to walk in that direction this morning.

I paused beside the front window of Amish Bread Bakery. Behind the counter, Esther Yoder's maple-colored hair shimmered like a halo around her white prayer cap. She handed a shopping bag to a man in a business suit.

There was no sign of the bishop's daughter, Sadie Hooley, who usually worked alongside Esther. After church, Becky had not spoken about Hannah's announcement of Esther's upcoming wedding to Isaac Glick.

Esther gave the businessman his change and spotted me peering through the window. She glared at me until I slunk away. I shuffled down the street. *Was the bishop's daughter, Sadie, the one whom the women at church spoke of?* It had to be. She was the only one of Bishop Hooley's daughters who worked at the bakery.

I frowned. How was Sadie attacked? Was she hurt? Enough to miss work? I didn't know Sadie well, but she had helped me during the summer when she didn't have to. She was a sweet, unassuming girl.

I was lost in thought when an Amish teenaged girl in a long, black cloak came around the corner and bumped me in the shoulder. "I'm so sorry." Her voice was breathless. A black bonnet covered her face.

I recognized the voice. "Sadie?"

She looked up. Her brown eyes were red-rimmed behind her glasses. She blinked at me.

"I'm Chloe Humphrey. We met a few months ago."

She wouldn't meet my eyes. "I remember."

"Is something wrong?"

Her expression crumbled. "I have to go. I'm terribly late for work. Esther must be angry."

"Is everything all right?"

"I'm late." Her eyes darted in every direction except for my face.

"I . . . I heard you were attacked."

She spun around. "Who told you that?"

That was tricky to answer. Did I admit I heard women gossiping about it at church? "Are you hurt?"

She licked her lips. "Did the police put you up to this?"

I stepped back. "The police? No."

Tears gathered in her eyes. "I have to go." She hurried in the direction of the bakery.

I chewed on my lip. If the police were involved, that could only mean Chief Rose was too.

Chapter Seven

On campus, students crisscrossed the grounds making their way to eight a.m. classes. The mood in the air was light as it was only a two-day school week. The college would close Tuesday evening for Thanksgiving. As much as I looked forward to the time off, I didn't dwell on the holiday. This would be the first year I wouldn't spend Thanksgiving with my father.

I surprised myself by missing it. I never looked forward to spending Thanksgiving with him and his new family. During the visit, my stepmother Sabrina only spoke to me when she found something lacking, which was often. My father didn't speak to me at all. This year, my father, my stepmother, and my half brother and half sister were on a cruise off the western coast of Mexico. Their ship may have already left port.

Going home to Cleveland didn't seem right either. After my father and stepmother moved to California when I fifteen, I lived with my best friend, Tanisha, and her family through the rest of high school. The Greens became the stable family I never had.

However, Tanisha was in Milan, Italy, and would be for the next two years teaching English as a second language. Her parents and younger brother invited me to spend Thanksgiving with Mrs. Green's family in Georgia, but I said I'd rather stay in Appleseed Creek and get some work done. As much as I loved Tee's family, it wouldn't be nearly as much fun without her there.

I didn't know how the Troyers celebrated Thanksgiving or what their plans were. I tried to work up the courage to ask. How pathetic would it be to invite myself to their Thanksgiving gathering? I didn't even know if, not being Amish, I could be included. What if it was some kind of church-related holiday for the Amish? If that were the case, Timothy and Becky would also be excluded.

Then there was the issue of Isaac Glick's wedding, which would be held on Thanksgiving Day. Would the Troyers attend? I doubted Becky would go. She wouldn't want to, nor would she be welcomed.

I stepped into the computer services office. My media specialist, Jonathan Clark, an African-American with the build of a former athlete, sat across the conference table from Darren Miller, the department's scrawny, constantly fidgeting programmer in his early twenties. Miller reminded me of a mouse as he scurried around the department from task to task.

Miller fumbled with his computer parts more than usual. The programmer looked like he was receiving electroshock treatment.

I turned to Clark, who rocked back in his office chair. He clicked his mouse on the tabletop as he moved it around his computer screen. "Have you seen the Mount Vernon newspaper?"

"No."

He pointed to it, neatly folded on the edge of the conference table and as far away from Miller as possible without actually being on the floor. Mount Vernon was the Knox's county seat and the only town to boast a newspaper. The front page headline read, **Appleseed Creek Amish Community Terrorized by Shears.**

I arched an eyebrow at Clark.

He moved his mouse around the tabletop and clicked. "Keep reading."

The article went on to say that four young Amish women had been attacked in the last week. They were jumped from behind and held down by their assailants while someone cut off their long hair. Except for a few minor scrapes and bruises during the attack, there were no other injuries.

Chloe read on.

> Haircutting is a serious offense in the Amish community. The Amish believe a woman's hair is her crown jewel and should not be cut. Appleseed Creek Chief of Police, Greta Rose, says she's taking this case extremely seriously. Rose said, "For religious reasons, Amish women don't cut their hair. If anyone attacks them and cuts their hair that can be considered a form of religious persecution and a religiously-motivated hate crime in the court of law."

I placed the paper back onto the table. "This is awful." Sadie Hooley came to mind. *Had her hair been cut? Is that what the ladies meant when they said she had been attacked?*

Miller dropped his wireless mouse on the floor and the battery popped out. He leaned over to pick it up and smacked his head on the edge of the table.

I winced. "Are you okay?"

Tears sprang to the programmer's eyes, and he jumped up from the table, dropping the mouse onto it and fleeing the office. The mouse sat in pieces on the tabletop.

Clark covered the mouse pieces with his large hand and pulled them toward him like a bear collecting pinecones.

"What's wrong with Miller? Is he upset by the story?"

Clark snapped the AA battery back into the mouse and replaced the cover. "His cousin was one of the victims."

I fell into a chair. "His cousin? Miller's Amish?"

Clark set the mouse beside Miller's abandoned laptop. "No, but his uncle married an Amish woman. He's Amish and all of his children are."

"What's the name of Miller's cousin?"

"Leah. He's spoken of her before, so I think the two are pretty close. You know for Miller to speak about anything other than SQL or C++ is a big deal."

Now that Clark mentioned it, I'd never heard Miller talk about his family or anything unrelated to Harshberger or computers. I tapped the cover story with my nail. "I understand why he's so upset by it. This is awful. I'm glad the police are investigating."

"They are to some extent, but Miller is the only one who will talk to Chief Rose and her crew. The Amish won't talk to her at all. The powers that be want to settle this within the district."

The powers that be? *The Amish bishop.*

I wondered why the chief hadn't mentioned the attacks Sunday morning when she told Timothy, Becky, and me about Curt and Brock being back in town. A knot formed in my stomach as another thought hit me. Could Curt and Brock be behind the attacks? They were the culprits behind vandalism in the district earlier in the year, which was one of the reasons they ended up in jail. Chief Rose implied they held a grudge against Becky and me. Perhaps they held a grudge against the entire Amish district. Curt, for one, had no use for the Amish.

"Actually," Clark went on, "Miller called the paper about the attacks. He's frustrated the Amish aren't speaking out."

I pursed my lips. I knew what that was like. During the summer when Becky had been falsely accused of a crime, it had been almost impossible to convince the Amish to tell the police what they knew.

"How did his uncle take Miller talking to the paper?"

Clark shrugged.

I circled the headline with my fingertip. "It says four Amish women were attacked. Who are the other three?"

"I don't know. You can ask Miller, I guess, but I would give him a minute." Clark rubbed his head covered in close-cut hair. "You seemed awfully interested. Are you planning to get involved?"

I took a step back. "Involved? Me? Why would I do that?"

A small smile played on his lips. "You were involved in that murder last summer. Almost got yourself killed, if I remember correctly."

I placed my shoulder bag on the table and removed my coat, hanging it on the hook by the office door. "That situation was completely different. Becky had been involved."

He shrugged. "If you say so."

Clark knew me better than I knew myself. If I had no plans to snoop into the haircutting attacks, what had I been doing walking by the Amish Bread Bakery this morning?

I watched the door, counting the minutes until Miller came back into the office.

Chapter Eight

By sheer willpower, I waited until Clark went on his lunch
hour before approaching Miller about the news story.

The programmer hunched over his computer and
tapped away at the keys. He typed code in the command prompt
line. I hated to interrupt him, but Clark would be back from the
cafeteria soon. I didn't have much time.

I sat across from him at the conference table in Clark's usual
spot. Miller didn't even notice me. "Miller?"

Nothing.

"Miller?"

He raised his head and blinked owlish eyes at me.

"Can I talk to you about the newspaper story? About your
cousin Leah?"

He gripped his mouse. "How do you know about Leah?"

"Clark told me. One of the girls who had their hair cut was
your cousin?"

He tugged at his spiky blond hair. "Why do you want to know
about it?"

I was almost certain that Sadie was another victim of the hair-cutting. "I have a friend." I paused because that was a stretch. "I know an Amish girl, Sadie Hooley, she's the bishop's daughter."

"I know that."

"I think her hair was cut too. The article mentioned three other girls."

"I don't know about Sadie, but two of them are Leah's friends."

"What are their names?"

"I'm still not sure why you want to know," he said, his face pinched.

Because I want to know if Curt and Brock are behind this, I thought. Instead, I told him, "You know my roommate Becky is Amish, or was. I don't want something like this to happen to her."

He licked his lips. "It's a nightmare."

"Who are her friends?" I asked again.

"Abby and Debbie. I don't know their last names."

"That's all right." I wondered if I should tell him about Curt and Brock. "Did the girls see their attacker?"

He shook his head. "No. Each time he came up from behind, covered their head with a burlap bag, ripped off their bonnets, and cut off their hair. Each girl was alone when it happened."

"He?" I picked up Clark's pencil and tapped the eraser on the tabletop.

"They said they thought it was a man. Who else would be strong enough to do that?"

Good question. I shivered. "Other than their hair, were they hurt?" I was afraid to hear the answer.

Miller turned slightly green. "No. Thank goodness."

"What did he use to cut their hair?"

He shook his head. "I don't know. Leah said it all happened in a matter of seconds. She doesn't know either. The guy was behind her."

I dropped the pencil into a utensil cup. "There was only one man?"

"Leah thought so."

Maybe it wasn't Curt and Brock after all. They typically worked as a team. If they were the ones cutting off Leah's hair, I couldn't imagine they were quiet enough for her not to notice a second culprit.

He frowned. "I hope the police do something. Leah could have been seriously hurt or worse. Whatever the guy used to cut their hair had to be sharp. Leah's hair is like rope. The person could have slipped and . . ."

"I'm sure Chief Rose is doing everything she can to find out who did this. She called it a hate crime in the article."

"It doesn't do any good if the Amish won't talk to her about it." He shook his head. "I don't understand. Why don't they ask for help when they need it?"

It was a question I'd asked myself many times since moving to Knox County.

Clark ambled into the office carrying a half-eaten corn dog. "Corn dogs in the caf today. You two better hustle if you have any hope of snagging one. I just saw a freshman walk out with ten. He said they were for his classmates in his economics class, but I'm suspicious. What do corn dogs have to do with economics, anyway?"

A small smile played on Miller's face. "Supply and demand."

Clark grinned and gave Miller a high five.

I let Clark have his chair. "I'll pass." Corn dogs were not on my diet plan.

Later that afternoon, I was on my way out of the office when my cell phone rang. "Chloe," Becky said. "The chain on my bike broke. Is there any chance you can pick me up from work tonight? I'm off at seven. Timothy's here working in the pavilion, but he said he's not leaving until nine or ten. I don't want to be stuck here that long."

I repressed a sigh. Carting Becky around town was getting old. "Sure. I'll be there."

As I walked up the driveway toward my house, I sensed something was off. I couldn't place it. The house looked like it had in the morning when I left. I stepped back from the house and took it in. Then, I saw what was bothering me. The light was on in my bedroom. I had turned it off when I left the room that morning. *Would Becky have gone in there and left the light on?* It was possible.

A shadow moved crossed the window. Someone was in my room, and it wasn't Gigabyte. I pulled my cell phone from my coat pocket and called Chief Rose.

She was there within two minutes. The village police station was tucked into a corner of the town hall on the square. She climbed out of her cruiser and found me standing on the sidewalk watching the house. "You have a prowler."

"Maybe." I was beginning to have my doubts. I hadn't seen the shadow a second time. "I think someone's in my bedroom." I pointed at the window. "See, the lights on. I know I turned it off this morning."

"Becky may have turned the light on and forgot."

I bit my lip. "It's possible, but . . ."

"I know, I know, with Curt and Brock running around we can never be too careful." She pulled her gun from her utility belt. It was the first time I'd seen her handle it. "I'm surprised you called me instead of Timothy."

"Timothy is working on a project at Young's Flea Market today. I figured you'd get here faster."

She nodded. "You figured right. Is the door locked?"

"It should be. Becky wouldn't forget to do that."

"I'll need your key, then. I don't think you want me to break it down."

I handed her my computer mouse-shaped keychain. She didn't comment on the keychain and kept her gun pointed downward. "Stay here, and I will check it out." She moved up the walk.

"Don't shoot my cat!" I called after her.

She rolled her eyes at me.

As the cold seeped into the fabric of my thick coat, I hopped from foot to foot on the sidewalk. I must have resembled Miller as I moved back and forth.

Five minutes later—which felt more like five *years*—the front door opened. Chief Rose walked a man out of my house, holding him at gunpoint. His hands were up, and his eyes were the size of duck eggs.

"Dylan?"

Chapter Nine

C hief Rose walked Dylan down the porch stairs. Despite the cold, a bead of sweat drew across the biologist's face as he stumbled on the last step.

"Watch your footing," the chief of police barked. She used the barrel of her gun to point to the middle of the lawn. "He claims he's your landlord."

I cleared my throat. "He is."

Dylan wore short sleeves and began to shiver. "See, I told you." He wrapped his arms around his torso.

She watched him, her expression stern. "I don't want to hear anything out of you."

"Dylan, what were you doing inside my house when no one was there?" I buried my hands deep inside my pockets.

"Fixing the window in your bedroom. The one that is painted shut."

"Timothy will fix it when he has time," I said.

Dylan's glasses slipped down his long nose. "I know, but like I told you and Becky yesterday, I plan to renovate the house. I don't have any afternoon classes on Mondays, so I thought this would be the perfect time to get started."

"How did you get in?" I asked.

He reached into his jeans pocket. "I used my key."

"No sudden movements," Chief Rose ordered.

Dylan's hand froze in midair. "Please ask her to lower the gun."

I glanced at her. "Chief . . ."

Chief Rose holstered her gun. "Fine."

My face grew hot. "You may be my landlord, but you can't go into my house whenever you like." He said he was fixing the window, but what else could he have been doing while he was in there?

"She's right, you know," Chief Rose crossed her arms. "You need to notify tenants at least twenty-four hours before entering their home. I can get you copy of the Ohio Revised Code if you want to see it."

Dylan turned to me. "I told you I planned to work on the house yesterday."

I folded my arms. "I know that, but you didn't say you'd be here today."

Dylan pushed his glasses up the bridge of his nose. "I'm so sorry. Truly, I didn't mean any harm. I let my enthusiasm for the house run away with me."

Chief Rose eyed Dylan. "I can still take him in. Run him through the paces."

I wasn't entirely sure what "run him through the paces" meant, but it didn't sound pleasant. "No," I insisted. "You don't have to arrest him."

Dylan gave me a small smile. "Let me go in and grab my coat and tools, and I will be out of your way." He dashed back into the house before we could argue.

"The good news is it wasn't Curt or Brock." Chief Rose's radio crackled, but she ignored it.

"What's the bad news?"

"Your landlord is a nut."

Dylan reappeared, wearing his winter coat and a stocking cap. He carried a red metal toolbox in his hand. "I didn't finish fixing the window. I'll come back another time to finish the job."

"I'm sure Timothy would be happy to do it. He has lots of experience."

The strange look crossed the professor's face again. "I don't need his help. He's Amish and doesn't understand what I'm trying to do."

I pulled back.

Chief Rose placed her aviator sunglasses on the top her head. "Do you have a problem with the Amish?"

"N-no. However, their carpentry techniques aren't appropriate for this centennial home. It's paramount that the work and fixtures on this home are in keeping with the house's original plans and design."

Chief Rose appeared unconvinced. I'm sure I looked much the same.

"I'm sorry." He shifted his toolbox into his other hand. "I'm still a little shaken up from being held at gunpoint."

Chief Rose refrained from comment but stayed with me until Dylan climbed into his beige sedan, parked two houses down, and drove away.

After the chief left, I stepped into the house, Gigabyte yowled at me. His typically short fur stood on end. I stroked his back and smoothed his coat down. "That upset you, didn't it, buddy."

He yowled and wove in and around my legs.

"It upset me too."

Inside my bedroom, everything looked how I left it that morning. Everything except the second window. The edges of the windowpane were scraped where Dylan had chipped away the paint.

Flecks of light blue paint lay on the windowsill. I hoped that it wasn't lead paint but judging from the age of the house it could be. I made a mental note to ask Timothy to take a look at it no matter what Dylan may want. The latch lay in pieces under the window.

I tried to open the window, and it rose easily. With the latch in bits on the floor, the window couldn't lock. My bedroom was on the second floor and there were no trees near this end of the house, so no one less than Spiderman could scale the house's siding and enter through my window. But the unlocked window made me uneasy. Curt and Brock were free, and now, I had renovation-happy Dylan Tanner to worry about too.

I checked my cell phone. I would have to worry about this later. It was about time for me to leave and pick up Becky at Young's.

After I parked my new car—a VW Bug I purchased a month after my car was totaled in Becky's buggy-auto accident—I got out and poked my head inside the kitchen. A waitress in a navy blue plain dress and white apron, the uniform for the women who worked at Young's, smiled at me. I stopped. "Is Becky here? She called me and said she needed a ride."

They were in the middle of the dinner rush. Waitresses and busboys flew in and out of the bustling kitchen trading empty plates for freshly made meals. The waitress picked up a tray loaded with soft drinks and mugs of coffee. "Becky said she was going to the pavilions to wait with her brother until you got here. She knew if she hung around the kitchen too long, Ellie'd put her back to work."

I thanked her and slipped back outside. The only lights to guide me to the pavilions were the lampposts scattered around the parking lot and the ambient light from the restaurant's windows. I stepped carefully as I made my way to the second pavilion, taking Timothy's warning from the day before seriously. I didn't want to step on a stray nail.

The job site was quiet. I bit my lip. If Timothy had to work late, why would it be so quiet? Shouldn't I be hearing hammering, sawing . . . something?

Since the waitress said Becky waited with Timothy, I figured they were in the second pavilion, the one Timothy showed me the afternoon before. I stepped through the clear tarp. Orange extension cords snaked along the cement floor. Gingerly, I moved around them.

One of the extension cords tangled around a wooden sawhorse. I sidestepped it, and my foot bumped into a work boot. I blinked several times. The person wearing the boot was prostrate on the ground. A gasp escaped me. Ezekiel Young lay on his stomach, his neck twisted. His glasses and shorn beard lay next to him on the sawdust-covered floor. The handle of peculiar-looking shears stuck out of his back.

I stumbled backward and tripped over the legs of the sawhorse and a nest of extension cords, landing flat on my back. Breath whooshed out of my lungs. My head had connected with the cement floor, and stars danced in my eyes. I lay there for half a second, scrambled to my feet, and ran.

I burst into the restaurant's kitchen, clutching the back of my head. The mouths of the Amish women working there fell open. The kitchen's fluorescent lighting blinded me, and I held up a hand to block the light.

I pointed behind me. "Pa-pavilion."

The women whispered in Pennsylvanian Dutch.

"He's in the pavilion." My legs felt weak. I grabbed at the prep counter to steady myself and knocked a tray of mashed potatoes to the floor. The ceramic dish shattered. Potatoes flew everywhere, and I passed out.

Chapter Ten

Timothy supported my head. "Chloe?" His blue eyes grew wide, and I saw fear there.

I tried to sit up. The room swung around me as if suspended from a bungee cord. The pain throbbed from the base of my neck forward to my forehead.

"Don't move. You could have a concussion."

Timothy's blue eyes came into focus again. Above him, Becky's pale heart-shaped face peered down at me. Tears ran down her cheeks.

The image of Ezekiel's shorn beard hit me like a punch to the jaw. "The pavilion. Ezekiel is in the pavilion."

Timothy's brow furrowed.

"He's dead," I said.

A keening cry went up in the room. Someone threw open the back door, and I felt the rush of air as people ran outside.

"Becky," Timothy barked. "Stay with Chloe." Gently as possible, he placed my head back down on the white-tiled floor. He jumped up and followed the others out of the kitchen.

Becky knelt beside me. The cotton fabric of her navy plain dress floated to the floor. "Chloe, are you all right? What happened?" She twisted her white apron in her hands.

I started to sit up again.

"No." She pushed on my shoulder to force me to lay back down.

I brushed her hand away. "Help me up or I'll get up on my own."

She supported my elbow as I stood. The room spun. Somehow, I stayed upright.

The back door to the kitchen was open, and the chilly air cut through the room. Fallen leaves blew in and danced over the tiled floor. No one seemed concerned. The Amish women who worked in the kitchen whispered to each other in their own language. The only word I understood in my foggy state was *Englischer*, in reference to me I was sure.

Sirens broke through the sound of their conversations.

"Chloe, what do you want to do?" Becky gripped my elbow as if her grasp was the only support keeping me from tumbling back down to the floor. I took a wobbly step. She may be right about that.

"Sit down."

My head spun like a Tilt-a-Whirl.

"There's a break room on the other side of the kitchen."

She led me from the room. My eyes blurred, and I concentrated on my steps, trying to forget Ezekiel Young's face. The small break room held a sofa and a round table surrounded by cane chairs. I lowered myself onto the sofa and fatigue washed over me.

Becky voice broke through the fog. "Chloe, aren't you supposed to stay awake in case you have a concussion?"

She was right, but what could it hurt to rest my eyes for a minute?

"Miss, miss? What's your name?"

My eyelids fluttered open.

A burly EMT with black hair curling around his ears shone a penlight in my face. I blinked. I turned my eyes away. Chief Rose watched me from over his shoulder.

"Your name?" the EMT asked again.

I shook the cobwebs from my head. *Ouch*. Shaking my head was the last thing I should be doing. "Chloe Humphrey."

"How many fingers am I holding up?"

"Three."

He smiled. "Good answer, Miss Humphrey, though I'm afraid you might have a concussion. We're taking you to the hospital."

I felt sick to my stomach. I hated hospitals, and I had ever since my mother died in one. "I feel fine. It's a little headache."

He squinted at me. "It's a big headache, and this isn't up for debate. The ambulance is outside ready to take you. Do you think you can walk there?"

I nodded and immediately regretted it.

He helped me to stand.

"Hold on, Nate. She's not going anywhere until I ask her a few questions." Chief Rose's tone was firm.

Irritation flashed across the mild-mannered EMT's face. "You can talk to her at the hospital."

I started to sit back down. "No, I want to talk to her here." The sooner I spoke with Chief Rose, the sooner I could forget the image of Ezekiel Young. At least I hoped so.

A smile spread across the police chief's delicate features. With her petite frame and short poodle-like hair, she looked like the girl next door, not a seasoned police officer. I knew better than to underestimate her. "I'm surprised to see you again so soon, Chloe. You've had an eventful day."

My forehead creased, then I remembered Dylan and the broken window latch back in my bedroom. That seemed so long ago. Could it possibly be the same day? What day was it? I didn't dare ask Nate. He would cart me off to the hospital that very minute.

She pulled a chair in front of the sofa. "Tell me what happened from the beginning."

So I did.

The police chief didn't take any notes. *Does she have a photographic memory or something?*

She leaned back in her chair. "Shame about the sawhorse tripping you."

My throbbing head agreed. "Do you think this could be related to the other haircutting incidents in the county?"

She arched her brow.

"There was a story in the paper. Ezekiel's beard was cut off." I shivered at the memory. "I doubt I will be the last person to make the connection."

Chief Rose frowned. "Cutting off hair is one thing. Murder is something entirely different."

I thought for a moment. No easy feat considering the pounding in my head. It was like someone was doing the Irish jig on my frontal lobe. "Do you think Curt and Brock could be behind this?"

The chief's peridot eyes flashed. "Cold-blooded murder would be a big step for those two."

Not that big of a step.

"I'll have one my officers find out what they were up to at the time of the murder."

I placed a hand to the side my head. "Please don't mention my name."

"I don't plan to, but Curt and Brock have a grudge against you, and they might figure it out, especially since the Amish are involved."

Nate shuffled his feet. "Is that all, Chief? It's time for Chloe to go."

Chief Rose glanced at him. "That's all for now." She helped me to my feet and the world didn't tilt on its axis as it had before. My stomach turned.

Was I nauseous because I was headed to the hospital or from something more?

Chapter Eleven

Becky readjusted the sofa pillow behind my back. She touched me on the shoulder. "Sit up."

I sat up, and she rearranged the mound of pillows for the third time. She stepped back and cocked her head. "It still doesn't look comfortable." She took a step toward the sofa.

I held up my hand to stop her. "It's fine."

Now out of her plain Young's uniform, she wore a neon pink sweat suit. She perched on the edge of our living room coffee table. "I'm sorry. I'm being a nuisance."

"You're not, but the pillows are fine."

Timothy walked in from the kitchen, carrying a tray of chicken soup and hot tea. Gig followed him expectantly. He loved Becky's chicken soup. Becky moved from the table to the couch, and Timothy set the tray on the table.

I scooted up in my seat. "You two don't have to dote on me like this. The doctor said I don't even have a mild concussion." Gingerly, I touched the goose egg forming on the back of my skull. "Just a nasty bump."

Timothy stirred the soup and handed it to me. "I don't think you should go to work tomorrow."

The bowl warmed my hands. "Why not?"

His jaw twitched. "You're not up to it. You should rest."

I suppressed a smile, secretly pleased he was so concerned. "I'm up to it. The doctor gave me the okay to go. Tomorrow's the last day before Thanksgiving break. There's so much work to be done before the college closes for the holiday."

Timothy's brow furrowed. "I don't like it." He blew on the cup of tea and glanced at his sister. "Becky, I forgot to bring a napkin. Can you go grab one?"

She jumped out of her seat like a shot.

Timothy watched her go. "Chloe." He took the soup bowl from me. "I want you to be careful."

I searched his concerned eyes.

"Whoever killed Ezekiel is dangerous. I couldn't stand it if you were hurt or . . ." He swallowed. "When I saw you lying on the restaurant's kitchen floor, I—"

"I got them." Becky waved the napkins in the air.

No, no, no. Keep talking, Timothy. What did you think when you saw me lying on the floor?

Timothy stood. "It's late. I'll let you girls get some rest."

I grabbed his arm. "There's one more thing."

A lock of white-blond hair fell over his eye. "One more thing?"

"Can you fix the window latch in my bedroom?" After my discovery in the pavilion, I would never be able to sleep in that room with a window that could not lock.

"What's wrong with your window?"

I bit my lip and told him.

Timothy stepped back, and I lost my hold on his arm. "Dylan was in your house when you weren't here?"

"He's the owner."

Timothy's face was thunderous. "I don't care if he's the president. He can't enter your home uninvited. I knew there was a reason I didn't like the guy."

"Chief Rose told him he needs to give us twenty-four-hour notice in the future."

Timothy pursed his lips.

Becky folded the paper napkin in her small hands. "Sounds to me like he was trying to help."

Timothy shot his younger sister a look. "Don't defend him." He sighed. "My toolbox is in my truck. Let me go grab it, and I'll fix the window." The door slammed after Timothy.

Becky handed me the napkin. "You know he's mad about Dylan because he's jealous."

I stirred my soup. "Jealous of Dylan?"

"He saw how the professor watched you yesterday."

"What do you mean?"

"It's no secret my brother likes you. I can tell. Everyone can."

"Everyone?" A knot formed in my stomach. "How do you feel about it?" I figured it was a safer question than asking how her parents felt about it. I wasn't sure I wanted to know that just yet.

"Fine." She said with a shrug and then grinned. "If you get married, we'd be sisters."

"Who said anything about getting married?"

"The more important question is how you feel about it."

The front door opened, which saved me from answering. Timothy went straight up the stairs, and Becky turned on a television cooking competition show.

I'd just finished eating my soup when Timothy came back downstairs. "I fixed it. Dylan sure did a job on that latch. He mangled it. Luckily, I had an extra latch in my box." He blushed. "I'm sorry I blew up. I'm not comfortable with this guy coming around the house. Do you know anything about him?"

I shook my head. "I could ask around. Maybe Miller or Clark knows something. They've worked at Harshberger a long time."

Timothy nodded. "At least Greta told him he can't come into the house again without letting you know."

Gigabyte bumped his velvety head against my shoulder, and I scratched him behind the ear.

Timothy set his toolbox on the floor. "Are you sure you are up to going to work tomorrow?"

I forced a smiled. "Yes," I said not feeling sure at all.

"Rest when you get home. I want you to feel well for Thanksgiving."

"For Thanksgiving?" I squeaked.

"Your father's not flying you out to California this year."

"No, he's not."

"That's good news." He grinned. "You can have a real Troyer family Thanksgiving. I already spoke to my parents about it, and they are happy to have you."

"Even your dad?" Mr. Troyer followed the rules of Old Order district. Becky and Timothy left the Amish way during their *rumspringas*—running around time—and before they were baptized, which is why they weren't shunned and the family can interact with them. I knew Mr. Troyer secretly wished his eldest son and daughter would change their minds and return. My friendship with the siblings was in the way of that wish.

"Even *Daed*."

Becky scrambled to her feet. "Chloe, you have to come. You're practically part of the family. The *kinner* would love to see you, and *Grossdaddi* would never forgive us if we show up without you."

Did this mean that the Troyers weren't going to Esther and Isaac's wedding? I knew that Amish weddings were a big deal in the district, and typically, everyone attended.

"I'd love to go." I settled back into the pillows. *A Troyer family Thanksgiving is just what I need.*

Becky clapped her hands. "Perfect. This year I'm bringing some dishes of my own. I've been watching all the Thanksgiving food shows on television and collecting recipes from the Internet. The hardest thing will be deciding what to cook. Will you make anything, Chloe?"

I laughed. "I don't think anyone wants food poisoning this holiday."

Becky shook her head. "Chloe, you need to get over your fear of cooking."

"Why should I bother if you're so good at it?"

There was a twinkle in her blue eye. "You may have someone to cook for."

I stole a look at Timothy. He grinned, and a blush crept up the back of my neck.

Chapter Twelve

The next morning, the worst of my headache had subsided, but I still felt dizzy as I dressed for work. The bump on the back of my head was the size of a walnut. The hair on top of it stuck out just a little, giving the illusion of a temporary cowlick. Slow and steady would be the plan for the day. Thankfully, a holiday weekend was right around the corner.

Clark eyed me as I walked into the office. "Moving slowly today, boss? What happened to you?"

Miller peeked over the top of his laptop. His spiky hair looked like it received an extra dose of styling gel this morning.

I eased into a chair at the conference table. "I guess it wasn't in the paper yet."

Clark wiggled his brows. "What's up?"

"You are probably going to hear about it soon enough . . ." I told them about my discovery at the flea market, and my voice only shook a little. I wished that the bump on the back of my head erased the memory of the shears sticking out of Ezekiel's back.

Miller closed his laptop lid and gawked at me.

"Are you okay?" Clark asked.

I nodded. Again, not the best idea. I needed to remember not to make sudden movements. "I have a bump on the back of my head. That's all."

Clark looked dubious. "The murderer could have still been in the pavilion when you found the Amish dude."

My chest tightened. That was something I hadn't thought of before. In a place as large as the pavilion, there would have been many places for the killer to hide. He may even have seen me fall.

"His hair was cut off," Miller whispered. "That's like Leah."

"Not exactly like Leah," Clark jumped in. "Her hair was cut off. He lost his beard."

Miller narrowed his eyes at his coworker. "I know that but the message is the same to the Amish. It's still targeting the Amish and their beliefs." Miller squinted as if holding back tears.

Clark's eyes drooped. "Man, are you okay?"

"I'm fine," Miller said gruffly. He jumped out of his chair. "I'm going to run to the caf for some coffee. Do either of you want anything?"

"No," I said, careful not to shake my head.

"I'm good," Clark said.

Clark pointed to the full coffee pot in the department's tiny kitchenette. "Something tells me he's not really on a coffee run."

Inside my office, I was tucking my shoulder bag into my desk drawer when I heard Clark holler. "Chloe, you got a present."

A present?

I slammed the desk drawer and poked my head out of my officer door. A tiny undergraduate teetered under the weight of an arrangement of fall-colored mums, the arrangement so large I could only see the student's jean-clad legs and riding boots.

"Whoa," Clark said. "Let me take that from you before you fall over."

The student grinned. "Thanks. This came into the mailroom this morning for you, Ms. Humphrey."

Did Timothy send me flowers?

"Who are they from?" Clark asked as Miller walked back in the office with the largest cup of coffee I'd ever seen. Surely, the college cafeteria called the size "bucket." Instead of sitting at his usual post at the conference table, Miller slipped behind the partition that marked off his cubicle.

"Oh," the student snapped her fingers. "I have the note that came with it."

She checked her coat pockets and frowned. She emptied her jeans pockets and frowned even harder. "Uh-oh. I must have dropped it between here and the mailroom." She shrugged. "Sorry."

"Did you read the note?" I asked. "Do you remember the name on it?"

Her eyes grew wide. "No, I would *never* do that. That's like breaking the mailroom code or something."

"If you read the note, it's okay. We're not going to report you to the mailroom police."

"I really didn't read it." She smiled brightly. "Just pretend it was from a secret admirer. For all we know that's who sent it. Gotta go. I'm late for class."

Clark shook his head as he watched the undergrad flounce out of the room. "I find the students' energy exhausting."

I inspected the flowers. They were beautiful, a deep array of orange, red, yellow, and plum. They had to be from Timothy—who else would send me flowers? He must have sent them to cheer me up after what happened last night. A smile formed on my lips.

"What should we do with them?" Clark asked. "Want me to put them in your office?"

"They'll never fit." My office was the size of a glorified closet. "Just leave them on the conference table."

Clark stood up. "I'd love to stick around and investigate this mystery, but I just got an e-mail from a psychology prof who says the video camera I lent him isn't working."

I touched the petals on a purple mum. "Did he take the lens cap off?"

Clark scanned the e-mail. "According to this, yes, but I'll believe it when I see it."

After Clark left to help the professor, I tapped on the partition around Miller's workspace. "Can you talk for a sec?"

He flinched.

"I've been thinking about it, and I'd like to talk to your cousin."

"To Leah?"

"Yes. I think the murder and haircutting are related. Maybe she can tell me something that can connect them."

"Why?"

"What do you mean *why*?"

"I mean why do you care?"

"I—I found his body. I'm curious . . ."

"Curiosity isn't going to help that dead Amish man—or my cousin."

"I know that. I can't stop thinking about it." I tried to push the image to the back of my mind.

He spun a ballpoint pen on the tabletop. "She spoke to Chief Rose, but only because I asked her to."

"Do you think she will talk to me?"

The pen fell on the floor, and the programmer didn't bother to pick it up. "I don't know. My aunt and uncle won't like it. They take their privacy seriously. They are furious at me already about the newspaper story. But how is it going to stop if people don't know about it?"

"Where can I find Leah?"

"She works at one of the little gift shops on the square, The Apple Core. My aunt and uncle own it, but Leah pretty much runs the place. That would be the best place to talk to her. Debbie and Abby help out at the shop sometimes too. You don't want to go to the family farm. My uncle wouldn't like that." He picked up a stress ball in the shape of a computer monitor and began to squeeze it. "I can tell her you might stop by."

"Thank you, Miller." I paused. "Happy Thanksgiving."

"You too." He turned back to the line of code running across his computer screen, and I went to my office.

"HELLO, HELLO," DEAN KLINK called as he entered the computer services department in the early afternoon. I peered out of my office door, blinking my eyes, sure I looked as owl-like as Miller had earlier in the day.

The dean wasn't alone. An attractive, smartly dressed woman in a knee-length navy suit and matching pumps stood beside him. She had perfectly straight, glossy, ebony hair and makeup so expertly applied it was as if Mary Kay had swooped down and done it herself.

Clark wiggled his eyebrows at Miller, who gave him the smallest of smiles in return.

I stepped out of my office. "Good afternoon, Dean."

"Chloe, you're just the person that I'm looking for." He clapped his hands. "My, what gorgeous flowers! Whose are they?"

"They are from Chloe's secret admirer," Clark replied.

Inwardly, I groaned.

"A secret admirer?"

"It's not a secret admirer. The student who dropped it off lost the card, so I don't know who sent them."

"A mystery, then. I love it." The dean beamed.

The sleek woman cleared her throat.

"I'm sorry," the dean said. "I'm taking Collette on a tour of campus. Collette Williams, this is Chloe Humphrey, Director of Computer Services, and her staff, Clark and Miller."

"Nice to meet you all." The woman replied in a faintly British accent. I couldn't decide if it was authentic.

"Collette is our new Director of Marketing."

I held out my hand. "It's nice to meet you."

"She started a few weeks ago and has already brought a new energy to the college."

Now that Dean Klink mentioned it, I remembered seeing an e-mail about Collette's arrival not long ago. However, I still didn't understand what that had to do with me. "Is something wrong with your computer accounts?" I asked.

The dean laughed. "Chloe, you act like the only time someone stops by this office is to complain. We have exciting news to share with you."

Clark stifled a snicker, and Miller ducked behind the safety of his partition.

The dean gestured toward an office chair. "Please have a seat."

I slipped into a conference chair, and the dean and marketing director followed.

"If it's not a computer issue," I said, "what can I do for you?"

The dean grinned. "That's why I like you, Chloe. You are always willing to pitch in where we need you."

"Where do you need me?"

"Collette?" The dean motioned for her to proceed.

Collette folded her hands on the tabletop. Her nail polish was without nick or bump. "One of the ways to attract more students to Harshberger is to be more attractive to the town of Appleseed Creek and neighboring communities. So this year we have entered a float in the town's holiday parade."

I didn't like the sound of that.

The dean peeked around the flower arrangement. "Bad news. Tony Rather threw his back out. He fell on a patch of black ice on his driveway and slipped a disc."

"That's horrible. Will he be okay?"

"He's spending the holiday in traction. He'll be fine."

I didn't consider spending Thanksgiving in traction as okay.

Collette's perfect brow drooped. "The worse news is he was supposed to be one of the faculty members on the Appleseed Creek holiday parade float from the college."

Clark could no longer suppress his grin. "That's too bad. The parade is only three days away on Black Friday. Where will you find a replacement?"

I shot Clark a look.

"That's why we're here! Chloe, I think you are a perfect choice for the float."

"You want me to ride on the float?"

"I can't think of anyone better."

I could. I turned to Clark. "Clark, you like parades, don't you?"

A knowing smile spread across the media specialist's face. "I love a good parade, but I'll be in Cincinnati visiting my wife's family for Turkey Day. Too bad. I'll have to pass."

The dean's brow furrowed. "You are going to be in town this weekend, aren't you?"

"Yes," I said slowly, regretting having told the dean that several weeks ago.

"Then, why not? You'll be at the center of an Appleseed Creek tradition! It's an honor to be on our float. Collette has everything planned down to the minute. You won't have to do anything but show up."

"I don't want to take away the spot from a professor . . ."

Collette nodded. "In the end, I think it would be best to have a nonfaculty member, like you on the float. We don't want to look elitist to the community."

Dean Klink waved a dismissive hand. "Besides, they've all had their chances to volunteer. Can you believe I brought this problem up at the faculty meeting today, and no one offered to take Tony's place?"

I could believe it.

"Will you be on the float, Dean Klink?" Clark asked.

The dean licked his lips. "Well, no, I'm leaving on a flight tonight to go to my daughter's."

I sighed. "I . . . well . . . what would I have to do?"

A grin broke on the dean's face. "I knew I could count on you, Chloe. You always pull through."

I was beginning to think that pulling through wasn't always a good attribute.

He tapped his fingers on the tabletop as if playing piano keys. "All you will have to do is show up, stand on the float, and wave." He stood. "Collette will e-mail the details of where you should be and when."

Sounded simple enough.

I made one more valiant effort. "Since this is Collette's idea, maybe she would like to ride on the float." I turned to her. "You should be recognized for all your hard work."

She smiled coolly as if she knew what I was up to. "Thank you for thinking of me, Chloe, but I will be too busy supervising the float to ride on it."

Dean Klink stood. "One more thing . . . each year the parade has a theme. This year it's winter wonderland."

I didn't like the sound of that.

A smile curved on Collette's face, reminding me of Gigabyte

when he was up to something. If she started purring, I was out of there. "That sounds like a nice theme," I murmured.

"It is," the dean replied. "Who would have thought we'd have actual snow this Thanksgiving. Everything will look spectacular."

Collette stood as well and brushed nonexistent specs from her skirt. "Chloe, in keeping with the theme you will have to dress up like a snowman."

A snowman? Did I hear that right?

The dean chuckled. "If we had more time and knew we were making the switch, we would have had the costume changed to a snow woman." He smacked the table and stood.

The marketing director inspected her manicure. "There is also something else I'd like to talk to you about, a special project for the good of the college. I'm sure you're the best person for the job."

"What is it?" I asked.

She glanced at Clark. "We'll discuss it later."

Why do I have a bad feeling about this?

Dean Klink and Collette left the office.

Clark looked as if he were about to burst. "Remember, when you wave to your public to move your hand back and forth like you are screwing in a lightbulb."

"Thanks for the advice." I returned to my office.

Chapter Thirteen

I stumbled out of Dennis, the academic building that held the computer services department, carrying the jumbo mums. It wasn't until I shoved the flowers into the backseat of my car that I realized I'd forgotten to ask Clark and Miller what they knew about Dylan Tanner. I had promised Timothy I would. No time to worry. Both men were long gone and I was late for my appointment at the elementary school. I promised Becky I would be there for the end of her site visit with her probation officer.

It was 4:15 already, so the after-school art program was wrapping up. Thankfully, the elementary school was only a block away from Harshberger.

I pulled into the back lot of the elementary school. Parents sat in their cars with motors running waiting for children to emerge. One by one, fourth and fifth graders stepped out of the school carrying newly fired clay pots and lopsided vases. I moved against the tide of children in the direction of the art room.

Two children remained in the room along with Becky and the art teacher, Ms. Snow. Becky sat across from a freckle-covered eleven-year-old boy. "If you press down on the brush, do you see how the stroke gets wider? The harder you press, the wider your stroke."

The child nodded and stuck out his tongue a little as he painted a red line the width of his vase.

A voice rumbled behind me. "She's doing a great job,"

I spun around to find Carl Fisher, Becky's probation officer, sitting on a stool in the corner of the art room as if the teacher had sent him there for bad behavior. Carl was the size of a lumberjack and had the bushiest eyebrows I'd ever seen. I was sure those eyebrows, not to mention Fisher's size, could be intimidating when he got angry, which came in handy in his profession. He'd never used them when speaking of Becky. He held a clipboard and made notes on an evaluation form.

"I'm glad to hear it," I replied.

He eyed me. "I heard about Ezekiel Young."

I wasn't surprised the probation officer knew about the murder.

Fisher squinted at me. "You okay?"

"I'm fine." Instinctively, I touched the bump on the back of my head. It felt smaller. "I feel horrible for the Young family though. I know how much they relied on Ezekiel to run the business. Ellie, his mother, must be heartbroken."

"It's a horrible thing to lose a loved one to murder." He said this as if he knew something about it. "Who does Greta suspect?"

"I don't know. She hasn't told me, not that I thought she would." I shot a quick glance in Becky's direction to make sure she wasn't listening to us. "Curt and Brock are a possibility. They were released from prison."

"I heard that too," Fisher said.

What hadn't the probation officer heard?

He folded his arms. "I was Curt Fanning's PO a few years back. That boy is as bad as they come."

"Chief Rose doesn't think Curt and Brock would resort to murder."

"I wouldn't be so sure of that," the probation officer murmured. "You and Becky need to be careful. Lock your doors and pay attention to who is around you at all times."

My pulse quickened as his warning sunk in.

Becky waved at us. "Pack up," she told her student. "Your mom's waiting for you outside."

The boy frowned as if he could listen to Becky's instructions forever, and reluctantly began packing his backpack.

"I wish I had a dozen Beckies," Fisher said.

Ms. Snow, a petite woman in her mid-forties, joined us. She wore a tie-dyed T-shirt and a peasant skirt. "I do too. I've noticed a big increase in the numbers of boys interested in the after-school art program since Becky started helping out." She signed the form on Fisher's clipboard.

The other student left the room, and the freckled boy and Becky walked to the classroom door. "Bye, Miss Troyer," the boy said with a slight blush on his cheeks.

Becky smiled. "Bye, Cameron. Happy Thanksgiving."

He grinned back at her and disappeared through the door.

Fisher stood up. "Becky, Ms. Snow tells me you are doing an excellent job, and I can see it with my own eyes. You only have three hundred hours of community service left. I'm sure you will finish that in record time between this and the other places you are volunteering. When you do finish, I'll recommend to the judge that he grant you an early release from probation for good behavior."

Becky's face lit up. "Really?" Her original probation sentence was for one year and wouldn't expire until August of next year.

"I completely support that," Ms. Snow said, giving Becky a little squeeze. "You're doing great and will make a wonderful art teacher one day."

Becky beamed.

Fisher held out his clipboard and a pen. "Sign here to say you received your monthly evaluation."

I found myself smiling. Becky left the Amish to pursue her art as she saw fit. Finally, she received praise for her talent instead of criticism as she had from the leaders in the district.

Fisher set his bowler hat on his head, which made him look like a 1920s mobster, and tipped it at us before leaving the room.

Ms. Snow smiled at Becky. "I want you to seriously think about teaching art, Becky. You're a gifted artist and good with children. That's a hard combination to come by. You will make the perfect art teacher."

"I will think about it," Becky promised.

Ms. Snow nodded. "Good. Now, the classroom door is locked. Just pull it shut when you leave after you finish cleaning up."

"I know what to do."

Ms. Snow nodded at me. "Nice to see you again, Chloe."

I offered to help Becky clean up. We made short work of emptying dirty water cups into the stainless steel sink and rinsing out the paint brushes.

Becky's cell rang. She pulled it out from her pocket and checked the readout. "It's Timothy. I'll get it."

"Go ahead." I held up a blue-tipped paint brush. "This is the last one." I almost asked her to thank him for the flowers but stopped myself. I thought they were from Timothy, but what if they weren't?

I heard the low murmur of Becky's conversation on the phone, but with the water coming full force out of the faucet I couldn't make out the words. I turned off the water and reached for a paper towel to dry the paint brush. I faced Becky, and she looked like someone had just told her *Iron Chef America* was canceled.

I blotted the brush on the paper towel. "What's wrong?"

She swiped a tear from her cheek. "It's *Grossdaddi*."

The throbbing began again in my head. "Is he all right?"

"No. He's at the hospital."

I dropped the paint brush onto the linoleum floor. "What happened?"

"Someone cut off his beard," she whispered.

Chapter Fourteen

When we arrived at the county hospital in Mount Vernon, both the Troyer family buggy and Grandfather Zook's stood tethered to the hitching post. Sparky, Grandfather Zook's beloved horse, wore a forest green horse blanket and neighed at Becky and me as we walked by.

Dear Lord, please let Grandfather Zook be okay.

The automatic emergency room doors opened. Inside the waiting room, Timothy sat with his parents. Mrs. Troyer huddled in her heavy cape and winter bonnet. Her husband wore a black stocking cap pulled down over his ears and a frown. Timothy murmured to his parents before walking over to us.

Becky hugged her brother. "Is he okay?"

Timothy stuck his hands into his jeans pockets. "He will be. He only has a few scrapes and bruises."

Tears gathered in the corners of my eyes. *Praise the Lord*, Grandfather Zook would recover. I felt like I could breathe again. On the drive to the hospital my mind played tricks on me. I had envisioned Grandfather Zook in Ezekiel's place, dead in the pavilion. Although I knew it wasn't true, the image was branded in my mind and would be there until I saw Grandfather Zook alive and well with my own eyes.

"What happened?" I asked just above a whisper.

"*Grossdaddi* was outside of the grocery store when someone jumped him."

Becky gasped.

Timothy shot a glance at his mother, her face buried in a handkerchief. "*Maam* asked him to go pick up a few things for the evening meal."

"How did someone jump him?" I asked.

"He did it while *Grossdaddi* covered Sparky with a horse blanket. The person came up behind him, threw a bag over his head, smashed him against the side of the buggy and cut off his beard."

Becky chewed a layer of lip gloss off of her lower lip. "He could have been killed. Why would anyone do that?"

Timothy shook his head.

"Did the person take his money?" I asked.

"No." Timothy glanced over his shoulder to his parents who whispered to each other in Pennsylvania Dutch. Mrs. Troyer wiped at her eyes, and her husband placed a hand on his wife's arm.

Becky wagged her head. "Who would attack a sick old man like that?"

Who indeed? Curt and Brock came to mind, especially now that the Troyer family was involved. Chief Rose didn't think Curt and Brock would resort to murder, but Probation Officer Fisher did. Since Fisher used to be Curt's PO, he knew Curt better than the chief did, didn't he?

The attack on Grandfather Zook and the three Amish girls must be related to Ezekiel Young's death. Could there be more than one person loose in Knox County cutting off Amish hair? It seemed unlikely. If it were Curt and Brock, why risk going back to prison? Curt, whose father died in the First Iraq War, particularly despised the Amish culture. He felt that the Amish were disloyal to the country by being conscientious objectors. His hatred led him and Brock to harassing the Amish last summer, which ultimately landed the pair in prison. Would they do it again? And so soon?

I removed my winter hat. "Is Chief Rose here?"

Timothy nodded. "She's been here and gone already. She got a callout right after she spoke with *Grossdaddi*."

Becky fingered her braid. "I want to see him."

"The nurse said they'd bring him out as soon as his paperwork for the hospital is complete. It shouldn't be too long now."

Mr. Troyer removed his hand from his wife's arm and stared straight ahead. Through his granite-like expression, it was impossible to know what he was thinking. I felt a twinge of sympathy for him. All he wanted was a simple life and his children to live the Amish way. Instead his two eldest children had left the culture, putting him in a precarious position with the church. Now, his father-in-law had been attacked in a way that seemed so specifically insulting to the Amish life Mr. Troyer loved.

Becky watched her parents. She leaned close to her brother and whispered, "How are *Maam* and *Daed*?"

Timothy's jaw twitched. "*Maam* is a wreck, and you know *Daed*. You can never quite know what he's thinking."

A nurse's aide appeared in the waiting room, pushing Grandfather Zook in a hospital-issued wheelchair. The elderly Amish man clutched his aluminum crutches in his hand. When Grandfather Zook was a child, he had contracted polio during the epidemic. As he aged, his symptoms worsened, and he became more and more dependent on the crutches to walk, and at times, even used a wheelchair. It wasn't often that I would see Grandfather Zook in his wheelchair. He was far too stubborn.

More striking than the wheelchair was the absence of his white, fluffy beard. The beard had once hung down to the middle of his chest and been reminiscent of untreated cotton. Jaggedly cut whiskers hung only an inch from his chin.

Mrs. Troyer jumped from her chair and hugged her father. She spoke to him in Pennsylvania Dutch at breakneck speed. In English, she said, "*Daed*, your beautiful beard. What would *Maam* say?"

He shook his finger at his adult daughter. "Your *maam* would be upset, yes, but not put on such dramatics like this."

His reprimand dried up her tears.

He grabbed her hand. "I'm sorry, *kinner*. I know you are only worried. You have your *maam's* big heart." He plucked at the short whiskers. "This is only hair. It will grow back."

Mrs. Troyer wrung her hands.

The nurse's aide let go of the wheelchair handles. "Do you need help getting him into the car, *er*, buggy?"

Timothy smiled at her. "We got it."

She nodded and left.

"Chloe!" Grandfather Zook's eyes sparkled as they fell on me. "You and Becky didn't have to come all the way to the hospital."

I gave him a hug. "Of course we did. We had to make sure for ourselves that you're okay."

His eyes twinkled. "It's going to take more than a pair of scissors to stop me."

"Were you scared?" Becky held her grandfather's hand.

"It happened too fast to be scared. I was throwing the blanket over Sparky's back and the next thing I knew my face was up against the side of the buggy." He rubbed his cheek. A bruise had begun to form on his right cheekbone. "The good news is Old Spark got a piece of him before the perp got away."

"Perp?" Becky's brows shot up. "Where did you learn that word?"

"That lady police officer said it. I rather like it. It seems fitting for the scoundrel who did this."

"What do you mean he got a piece of him?" Timothy asked.

"Sparky took a bite out of the man's shoulder. You should have heard him scream. Horse bites hurt, and Sparky made this one count. He came away with a mouthful of the perp's coat too."

"Where's the piece of coat?" Timothy asked.

"The lady police officer took it. She said it was evidence."

"I can't believe this is happening." Becky let go of her grandfather's hand and twisted her braid. "First Chloe finds a dead body, and now this."

Internally, I groaned.

Mr. Troyer's head whipped around to his eldest daughter. "What?"

Becky's mouth fell open as she realized her mistake.

"Ezekiel Young is dead." Timothy went on to explain the events at the flea market the day before.

Grandfather Zook paled. "How's Ellie? She must be heartbroken." His eyes narrowed. "Why didn't you tell me about this, *grandkinner*?"

Timothy's brow creased. "I'm sorry. I thought you would have heard it from a neighbor in the district by now."

Mrs. Troyer touched her husband's coat sleeve. "Why didn't we hear this from our neighbors?"

He said something back to her in their language. Mr. Troyer was more comfortable speaking Pennsylvania Dutch, but I knew sometimes he spoke it when he didn't want me to know what was going on.

Becky gave me a tiny, lopsided smile as if she knew what I was thinking.

Grandfather Zook stamped his crutches on the ground. "That's Deacon Sutter's work. He—"

"Let's not speak of this here." Mr. Troyer's tone left no room for debate. "My wife has an evening meal waiting for us back home."

Mrs. Troyer patted my shoulder. "You, Timothy, and Becky are welcome to join us." She seemed more at ease now that she would have the opportunity to feed her family. She was much like Ellie in that way. However, that was the only characteristic shared by the quiet woman and the flamboyant restaurant and flea market owner.

Timothy took hold of the wheelchair's handlebars. "Let's get you to the buggy."

"I can walk." Grandfather Zook pushed himself out of the chair and toppled forward. Mr. Troyer and Timothy steadied him. "Whoa," Grandfather Zook grunted. "I must be more shook up than I thought."

Because of the cold, Grandfather Zook rode with Timothy in his truck. Mr. and Mrs. Troyer went home in their buggy, and Becky drove Sparky and Grandfather Zook's buggy home. I left my car in the hospital lot and rode with Becky.

The hot brick Grandfather Zook placed at his feet for warmth had long since lost its heat. I piled lap blankets over Becky and me and pulled my stocking cap farther down over my ears.

Becky flicked the reins and we backed away from the hitching post. She eased the buggy onto Coshocton Avenue, which was the center of shopping and businesses in the county. "This feels strange."

"What happened to Grandfather Zook?"

"Yes." She pulled Sparky to a stop at a traffic light and in front of a McDonald's. "But I meant driving the buggy. I've driven this buggy hundreds of times but not in months and never wearing jeans."

The light changed, and she made a clicking sound at Sparky. "Until I sat on the seat, I didn't realize how much I missed it."

"That can't be the only part of being Amish you miss."

"It's not. I miss seeing my family every day and *Maam*'s meals. I even miss milking the cows." She laughed. "I don't miss the cows that much, but I guess I miss the routine. The cows were always there needing to be milked twice a day. It was something I could rely on. Now, everyday is different."

"Is variety a bad thing?"

"No, just different." Street light reflected off her teeth when she grinned. "And now that I found the cable television, I don't know how I could ever go back to being Amish."

I laughed and snuggled deeper under the blankets. "What's Thanksgiving like at your house?"

"It's the best." Becky went on to describe all the food, detailing the ingredients and preparations for each dish.

We stopped at the final traffic light on Coshocton, and Sparky knew his way home and pulled the buggy into the left turn lane. A pickup pulled up next to us in the right turn lane. It was green. I grew still as Becky chattered about pickling.

I felt the driver of the green pickup watching me. As if my neck had a will of its own, it turned my head.

Curt Fanning stared back at me. His dirty goatee was scruffier than before, and the features of his angular face were sharper as if he had both lost weight and aged beyond his twenty-five years while in prison. The red glow of the traffic light reflected off of his father's dog tags hanging around his neck.

A slow smile spread across Curt's face. He puckered his lips and made a kissy at me. I recoiled. He turned right on red and was gone.

I stared straight ahead. The light changed and Sparky took the left turn. Blissfully unaware, Becky was describing the proper consistency of turkey gravy.

My heart felt like it would beat out of my chest. I inhaled and exhaled long, deep breaths as quietly as I could.

Chapter Fifteen

I n the Troyer horse barn, Becky covered Sparky with a wool horse blanket. She scratched the white star in the middle of his forehead, and he leaned into her touch like a cat. "You did *gut*, Spark. You probably saved *Grossdaddi* today. You deserve a big bag of carrots."

Sparky whinnied.

We entered the Troyer home from the back door, which opened into a small mudroom. On the other side of the mudroom was the center of the home, Mrs. Troyer's kitchen. The Amish mother spent the majority of her day in this space. It was where she cooked, baked, canned, ironed clothing, and sewed at the large table. Now that I thought about it, every time I visited the Troyer farm, Mrs. Troyer was in the kitchen working, no matter the time of day.

The kitchen had all the appliances an Amish woman, or an English woman for that matter, would need. The refrigerator and stove were powered by propane. The sink had running water. Jars of canned goods lined the shelves of the beautifully-made Amish hutch in the corner of the room, and hand-embroidered tea towels hung from the oven door handle.

While Mrs. Troyer was at the hospital, Ruth, Becky's thirteen-year-old sister, kept the evening meal warm on the propane stove. The girl, who looked more like Becky every day, stirred what looked like stew in the huge cast iron pot on a front burner. Although her light blonde hair and features were like Becky's, her expression resembled her father's stony glare.

I pulled off my gloves. "Hi, Ruth."

She only nodded.

My forehead creased.

Thomas zoomed over to me and took my coat. "Chloe, you came. *Gut!*" He took Becky's coat too.

A smile broke out on my face. The seven-year-old bounced out of the room, dragging our coats on the floor. He was back before I could take another step.

"Thomas, don't run," Mrs. Troyer admonished the boy. Thomas slowed his pace just a tad as he fell onto the bench next to Grandfather Zook at the family's long kitchen table. The table had pine benches on either side and paddle-backed chairs at the ends. The table ran the length of the kitchen, the largest room in the Troyer home, and could seat up to twelve people. Grandfather Zook sat at one end of the table, warming his hands on a large mug of coffee. The jagged edge of his beard had already been trimmed. "What took you two so long?"

Becky rolled her eyes and gave her grandfather a hug before helping Ruth and her mother finish preparing the meal.

Mrs. Troyer moved around her kitchen with confidence she never displayed outside of the safety of her own home.

"Can I help you?" I asked.

Like I knew she would, she shook her head. "You're a guest."

I wondered if there would ever be a time when I would no longer be considered a guest.

Timothy sat closest to the wall, and I was struck by how well he seemed to fit in to this place. I bit my lip. Did he miss being part of the Amish like Becky did? Would he ever want to go back? As much as I cared for him, I knew a transition from English to Amish was one I could never make.

Naomi, the youngest Troyer, who had just turned four, was curled up on Timothy's lap. She looked up at me with watery blue eyes. She clutched her faceless doll under her arm and said something in Pennsylvania Dutch to Timothy. She was still a year from school. The little English she knew she learned from her brothers and sisters. When I visited the Troyer farm, they often spoke English so that I could understand. She gave me a small smile and murmured, "Chloe here."

My heart melted.

Ruth and Becky buzzed about the room, setting the table. Mr. Troyer was absent.

"My son-in-law is checking on the cows," Grandfather Zook said as if he read my mind. He patted the empty bench seat next to him. "Chloe, you sit right here next to me. The women will knock you down if you get in their way."

Ruth flew by me with a crock of stew. Grandfather Zook was right.

Thomas wiggled in his seat. "I'm glad that Sparky took a bite out of the perp."

I couldn't help but smile. Apparently, Grandfather Zook had shared his new favorite English word with the children.

"Thomas!" Mr. Troyer's voice cracked like a whip as he stepped into the room. "There will be none of that. The Lord commands us to forgive."

Thomas dropped his head. "*Ya, Daed.*"

Mr. Troyer held the door open as he removed his work boots in the mudroom. A cold burst of wintry air blew through the kitchen.

A paper napkin on the table took flight, and Naomi giggled into Timothy's shoulder. He whispered something to her in their language, and her giggles increased.

The door slammed shut after Mr. Troyer entered room. He washed his hands at the sink.

"How do you think my trim looks?" Grandfather Zook scratched his chin and turned it back and forth, so that I could have a good look at it. "My beard hasn't been this short since I was Becky's age."

"You look distinguished," I whispered, knowing that Mr. Troyer would not approve of my praising the shorter beard.

He grinned. "I think so too. It will grow back better than ever." He lowered his voice. "I do have one of the best beards in the county. This is probably why I was singled out. Beard jealously."

I smiled, but my tone was serious. "Are you sure you weren't hurt? It must have been frightening."

"It was a shock, that's for sure. I only have a few bruises, nothing a pack of ice and a hot water bottle can't mend."

Ruth slammed a basket of rolls on the table between Grandfather Zook and me. Several fell out of the basket, and I quickly put them back. I raised my eyebrow at Grandfather Zook. He shook his head.

Carefully, Becky placed a large tureen of stew in the middle of table, and the Troyer women took their seats. Mr. Troyer said grace in their language, and Becky whispered the translation into my ear, "And comfort the Young family during this time of loss." Stew, rolls, biscuits, and mixed vegetables were passed around the table.

Ruth's smooth brow crinkled. "What's wrong with the Young family?"

Mr. and Mrs. Troyer shared a look across the table. "Ezekiel Young passed away yesterday."

Ruth frowned. "I didn't know he was sick. I saw him a few weeks ago when I delivered cheese to Young's and he was fine."

"He wasn't sick," Becky said.

Ruth's head snapped around in her sister's direction. "What would you know about it?"

Becky gripped her spoon. "I work at the Young's restaurant and saw Ezekiel almost everyday. He wasn't sick."

"Then, what happened?" Ruth looked to her parents for the answer. "Was there an accident?"

"Let's not speak of it in front of the younger children," Mrs. Troyer said.

Ruth's lower lip protruded from her mouth. "We can never speak of anything because of the children."

"Ruth," her father's voice cut through the air like a knife. "That is enough."

Tears welled in her eyes. "No one will talk to me about anything. I'm tired of it."

Her father slammed his coffee mug on the table. "Ruth, you're excused from the table."

She opened her mouth and then closed it. "Fine." She picked up her dish, walked it over to the sink, and stalked from the room.

We ate in silence for several minutes. Both Naomi and Thomas kept their heads down. Mrs. Troyer touched her youngest son's arm. "If you're finished, take Naomi upstairs to play."

He nodded and pulled his little sister from the room. Before they left, Naomi gave Becky, Timothy, and me each a goodbye kiss.

Mrs. Troyer began to clear away the children's dishes. She had barely touched her food.

"Why is Ruth so upset?" Timothy asked.

Mr. Troyer's brow furrowed.

Grandfather Zook buttered a roll. "Anna Lambright's parents won't let the girls see each other."

I frowned. Anna was Ruth's best friend.

"Why not?" Becky asked.

"The bishop believes our family is a poor example to the district." Grandfather Zook broke off a piece of his roll and held it. "And we may lead others away from the Amish way." He tossed the bite of roll into his mouth.

Becky's mouth fell open. "Who have you led from the Amish way?"

"You."

Becky's head jerked back.

Grandfather Zook sighed. "And Timothy. Had we have been a more Amish family, you would not have chosen to leave."

"Are you being shunned?" Timothy asked.

"*Nee*," Mrs. Troyer said as she retook her seat.

Becky's forehead creased. "What does the bishop expect of you? Does he think we will come back?"

Mrs. Troyer moved food around her plate with the back of her fork.

"No," Mr. Troyer said. "But he wants us to be more Amish."

"How much more Amish could you get?" Becky asked.

Mr. Troyer sipped his coffee. "The first step is distancing ourselves from you and Timothy." He glanced at me. "And Chloe."

Tears welled in Becky's eyes. "What?"

Mr. Troyer's typically stern face softened. "I'm sure this is only temporary until the new bishop finds his way. When he is in charge of the district for some time, he will see there's no danger in seeing *Englisch* children. Until then, we need to limit how often you come to the house."

Timothy gripped his spoon so tightly the edge made an indentation in his skin. "How long is temporary?"

"A few months, until we can prove to the bishop we have taken his guidance to heart." Mr. Troyer set the dinner roll he was about to take a bite from back on his plate as if he had lost his appetite. I knew I had lost mine.

Becky's eyes welled with tears. "It's because of me, isn't it? Even though I left the church, it's still trying to control me by hurting you."

Mrs. Troyer wrung her hands. "The bishop said—"

"It wasn't the bishop." Timothy clenched his jaw. "Deacon Sutter is behind this. He was with the bishop when he delivered the news, wasn't he?"

Since moving to Appleseed Creek, I'd received a crash course in Amish governance. The bishop was the head of the district and set the rules. Each district had its own bishop. Rules varied between districts depending on who the bishop was since everything was at his discretion. Much had changed in the Appleseed Creek district because Bishop Glick had been a relatively liberal bishop. Apparently, Bishop Hooley was not. The deacon was the district's enforcer. He was the one who made sure everyone followed the rules that the bishop established.

Timothy's mother wouldn't meet his eyes. "Your father is right. The bishop will relax his rules after a time. Bishop Glick never shunned anyone over seeing their *Englisch* children."

Becky gnawed on her lower lip. "I thought you said you weren't being shunned."

Her father's brow furrowed. "We're not. Yet."

His announcement fell like a lead weight in the middle of the table. The implication being that the family would be shunned if Becky, Timothy, and I continued to visit them.

"We aren't dealing with Bishop Glick anymore." Timothy placed his hands on the table. "He's dead. Deacon Sutter will hurt our family anyway that he can. He is using Bishop Hooley as his puppet. He must be thrilled he finally has a bishop who will make the rules he wants to enforce."

Mr. Troyer glared at his son. "Don't speak of the deacon that way in my house."

"But *Daed*—"

"He's a leader in the community and deserves respect." His father's face softened. "*Gott* will help us, but we must obey the rules even if we don't agree with them."

"What about Thanksgiving?" Becky cried.

Mrs. Troyer dropped a dish, and it shattered on the floor. "*Es dutt mir leed*," she apologized and knelt on the floor to began picking up the ceramic pieces.

I sprang from my seat. "Let me." I crouched on the floor next to her.

"*Nee*, it is my fault."

I placed a hand over hers. "Please."

She nodded and stood.

Grandfather Zook stamped the end of his butter knife on the table. "Thanksgiving is different. You will come here. Martha makes a meal like no other."

Mr. Troyer gripped his coffee mug. "The bishop . . ."

"I don't care what the bishop said. It's a holiday. We can start obeying his rule after Thanksgiving." The older man folded his arms across his chest as if the issue were settled.

Mr. Troyer's brows knit together and his nostrils flared.

Grandfather stirred milk into his coffee. "Besides the Glick-Yoder wedding is on Thanksgiving. The whole district will be there. They'll be too busy to worry about us."

"You're not going to the wedding?" Timothy asked.

"No, we're not." Mr. Troyer's voice clearly said he didn't want to talk about the Glick-Yoder wedding.

Mrs. Troyer stared at her husband as if pleading with him. His stern expression softened just a tad. "Fine. They can come for Thanksgiving." He didn't look at me but added, "Chloe too."

A grin spread across Grandfather Zook's face. "Chloe, will you help me into the living room? I'd like to sit a spell."

I stood and helped him into his crutches, then took his elbow as we shuffled into the adjoining room. I set him on a gray armchair and placed his feet on an ottoman. He settled into the seat. "Much better."

"Grandfather Zook, can you tell me anything more about the person who cut off your beard?"

"What do you want to know?"

"You said Sparky bit the man's shoulder. You think the attacker was a man?"

He touched his short whiskers. "Yes, it sounded like a man when he cried out."

"How big was he?"

"I can't say. Are you helping the lady police officer again?"

I didn't answer his question directly. "Could what happened to you be related to Ezekiel's murder and the attack on the four Amish girls?"

He took my hand. His cool and dry grasp felt like crepe paper. "Don't put yourself at risk on my account. I don't seek vengeance for what happened. *Gott* will use this for *gut*."

I squeezed his hand but couldn't help wondering if that were true. I swallowed, gathering courage to ask my next question. "Will the family be shunned?"

He settled back into his seat. "I can't say. I know things are changing in the district, and change puts folks on edge. Hooley has a tough job stepping into Glick's shoes. There wasn't a more beloved bishop in the district than Glick. Perhaps Hooley believes he needs to flaunt his authority by being strict to get folks to give him respect." He took my hand again. "Don't worry about that. *Gott* knows we've done nothing wrong. Everything will be as the Lord wants it in the end."

His response did little to alleviate the guilt I felt by putting the Troyer family in this position with the district. On Thanksgiving,

I would allow myself one final day to be with all of them, but after the holiday, I would stay away from the farm.

Timothy drove Becky and me back to the hospital to collect my car and then followed us home. The moment I parked in the driveway, Becky ran into the house, leaving me to struggle with the monster mums.

Timothy got out of the truck and held the car door open for me. "What is that?"

My heart sank a little at his question. If he didn't know what the mums were, he didn't send them. "Someone sent flowers to my office today."

Even in the dim light, I saw his brow wrinkle. "Who would do that?"

My heart sank a little further. I gave the flowers one final yank, and they popped out of the Bug. I stumbled back, and Timothy placed a hand on my back to steady me.

He took the flowers from my arms, which hid his face. "Where's the note?"

"The student who delivered them lost it, and before you ask, she didn't read it."

"Why would someone send you flowers?" The pitch of his voice rose, as if he were confused.

I slammed the Bug's door. "Is it hard to believe someone would want to send me flowers?"

"N-no." He dropped the arrangement a few inches so I could see his face. "Maybe they are from your dad?"

I snorted. My father could afford an expensive arrangement, but he certainly didn't have the time or desire to send it.

"Tanisha?"

"I doubt it. She barely has enough money to pay her rent." This conversation grated on my nerves. Maybe it was a secret admirer. What would Timothy think about that? Was that so impossible to

believe? It was time to change the subject. "Listen, I've been thinking about Grandfather Zook."

"We all have." Timothy walked the flowers to the porch and set
them by the door. He sat on the porch steps as if he knew this was
going to be a long conversation.

I turned up the collar of my winter coat to keep as much of the
cold wind off of my skin as possible. "Grandfather Zook believes
his attacker was a man."

Timothy stuck his hands deep into his coat pockets. "You think
a woman could have done that? Thrown him against the buggy and
cut off his beard?"

I gave him a crooked smile. "That was mildly sexist. Women
commit crimes as well as men, and there are some that are strong
enough to do that." I paused. "We need to talk to the other victims."

He sighed. "The other victims?"

"Of the haircutting."

Timothy's mouth formed a straight line.

"I spoke with Miller about it today."

Timothy's brow shot up. "Miller, why?"

"His cousin is Leah Miller."

"I know who Leah is. She's a couple of years younger than
Becky."

"She was one of the girls who had her hair cut."

Timothy grew very still. "And that's why you talked to Miller
about it."

I nodded.

"You want us to get involved again." His voice was soft.

"We are already involved. Look what happened to your grandfather today, and I found Ezekiel . . ."

He pursed his lips. "I don't like it. I don't want you to get hurt."

I grinned at him. "If you help me, you can make sure I won't."

He watched me. "You're going to do this whether I help you or not."

"Yep."

He shook his head. "Okay. But I think it's a bad idea, and so will Greta."

"That's the right attitude."

He rolled his eyes.

"I want to start tomorrow. Miller told me Leah works at The Apple Core downtown."

"I know. It's a gift shop that sells Amish trinkets to *Englischers*."

"Right. I plan to stop by there tomorrow morning and talk to her. Can you come with me?"

He shook his head. "I promised Uri I'd meet him at Young's first thing. He'd like me to check the pavilion job site to make sure that everything is okay now that the police are out of there. He can't bring himself to go back inside it."

"That's understandable. How is he?"

"He didn't sound good on the phone."

"He not only lost his brother, he lost his twin. It must be like losing a piece of yourself."

"Ezekiel and Uri were twins, but they were so different. You saw that Sunday at the dinner. I'm sure Uri is devastated, but the twins never struck me as particularly close. At least they weren't as close as other twins I know."

I shivered. "Something has been nagging at me."

"What's that?"

"If we take for granted that all the haircutting attacks are related, why was Ezekiel the only one killed?"

Timothy shifted into his seat. "That's a good question. Grandfather Zook didn't see his attacker, but maybe Ezekiel did and was killed so that he couldn't talk."

"If he saw him, Ezekiel would have fought back. He's not a small guy."

"Did you see any sign of a struggle?"

After two days of trying to forget what I saw, I forced myself to remember the scene. Images flashed across my mind: the orange electrical cords snaking across the floor, the air-compressed nail gun, the sawhorse that tripped me up, Ezekiel's beard and glasses covered in sawdust, the shears sticking out of his back, and the toolbox lying on the floor.

"There is something," I said.

"What?"

"A large tool box was on its side. Some of the drawers were opened and tools were on the floor."

"That's something," Timothy said. "Ezekiel was far too precise to treat his tools that way."

I buried my hands deeper into my pockets. "I wonder if Ezekiel had any other injuries, like defensive wounds."

"That's something we will have to ask the chief."

He was right. "It's probably best you can't come with me to The Apple Core tomorrow," I said, changing the subject. "Leah is more likely to talk to me alone. Woman to woman. I hope to meet the other two girls attacked too. Miller said their names are Abby and Debbie, and he said they work at The Apple Core too."

"They must be Debbie Stutzman and Abby Zug. You might want to talk to Becky. She went to the Amish schoolhouse with them."

"I will."

He touched my chin and turned my face toward his. "Promise me you will be careful."

I swallowed. "I promise." I would be willing to promise him so much more.

He let go of my face and stood. "You'd better go inside. It is too cold to sit out here."

I couldn't disagree more. Reluctantly, I stood.

Timothy picked up the flower arrangement while I opened the front door.

Becky lay on her dog pillow in the middle of the living room, watching yet another Thanksgiving cooking special. *Honestly, how many ways were there to cook turkey?*

Becky rolled over onto her back. "Do you think Daed would let us deep-fry a turkey this year?"

Timothy arched a brow at me. "You let her watch too much TV."

"Hey, she's an adult."

Becky grinned. "That's right."

"Where should I put this?" Timothy asked.

"By the front window is fine."

He set the pot down. "If you find out who sent these, let me know."

I shrugged. "Sure." I held back the question on the tip of my tongue. *Why do you care?*

Chapter Sixteen

The next morning, I woke up at six as I normally would on a work day. When I remembered the events of the last few days, I couldn't fall back to sleep. I lay in bed and listened to Becky dress for work. She had a long day ahead of her in the Young's pie shop. She said there were over six hundred pie orders for Thanksgiving Day.

Even though the Young family was devastated by Ezekiel's murder, the restaurant and shop had to stay open this week for Thanksgiving, one of the busiest weeks of the year for them. I wondered if Ellie would be at the restaurant. If it were me, I would stay at home and let the staff handle the preparations. Becky poked her head into my room to say goodbye. Her bike was out of commission, but she was getting a ride from a friend that morning.

I propped myself up on my pillows. Her prayer cap, which was part of her uniform, sat lopsided on her head. "Hey, before you go. What do you know about Leah Miller?"

"Leah?" She straightened her cap. "Why do you want to know about her?"

"I'm going to talk to her today. She's one of the girls who got her hair cut off."

"Really?"

"Why is that so surprising?"

"Well, Leah is about the last Amish girl I'd expect that to happen to. She was a couple of years behind me in school, but I remember she was bossy. She always wanted to be the leader in everything. If she didn't have her family's store to manage, I always thought she'd make a great Amish teacher. She'd certainly keep the students in line. She wouldn't spare the rod either."

"Even with a tough exterior, if someone came up behind her, that person could have overpowered her."

Becky twisted her mouth as if considering this. "I guess."

"What about her friends Debbie and Abby?"

"You must mean Debbie Stutzman and Abby Zug. They were always Leah's sidekicks, not the friendliest girls in the world, but more so than Leah. They were always together. So much in fact, our teacher called them the triplets."

Beep! Beep!

"That's my ride. Gotta go!"

I swung my legs over the bed. It was time to meet the triplets.

THE LEAVES HAD LONG since fallen from the large oak trees in the middle of the square, and I could look out over the grounds right into the Amish Bread Bakery. Inside, Sadie placed pie in the display window. I hoped I would have a chance to talk to her.

The Apple Core was on the opposite side of the square and catered to English visitors touring Amish Country. In the summer, it wasn't unusual to have three or four tour buses in town on a weekend day. At ten in the morning, a bus idled in front of the store, BUCKEYE COUNTRY TOURS, etched on the side of it. Two men sat outside the store on a park bench. One wore a gray ivy cap. The other wore earmuffs, his bald head red from the cold.

"You think I should go in there and see what damage my wife is doing to my credit card?" *Earmuffs* asked his companions.

"Nah," *Ivy Cap* said. "It's too painful to watch." He wiggled his bushy eyebrows at me. "Hi there, little lady. You from around here?"

Was I from around there? No, definitely not. "I live in town."

"Can you tell us where two old dodgers can get a cup of joe?" He hooked a thumb at the gift shop. "The women are in there blowing our Social Security checks. We'd like a warm cup of coffee before we climb on the bus to hear about all the wonderful Amish-made doilies they bought."

"I hate doilies," Earmuffs piped up. "I used one as a coaster once, and the wife went ballistic."

I suppressed a chuckle. "There is a bakery across the square. They have lots of good treats to eat and a small coffee counter."

Earmuffs smacked his lips. "Do they have cinnamon rolls? I heart those."

"*Heart?* What are you talking about, you nut?"

"That's what my granddaughter says. She hearts everything. I'm trying out the lingo, so I can connect with the young folks. I figure she's less likely to stick me in a home that way."

"You're cracked." Ivy Cap smiled at me. "Thanks for the tip, toots." The pair shuffled away.

Through The Apple Core's front window I watched ladies ooh and ah over a display of hand-painted Amish figures. Quilted placemats, Christmas ornaments, and even doilies filled their plastic shopping baskets. The men were right—their Social Security checks were toast.

The apple-shaped bell rang when I stepped into the store. At least twenty ladies crowded the shop.

One held up a faceless Amish doll that reminded me of Naomi's favorite toy. "Should I get this for my granddaughter?" she asked a friend.

Her friend scrunched up her face. "I thought she asked for a Barbie Princess."

"She did, but this is close enough."

"Your granddaughter might not agree."

A counter with a cash register was on the right side of the room. An Amish girl I suspected was Leah Miller stood behind the counter. She was petite with brown hair and a prayer cap on the top of her head. Her features were sharp and looked much like her cousin's. I stepped around a blue-haired woman in polyester pants and winter coat three sizes too large who examined a magnet display with such concentration that I doubted she would be able to make up her mind before Christmas.

I smiled at the young woman behind the counter. "Leah?"

The Amish girl nodded.

"I'm, Ch—"

The blue-haired woman knocked me in the shin with her cane. I jumped back. "Ouch!"

"There's a line, missy, and you better get to the end of it."

Her cronies agreed in angry whispers.

Leah gave me a tiny smile and accepted the two dollars from the woman for a magnet shaped like an Amish buggy.

As Leah placed the money into the cash register, a strand of hair fell from beneath her prayer cap. The lock's jagged edge dangled behind her ear. It was clear it had been cut.

The English woman squinted at her and pointed a bent finger. "Is your hair cut? Amish women don't cut their hair. I saw a special about it on public television." She turned back to a friend. "Her hair is cut. She's not Amish. She's an imposter." She slapped the magnet back onto the counter. "I don't want to buy an Amish magnet from a fake Amish girl."

Leah clenched her jaw.

I stepped up to the counter. "She is Amish."

The woman looked me up and down. "How would you know? You aren't Amish."

"I live in Appleseed Creek."

She sniffed. "I don't believe you. Amish women don't cut their hair. I saw it on television." She spun around, whacking me in the shin again with her cane and stomp-hobbled out of the door.

A middle-aged woman hurried to the counter. "I'm so-so sorry. Maureen takes her television programs very seriously." She lowered her voice. "She thinks the TV talks to her." Her face reddened as she grabbed two handfuls of Amish magnets. "Here, I'll take these."

The remainder of the women purchased their items and left the store. The bell jangled after the last one.

Leah pulled a bobby pin from her apron pocket and tucked the offending lock of hair back into place.

"I feel like I have to apologize for that." I adjusted my purse strap on my shoulder.

"Why?"

I smiled. "I guess because they are English from the city and I am too."

She shook her head. "I've heard worse. Unfortunately, I have to bite my tongue. Senior tour buses keep the shop open." A small smile formed on her lips. "No one from Appleseed Creek would buy that many magnets."

"I'm—"

"I know who you are. Darren said you would stop by the store today."

It sounded odd to hear Miller called by his first name.

"I'm sorry about your hair."

The tears flooded her green eyes, giving them a swampy appearance.

"Did Mill—Darren say why I wanted to talk to you?"

"He said you found Ezekiel Young's body."

I nodded.

"I'm sorry to hear that. What a horrible thing."

The memory came back to me—the cut beard and the shears sticking out of his back. "It was."

She smiled as if she appreciated the honest answer.

"His beard was cut off."

"Darren told me. I still don't know what that has to do with me."

I removed my scarf. "I can't help but think it's connected to what happened to you and your friends."

"It could be."

"Can you tell me about it?"

She squinted at me. "Why should I? Darren already made me talk to the police, which my parents didn't like, and he told the *Englisch* newspaper about it."

"I know, but I thought I could help too."

She touched her prayer cap as if to make sure it was still in place, and arched an eyebrow at me. "Because you found a dead person?"

"Something else has happened."

She moved down the counter and began putting the magnet display back together. "What has happened?"

"Grandfather Zook was attacked last night. Someone cut off his beard."

She dropped the plow magnet she held, and it clattered on to the glass counter top. "How is that possible?"

I shook my head.

"Why would anyone do that to a sick old man?"

I grimaced slightly, knowing Grandfather Zook would have
hated to be described in those terms. "You can see why I'm sure
curious about what happened to you now."

"I know you have an interest in the Troyer family. I know you
and Timothy are courting."

She did? We were?

She returned to tinkering with the display. "Grandfather Zook
is one of the nicest men in the district. I can't believe someone
would do that to him. Ezekiel Young is another story. He was an
old grouch. I'm sure there are many people who aren't shedding a
tear over his death."

"Like who?"

She slid back to her place behind the cash register. "I shouldn't
have said that. It was wrong. *Gott* forgive me."

"Do you know someone who may want to see Ezekiel dead?"

"I can't speak of it. It's wrong. I don't know anything for sure."

"But—"

"I said I won't speak of it," she snapped.

I stepped back. "Okay, I'm sorry." I paused. "Can you tell me
about your attack? And the ones on your friends?"

She licked her lips. "I will because Darren asked me too, and I
trust my cousin even though he is an *Englischer*."

"Thank you," I murmured. "Grandfather Zook believes his
attacker was a man. Do you think so?"

She watched the front door as if she were pleading with a tour
bus to arrive. "Yes. It was definitely a man."

"How do you know? Did you see him?"

"No."

"Did you hear him?"

Irritation flicked across her face. "No, but I know it was a man.
I could tell."

I decided to let that line of question go for now. "Can you tell me what happened?"

"What did Grandfather Zook say?" She stepped around the counter and began to straighten pamphlets that sat in a wire rack by the glass front door.

"He said someone came up from behind him, pushed him against his buggy, threw a bag over his head, and cut off his beard."

Her hands moved quickly through the pamphlet rack. It was a wonder she didn't get a paper cut. "Yes, that's similar to what happened to me. I was stopped on the side of the road. The chain on my bicycle fell off of the gears, and I was fixing it. I guess I was concentrating so hard I didn't hear the man come up behind me."

"Were you wearing a bonnet?"

"Yes."

"He put a bag over your head? It must have been large to fit over your bonnet."

She walked back behind the counter. "It was. It was a burlap potato bag that held thirty to forty potatoes."

"Where is it?"

"The bag?"

I nodded.

"I threw it away. I don't want something around to remind me of what happened."

That couldn't have made Chief Rose very happy. She would have wanted the bag for evidence.

"Is there anything that you remember about the man?"

She shook her head. "It happened so fast."

"I would like to talk to Debbie and Abby too. When will they be here at the store?"

Her eyes widened. "I don't think they will talk to you." She pulled a feather duster out from under the counter and began dusting around the cash register and displays. "I can talk to them for you."

"I think I should talk to them myself."

"Fine." She examined my face. "They'll be in after five helping me display the Christmas stock. You can talk to them while we work. There's much to be done, so I hope you won't take up too much of our time."

"Thank you." I nodded. "Have you spoken to Sadie Hooley?"

Her nose wrinkled. "What about Sadie?"

"She was also attacked. Maybe she can be here too for our talk?"

A strange look crossed Leah's face. "Sadie is not a close friend of mine. If you want to talk to her, you will have to do that yourself."

"You don't know her?"

"I know Sadie, of course. We were in school together but are not friends."

"Who are Sadie's friends?"

"Sometimes I would see her with Becky Troyer before she left the district. Mostly, she's by herself." She pursed her lips. "Her father is the bishop."

"Has Bishop Hooley spoken to you since the attack?"

Her mouth drew into a thin line. "Yes—to ask me not to talk about it. I guess I broke that rule. Just another of the dozens he's set on the district since being chosen bishop. My father says *Gott* chose him, but why would *Gott* choose such a weak man to lead? Everyone knows Deacon Sutter is telling the bishop what to do. Finally, the deacon got the power he wanted." She blushed. "I'm sorry. I spoke out of turn. I shouldn't speak that way about the bishop or the deacon, especially to an *Englischer*."

"I know much in the district has changed since Bishop Glick's death."

"Too much." She looked at the analog clock on the wall. "I must get back to work. Come back at five if you would like to talk to my friends."

"I'll be here," I said, hoping that she would keep her promise.

Chapter Seventeen

I left the store lost in thought. The attack on Leah sounded so much like what happened to Grandfather Zook. The attacker came up from behind both of them when they were distracted by a task and threw bags over their heads. I shivered. It would be good advice to all the Amish to watch their backs.

I paused in the middle of the sidewalk. If there was a burlap bag over the girls' heads, how did the attacker cut off their hair? Something about Leah's story didn't compute, and there wasn't a burlap bag near Ezekiel Young's body. His eyes were open and glassy when I found him. Of course, the attacker may have taken it with him. Ezekiel was stabbed in the back. Was it possible there were two Amish haircutters in the county? It was hard to believe. Timothy said nothing like this had ever happened in the district before.

"Red, if you think any harder, smoke's gonna come out of your ears."

I jumped away from the voice I knew too well. Curt.

He and Brock stood behind me, and I knew how they could sneak up on people without their knowledge. I started walking, unsure of where to go. I didn't want them to follow me home although they already knew where I lived.

"Where are you going, Red?" Baby-faced Brock sneered at me. In two steps he was beside me matching my stride.

"Leave me alone."

Brock shook his head. "I thought you would be happy to see us since we've been gone for a little while."

"As far as I'm concerned, you can go back to jail." I increased my pace, but it was still three strides to Brock's one step.

Curt came up on my other side. "That hurts."

My jaw twitched.

Brock cracked his knuckles. "Red still has all of her sauciness, Curt."

Curt gave a dramatic sigh. "I noticed, brother."

Brock rubbed his chin. "I heard you found a dead guy."

I swung around. "What do you know about it?"

Curt's eyes narrowed. "Nothing. Why would I know anything?"

I glared at Brock. "Do you know something?"

"Me. Nope. Nothing."

"It's not like you'd tell me if you did."

Curt sucked air in through his teeth. "Why would we? So you can run to your Amish boyfriend or the chief and turn us in?"

Brock frowned. "I'm bummed. I thought you'd be the forgive-and-forget type, Red. Isn't that what they preach in your church?"

"I'm out of here." I walked faster.

"Now, wait a minute." Brock stepped in front of me. "We want to talk to you."

I dodged around him and headed in the direction of town hall.

Curt stopped on the sidewalk. "Looks like she's walking us to the police station."

I kept going.

Brock stopped too. "I'd rather not run into the chief. She's hot and all but has an attitude worse than yours."

"See you around, Red," Brock called after me when I turned the corner of town hall. I stood outside the door to the village police station, trying to catch my breath. I bit my lip. *Should I go inside and tell Chief Rose I saw Curt and Brock?*

The navy blue metal door flew open and nearly missed my nose. The person on the other side pulled up short. "I'm so sorry." Her voice was breathless.

It was an Amish woman, her eyes hidden by a large black bonnet.

"Sadie?"

She peered out from under the bonnet's brim. "Hello." She skittered about me and disappeared around the corner of town hall.

I hurried after her, Curt and Brock nowhere in sight. "Can I talk to you for a minute?"

She blinked at me from behind her glasses. "I need to return to the bakery."

"What were you doing at the police station?"

She increased her pace. "I really must go."

"Sadie, please, I was the one who found Ezekiel Young's body."

She pulled up short and turned around slowly. Tears sprang to her eyes.

"Are you all right?"

"No," she whispered.

I pointed at a park bench in front of town hall beneath the American flag. "Let's sit for a minute."

She sank onto the bench as if her legs no longer had the strength to hold her up. I sat next to her and noticed a quarter-sized abrasion on her cheek for the first time.

A hand flew to her cheek. "It's getting better."

"Is that from the attack?"

She lowered her shaking hand. "It's from the bag that was over my head."

Then the bag part was true.

"Were you at the police station to talk about your attack?"

She nodded slowly as if it took effort to move her head up and down.

"Why?" I couldn't help but ask. "I thought you weren't willing to speak to the police."

"Ezekiel," she whispered.

"Because of Ezekiel's death?"

She turned to me. "We were going to get married, and now he's gone."

My mouth fell open. "Married?"

She removed a handkerchief from her sleeve and twisted it in her lap. "I went to the police to tell them what happened to me." Self-consciously, she touched the back of her bonnet as if to feel for the missing bun there. "I will do anything to help find the person who did this."

"What did Chief Rose say?"

"She was very kind. She will do what she can."

"Who knew you and Ezekiel were to marry?"

"No one knew. I wanted to take it slow because *Daed* is the bishop. I didn't want my family to deal with too much change all at once. I needed to be home to help *Maam* with the children. *Daed* is gone so much now. I told Ezekiel we could marry next year after life is calmer for my family. He was patient and agreed."

In my mind, I tried to place grouchy Ezekiel Young and timid Sadie Hooley together as a married couple. The picture didn't fit. "Did anyone in his family know? His mother?"

She shook her head.

"His twin brother?"

She worried her thumbnail. "No. Uri and Ezekiel were twins but not close."

I wondered how they could keep this a secret in such a small place like Appleseed Creek. I told her about Grandfather Zook.

Sadie dropped her handkerchief on the sidewalk as her hands fluttered her mouth. "This person has to be stopped, which is why I went to the police. If my father or the deacon knew, I would be in trouble."

I handed her the handkerchief. "I want to help the police find who's responsible too." I shifted in my seat. The chill from the cold, cement park bench crept into my back and thighs.

"The police asked for your help?"

I avoided the question. "Chief Rose has spoken to me about it." I didn't add that she was questioning me in relation to my discovery of Ezekiel Young's body. "Can you tell me what you told her?"

"There's not much to tell. It was early morning, a little before four o'clock. I was unlocking the back door to go into the bakery, the one in the alley. It was my turn to get the breads started for the day. Someone came up from behind me, threw a bag over my head and pushed me against the wall." She shivered. I didn't know if it was the result of the cold or the memory.

"Then what?"

"There are two steps in the alley to the back entrance. The person threw me off of the steps and pressed my face into the ground." She touched her cheek again. "That is how I got this mark. After that, it was a blur because I was just trying to breathe. I felt his knees in my back and he pulled the bag up in the back, ripped off my bonnet, and cut off my bun. I can still hear the sound of the shears ripping through my hair. I will never forget the sound." She folded and refolded the handkerchief in her gloved hands. "Then, I heard footsteps running away. I didn't dare move until I knew he was gone. I don't know how long I lay there frozen in fear. Esther found me."

"Was it a man who attacked you?"

"I don't know, but it must have been. The person on my back wore trousers. I would have known if the attacker had worn a skirt. I didn't hear a woman's skirts, which are always loud in the winter with all the layers."

I didn't bother to tell her that most non-Amish women wore pants. "Did the person say anything?"

"Not a word. I think that was one of the most frightening things about it." She gave a shuddered sigh. "The chief said I was helpful, but I didn't feel like I was."

"When the person ran away, what did it sound like?"

She closed her eyes as if she was picturing the scene in her mind. "Loud footsteps."

"More than one?"

"I—I don't know. Maybe." She frowned. "There was another sound. After the footsteps ran away, I heard a vehicle cut through the alley."

"After the footsteps stopped?"

She nodded. "It could have been completely unrelated."

Or it may have been the getaway car—or green truck.

"Did you tell Chief Rose all of this?"

"Yes." She held the handkerchief over her eyes. "It's too much . . ."

"I'm sorry about Ezekiel . . ."

"When my hair was cut, I thought that was the worst blow I could suffer. Ezekiel comforted me. He said it would grow back. But the last time I saw him we fought. I felt he should be more upset by what happened to me. He was sad of course, but not angry. I wanted him to be angry. He could become angry so easily over so many things. I thought this deserved his wrath." Her breath caught.

"I didn't know then that I would suffer a much worse loss. I would shave my head to have my beloved back." She buried her face in her handkerchief.

I placed a hand on her back. A large tour bus drove by on its way to the square. Tourists stared out the window at us, and I saw several iPhones and digital cameras pointed in our direction. What an interesting attraction we made. An English woman in jeans and a wool Old Navy coat comforting an Amish woman in skirts, cape, and bonnet. I suspected the shot would be floating somewhere on the Internet within seconds. In that instant, I understood why the Amish shied away from cameras.

She sat up. "Would you like to see?"

"Your hair?"

She nodded. "Maybe it will help you."

I didn't know how, but I agreed. She removed her bonnet. Instead of an elaborate bun there was a stubby ponytail, two inches long. Sadie had the bonnet off for only a few seconds. Thankfully, she replaced it before another tour bus made its way down the street.

"Thank you for talking to me," I said.

She stood and tucked her handkerchief back into her sleeve. "I know hatred is wrong, but I hate whoever did this. Please find them, and stop them."

A knot grew in my stomach. "I'll try." *How could I ever make such a promise?*

She thanked me and continued down the sidewalk. I watched her go. I needed to pay a visit to the Young family to see if Sadie and Ezekiel's engagement was as well a kept secret as they had thought.

Chapter Eighteen

When I stepped through the front door of my house, my cell phone rang. I checked the readout. It was a college number. "Hello?"

"Miss Humphrey, this is Collette Williams from Harshberger."

"Hi," I said, wondering how the marketing director got my cell number.

"Where are you?"

"At home," I said slowly.

"What are you doing there? You are supposed to be on campus."

"Campus is closed."

"I know that," she snapped. "You are supposed to be here for the float."

The float? I'd completely forgotten about that.

"I sent you an e-mail last evening." She sounded exasperated. "You need to stop by campus today to prepare for the parade."

"I haven't checked my college e-mail since I left work."

She sighed. "You should check your college e-mail every day. Holiday or no holiday."

I didn't bother to argue with her. "What time do I need to be there?"

"Now. The seamstress is here to fit you for your costume."

Inwardly, I groaned. I had forgotten the snowman costume. The only good part about it was I could take a photograph of myself and e-mail it to Tanisha in Italy. I'm sure it would make her week. "I'll be there as soon as I can."

I had planned to make a quick stop at home to grab my car keys and drive out to Young's Flea Market, but my plans had been foiled. Even though the college was within walking distance, I drove so that I could go directly to Young's after my fitting. I shivered at the thought. What woman wanted to dress up like a chubby snowman? Talk about giving someone body issues. Collette's special project also worried me.

The college grounds were deserted except for a handful of cars parked outside the gymnasium. A flatbed truck that looked like it had been on the receiving end of a snowplow sat in the parking lot. I couldn't remember the last time I had seen so much white outside of a National Weather Service certified blizzard. Quilt batting and cotton balls bought by the gross created the snow-like base. If it rained, the float would be waterlogged within seconds.

Billy of Uncle Billy's Budget Autos, an overweight man with bushy red hair, somewhere between the age of thirty and fifty, came around the side of the truck. He lumbered over as I exited my car and called to me as if we were old friends. "Chloe!" In a way, we were. Billy had loaned me a car when my last one was out of commission. It had been a deathtrap on wheels, but he'd meant well. He whistled. "How have you been?"

I smiled. "Okay."

He ran a hand over his red mustache. "Timothy was in the shop last week to buy a part for his truck. I asked him about you, and he got all red in the face. I had to tease him a little."

My own face turned warm although I was secretly pleased to hear about Timothy's reaction.

"Wow, look at your new wheels. A VW Bug. Nice! I had one of the older ones at the shop once. I tricked it out with duct tape strips. Got tons of compliments on that car too. I was bummed when I finally sold it." He walked around my duct tape-free Bug. "A few pieces of duct tape on the fender would really class it up." Billy's love of indestructible gray tape was legendry in the county.

"I think I'll pass. I prefer a duct tape-free car."

He shrugged as if it made no difference to him, then shot a thumb at the float. "Get a load of that."

"Nice. Did you make it?"

"Yep." He grinned from ear to ear. "The owner of the quilt shop in town almost had a stroke when I put in my batting order. I want it to be the best float of the parade." He tapped a four-by-four cube of Styrofoam to his right. "I'm working on the igloo right now."

Oh boy.

The gymnasium doors opened, and Collette stood in the gap. "Miss Humphrey, we need you now."

I turned to Billy. "Gotta go."

"Sure thing. See you Friday for the parade." He picked up an electric saw and started shaping the igloo.

Even on her day off, Collette was dressed to impress. She wore a cashmere sweater and charcoal pleated pants. I, on the other hand, wore jeans and a purple fleece sweatshirt. "I'm sorry I missed the e-mail."

She brushed her cashmere arm. "I'm not surprised. You didn't tell the dean yesterday about your adventure at Young's Flea Market."

I licked my lips wishing I had thought to put lip balm in my purse that morning. "My adventure?" Of course, I knew what she was talking about, but how much did she know?

"Yes. You found a dead body there. You should really inform the college about these sorts of events."

"Why?"

Her mouth puckered. "Because the college needs to know whenever an employee may be in the press."

"You want to use a man's death as publicity?"

She sniffed. "You make it sound like a bad thing when you put it like that."

And it's not a bad thing?

"The college can use stories like this to build up press, especially since there are Amish involved."

"What do the Amish have to do with it?"

"The dean says you have several Amish friends."

"Yes," I said slowly, annoyed she ignored my question.

"Good. We will talk later about my new idea."

I folded my arms. "What new idea?"

Collette pointed to the gym door. "The costumes are in there. We will talk about the Amish later."

Why does that sound like a threat?

I stepped inside the gym. Banners from basketball and volleyball titles and championships hung from the rafters. The bleachers were tucked safely into their bearings. If I thought outside was a winter wonderland, I hadn't seen anything yet. One quarter of the gymnasium floor looked like a cotton field. At this moment, I realized this parade was a big deal for the people of Appleseed Creek—and for the college.

A small Amish woman came up to me. "Are you Chloe?"

I nodded.

"I'm Mary Yoder. Your snowman is over here."

I turned to see an enormous snowman suit complete with carrot nose, buttons for eyes, and a red bow tie. "Oh, my!" In that thing, I would be larger than Billy.

She smiled shyly. "I made it myself." She looked from me to the suit and back again. "It's a little big for you."

No kidding. The history professor who was supposed to wear it was at least six feet tall. I was five foot four.

She twisted her mouth, and then her face cleared. "I know. I will take off the bottom tier. You will be a two-tier snowman instead of three. Will that work?"

I shrugged. "That's fine for me."

She knelt on the floor and took scissors to the lower half of the dress. The snipping and tearing as the scissors moved through the fabric reminded me of what Sadie said about hearing the shears. For the first time, I wondered what type of shears had killed Ezekiel. Knowing that might lead me to the killer. Were they ones of a hairdresser? A tailor? Mary moved to the other side of the dress. Or a seamstress?

"All done," she said. "You can try it on now."

I was afraid she would say that.

She helped me climb into the costume. I nearly tipped over. "It fits." Her voice was muffled.

This is what it must feel like to be inside of a pillow. I started to sweat. At least I wouldn't be cold on the float. That was for sure.

Mary removed the headpiece. "Was it comfortable?"

I wiped a hand across my damp brow. Not wanting to hurt her feelings, I said, "It was soft."

She gave me a smile and helped me step out of it. "I'm sorry to have rushed you. Collette said that she called you to remind you to come."

"She did. I missed the e-mail she sent about the fitting."

"It's okay. I could be here only a short time. I must go and finish putting the last touches on my sister-in-law's wedding apron. Also, there is much cooking and baking to be done. She's to marry tomorrow."

Yoder was like the name Smith in the Amish world, so I thought nothing of it when she introduced herself as Mary Yoder. However now that she mentioned the wedding, I knew she had to be a relation of Esther Yoder. There couldn't possibly be another Yoder wedding on Thanksgiving in Appleseed Creek.

"Esther is your sister-in-law?"

Her eyes brightened. "You know her?"

"From the bakery," I said quickly. I didn't want to reveal my connection to Becky. Mary may not know of me, but she would certainly know of Becky who Isaac was in love with until she left Amish life.

"Esther has waited for Isaac a long time." She placed her scissors into her sewing box along with her needles, thread, and seam ripper. "My favorite treat of the day will be the wedding fruit. It's one of my favorite treats."

"What's in it—"

"Chloe, I'm so glad to see you," Dylan interrupted us. He wore a spandex jumpsuit with enough sequins to cause temporary blindness. A pair of black ice skates, laced together, hung from his shoulder. "I'm an ice skater on the float." His cheeks flamed red. "It wasn't my idea."

"The snowman wasn't mine either." I gave Mary an apologetic smile.

"Oh, you will be on the float too?"

I was beginning to wonder if the history professor really threw his back out or used it as an excuse to get out of this circus.

Dylan smoothed down a sequin on his forearm. "Did you like the flowers?"

"The flowers?"

Mary fell silent as she finished collecting her things. The smile she wore while describing Esther's wedding was gone. She seemed to grow smaller as she packed her bags.

"The ones I sent to your office yesterday. I'd hope you'd take them as an apology and a peace offering."

I nearly dropped my snowman head. "The flowers were from you?" Mary took the fuzzy white head from me.

He frowned. "Didn't you read my note?"

"No. I never got it. The student who delivered the flowers lost it."

Dylan shook his head. "I wanted to apologize about confusion on Monday. The chief of police was right."

Confusion? That's what he's calling it?

"I shouldn't have been in your home without letting you know. This is my first rental property, and I'm still learning all of the rules." His smile fell just short of charming. "I don't blame you for getting upset."

"I appreciate that, Dylan."

"Good. I knew the flowers would work. They always did the trick on my wife."

"You're married?" I couldn't keep the relief out of my voice. If he was married perhaps all of this attention was really about the house, not me.

His face fell. "I'm separated."

"Oh." I didn't know if I felt more disappointed for Dylan or for myself.

He ran his finger along an ice skate's blade. "I would like to work on the house on Friday. Would that be an okay day for me to come over?"

"What were you planning on doing?"

"I need to finish fixing that window latch for you."

I shifted from foot to foot. "That's not necessary. Timothy did it."

Dylan clenched his jaw and blood rushed to his face. "I don't want Timothy to work on the house."

I put my hands on my hips "Why not?"

"Because I can't afford him."

"He doesn't expect to be paid. He did it as a favor to me as his friend."

He blew out a breath. "This house is an investment for me. I can't have Timothy mess up things."

I jumped to Timothy's defense. "He doesn't mess up things." *Should Becky and I look for a new place to live?*

He shook his head as if I couldn't possibly understand. "If the window is already fixed, I'd like to inspect the rest of the house, so I can compare it to the original floor plan. I may have a worker or two with me to help. How does one o'clock sound?"

"What about the parade?"

"That's long after the parade is over."

What could I say? It was his house, and he was giving me more than twenty-four hours notice. I sighed. "One o'clock is okay."

He grinned and thanked me before he left the gym. I scanned the room for Mary. I wanted to say goodbye to her and maybe glean more details about Esther's wedding. No such luck. Mary was gone.

Chapter Nineteen

O n the way to Young's, I called Chief Rose's cell phone number, the one she'd given me during the summer. The chief answered on the second ring. "Humphrey, what's going on?"

"Two things."

"I'm listening."

"I saw Curt and Brock."

She was silent.

"Nothing much happened. I bumped into them on the square. They left me when I headed to the police station."

"I didn't see you come into the station, and no one told me you were there."

"I didn't make it in. I ran into Sadie leaving the department and spoke with her."

"Uh-huh." She sighed. "What was the second thing?"

"What kind of shears were used on Ezekiel Young?"

There was a long pause, and I thought she wasn't going to answer my question. The chief took in a deep breath. "What do you mean exactly?"

"The ones he was stabbed with . . . what are they normally used to cut? Hair? Boxes? Rope? The type of shears wasn't in the paper."

"That's because I wouldn't let the press know. I have to keep some of the facts hidden."

"Will you tell me?"

She sighed. "Wool."

"Wool?"

"Yes. Wool shears used to shear sheep."

"Oh." I paused. "I have another question."

She sighed. "I think you are up to three things now."

"In the pavilion when I saw Ezekiel, I remember a toolbox on the floor." I moved the phone to my other ear. "Was there any sign of struggle? Did he fight back?"

The chief waited a few beats before answering. "Not much. We think that the killer snuck up on Ezekiel when he was working. Ezekiel didn't hear his approach over the sound of the nail gun's motor. The person stabbed Ezekiel in the back. The person either knew anatomy or got lucky, because the shears got him in the heart."

I shuddered.

"He didn't die immediately. It took a couple of minutes. We think as he was struggling, he knocked the box off of the workbench. There wasn't much blood because his coat absorbed a lot of it. There was a mark on the floor that indicated the killer flipped him over onto his stomach. The county crime lab thinks Ezekiel crumbled to the floor on his left side. While on his side, the killer cut off his beard." She paused. "Ezekiel may have even been alive while his beard was cut. He was in too much pain to fight back."

Bile gathered in my throat. "What about fingerprints, shoe prints, anything like that?"

"I can tell you've been watching television." She cleared her throat. "There weren't any fingerprints other than the workers who would have been in the pavilion. Timothy's were all over the place."

"You're not suggesting he—"

"I'm not. As for shoe prints, the killer was careful. It looks like he used a pine branch to wipe his prints in the sawdust as he left. We found one outside the pavilion covered in sawdust. Before you ask, there were no fingerprints on the branch." A tapping sound, like the chief's pencil against her desk, resounded through the phone. "My turn for questions. Why are you so interested?"

"I think Timothy and I can help you find out who did this."

She sighed again. "I won't bother to tell you to stop, but if you find out anything I might think is important, you tell me."

"Deal." I ended the call and turned into Young's massive parking lot. The restaurant part of the lot was filled with cars and buses as usual, and the hitching post had more horses and buggies than it normally did. The Buckeye Country Tour bus was one of the buses waiting at the back of the lot. I planned to avoid the lady with the cane.

I stepped inside the building. The pie and gift shops buzzed with happy activity as visitors made their selections. There was no indication of the tragedy that happened in the pavilion two days ago. Typically, Ellie stood at the hostess stand seating guests or telling the young Amish girls who worked for her how to do it properly. Instead Aaron Sutter, Timothy's best friend, was at the hostess station. From his wheelchair, he collected names from guests yet to be seated and handed menus to an Amish girl to lead the parties to their tables.

He shot me a grin, and his coal black hair fell over mischievous hazel eyes.

My shin ached when I saw his next customer—the lady with the cane.

"How long is the wait?" she croaked.

"Only twenty minutes."

"*Twenty* minutes? I can't wait that long. I'm hypoglycemic and need to eat now."

Aaron frowned. "I'm sorry to hear that, but the wait is twenty minutes. We have lots of treats in the pie shop you can purchase if you are hungry now."

She narrowed her eyes at him. "You're trying to get me to spend more money."

"No ma'am." The corners of Aaron's mouth twitched as he held back a chuckle.

"Do you want me to spoil my dinner?"

"Absolutely not. Young's has the best food in the county. I want you to enjoy it."

The lady with the cane cocked her head as if surprised by his friendly response. I suspect his was much different than the typical reaction to her disagreeable temperament. Finally, she hobbled in the direction of the pie shop.

There were no more customers waiting to give Aaron their names, so I walked up to his chair.

"One for lunch?" Aaron asked with a small smile.

"I'm afraid not, but it smells great. I'm looking for Ellie. Do you know where I can find her?"

"She's at home today because . . . well . . . you know why."

I nodded. "Are you working here now?"

He shook his head. "I'm helping out while the Young family makes arrangements. The bishop asked for volunteers, so here I am."

"That was nice of you."

Becky walked by with a tray holding at least a dozen huge glasses of pop and water. It was a wonder she didn't drop the tray on the floor. I know I would have. Aaron turned his head and blushed when he saw Becky. I suspected that Becky working in the restaurant was the deciding factor for Aaron to help out at Young's.

I stopped short of snapping my fingers to regain his attention. "Where's Uri?"

"The whole Young family is in Ellie's house, behind the pavilions, preparing for Ezekiel's funeral."

"When will the funeral be?"

"Typically, it would be tomorrow since that's three days after Ezekiel's death, but the police haven't released his body yet, so I don't know."

The restaurant's front door opened letting in a burst of cold air. A large group of people stepped inside, and behind them, I could see even more stepping off of the tour bus.

"I'll get out of your way," I said.

Aaron winked at me and greeted his next guest. Aaron had said that Ellie's house was behind the pavilion. In past visits, I had noticed a two-story home at the edge of the property and never thought much of it. I couldn't go there now and interrupt her grief. I left the restaurant through a side door and walked around the building toward the pavilions. Maybe as a team, Timothy and I could think of what to do next.

I followed the sound of power tools. As I rounded the first pavilion, I saw two Amish men, one I had never seen before, speaking in their language. The man had a brown and gray beard and silvery hair sticking out from underneath his black felt hat. His face was drawn and he wore glasses over small eyes. The second man I knew right away—Deacon Sutter. The deacon was a tall man with a black beard and hair, and a perpetual scowl on his face. I'd never seen Deacon Sutter smile.

I took a step back. The last person I wanted to run into, aside from Curt and Brock, was the deacon. I slipped on some loose gravel, and the deacon turned. "What are you doing here?"

"I'm looking for Timothy."

His dark eyes narrowed. "You are still bothering the Troyer

family." His lip curled. "I've warned the family about you." Deacon Sutter turned back to his companion. "This is the *Englischer* I told you about, Bishop. She is the one who found Ezekiel Young. She tempted Rebecca and Timothy Troyer from the Amish way."

Bishop? That made the other man, Bishop Hooley, Sadie's father.

The bishop's gaze met mine, his expression the same as Sadie's this morning—sad, afraid, and weary.

I held my ground. "Both Timothy and Becky had left the Amish before I met them."

The deacon swung back around, and his dark eyes narrowed. "But you insist on visiting the Troyers who are still Amish. You're trying to lead them all from the Amish way."

"No, I would never do that." I glared back at him. "The Troyers are my friends."

Deacon Sutter looked dubious. "Bishop Hooley made the right decision when he advised the district to keep their distance from the Troyers."

"You're shunning them."

His jaw twitched. "What would you know about shunning? What you read in a book? You know nothing."

My eyes flicked to the bishop. He didn't say a word. He looked everywhere but at my face, as if he were afraid to make eye contact.

Deacon Sutter continued to speak for the bishop. "The Troyers are not shunned. The bishop has only advised district members to limit their contact. However, if they continue to disobey the rules of the district, the bishop will have no choice but to turn them out from the People."

"Don't you mean your rules, Deacon Sutter?" I asked.

"It may be fine to speak to your elders like that in the *Englisch* world, but it's not in the Amish. If the Troyers are your friends, you would leave them alone. Instead you have chosen to be the reason they are alienated from the district."

His words felt like a slap across the face. Maybe I shouldn't go to the Troyers for Thanksgiving? Maybe it would push the bishop and deacon too far?

Deacon Sutter said something to the bishop in their language before the pair walked past me, gazes straight ahead, in the direction of the restaurant.

I stood there for a moment collecting myself. The Troyers were right. The deacon was in charge of the district now. The bishop had been too terrified to speak.

Now, I knew the truth. Becky thought she was the reason why her family was being ostracized. She wasn't.

It was me.

Chapter Twenty

Thorc you arc!" Timothy's voice broke through my black thoughts. He jogged up to me. "I was just inside the restaurant, and Aaron said you were here." He studied my face. "What's wrong?"

I bit my lip. I couldn't tell him exactly what the deacon had said. What would he think if he knew I was the reason his family suffered? "I ran into Deacon Sutter and Bishop Hooley."

Timothy made a face. "What did they have to say?"

"The bishop didn't say anything."

"No surprise there. Back when he was a preacher, and I was still in the district, his voice would shake when he preached. It was painful to sit through the services knowing he'd rather be doing just about anything else."

"Why is he the bishop, then?" My teeth began to chatter. The sun was shining, but it was much colder outside than it looked.

"You're shivering. Let's go inside and get something hot to drink. Aaron's in the break room."

Timothy led me in through the kitchen entrance. Amish women moved around the stainless steel appliances with ease and efficiency. I followed Timothy into the break room, the same spot Chief Rose interviewed me in after I found Ezekiel's body. The night of Ezekiel's death I had been too woozy to notice much about the room. It was a simple space with the same small, white tile found in the kitchen and one wall lined with shelves, which served as overflow for the restaurant's extensive pantry. There was a sofa there as well and a round table surrounded by six wooden chairs.

Aaron sat at the table eating a meat loaf dinner. "I could get used to this. Work a few hours and get all the food I can eat."

The meat loaf smelled heavenly, and I realized I hadn't eaten anything all day.

Aaron must have seen me drooling. "Want some?"

"I am hungry," I admitted.

Timothy laughed. "I'll go see if they have extra in the kitchen."

I sat next to Aaron while he cut his meat loaf into tiny, uniform pieces. "Hmm, I've never heard Timothy offer to get food for someone, especially for a pretty girl."

"He's just being nice."

"*Really* nice," Aaron said.

Timothy reentered the room carrying a waitress's tray of two meat loaf dinners with green beans, seasoned potatoes, and two glasses of Coke. "Order up!"

Aaron winked at me.

I thanked Timothy, and Aaron gave a short blessing over our impromptu meal.

I cut into the meat loaf, and it fell apart on my plate. "I met the bishop outside."

"How'd that go?" Aaron asked.

"He doesn't seem all that comfortable. Why didn't he turn the job down?"

Aaron forked a red-skinned potato. "He can't. He must do the work *Gott* has called him to do."

"The district had to know that Bishop Hooley wasn't comfortable with being a leader. Why didn't it choose someone else?" I wanted to ask why the district chose someone like Aaron's father to be deacon, but held my tongue. Father and son disagreed on many things, but Aaron was still the deacon's son and must care for his father. If he didn't believe that, wouldn't he have left the district like Timothy had? My eyes fell on his wheelchair. Maybe he felt he had no choice but to stay.

"The district doesn't pick the leaders of the church, which are the bishop, the deacon, and the two preachers. *Gott* chooses them."

My forehead creased. "How?"

"Each man that the district puts forward gets a copy of a songbook. Inside one of the songbooks there is a piece of paper with a Bible verse written on it. The man who receives that songbook is the man selected by *Gott*. It is as simple as that."

"It sounds a little like a game of chance," I said.

Aaron frowned, and I was afraid I went too far. "I can see why you would think that, but we believe it is the best way to know the will of *Gott*."

I thought about that. It seemed like a risky way to know God's will.

Timothy pushed green beans around his plate. "Your father was with the bishop when Chloe met him."

Aaron sipped from his coffee mug. "I knew they were here visiting with Ellie."

"Has your father said anything about the haircutting?" I scooped up a forkful of green beans.

"He talks about it often. He believes it's a church matter, and we should not involve the police. Now that there's been a murder, the deacon won't be able to keep the cops away."

"Do you think the haircutting and the murder are related?"

"Yes," he said, simply. "If they are not, then we have two crazies running loose in the county. I think the person doing this is Amish."

I almost dropped my fork. "You do?"

He nodded. "What *Englischer* would know the significance of cutting off an Amish person's hair? I suppose they could find that out in a book or from talking to someone, but that seems unlikely. To me, it seems like a particular insult given Amish to Amish."

I considered that. This certainly ruled out Curt and Brock. They couldn't be farther from Amish if they tried.

"You're going to a wedding tomorrow." Timothy said this as a statement, not as a question.

"I'll be there." Aaron's brow knit together. "Is Becky upset about the wedding?" He squinted as if bracing himself for the answer.

"She was upset when she heard the news, but I think she was more surprised that they are marrying so quickly." I smiled at Aaron. "But she's not upset Isaac is marrying. I don't believe she thinks of Isaac much anymore."

A grin spread on the young Amish man's face. "I'm glad to hear it." He pushed back from the table. "I'd better head back to work. I don't want to get fired. I kind of like working here. It might be a new career path for me."

Timothy grinned. "Is it the work or your coworkers you are most interested in?"

Aaron smirked.

Timothy held the door for Aaron as he rolled out of the room. He closed it after his friend, then turned back to me. "How did it go at The Apple Core?"

"I'm meeting with Leah and her two friends late this afternoon." I went on to tell him about my visit at The Apple Core.

"Do you want me to come with you?"

"No, I think they are more likely to talk to me if I'm by myself." I tucked my napkin under my plate. "I spoke with the chief."

"You've been busy. And?"

"I asked her about any sign of struggle." I went on to tell Timothy about how the crime scene techs believed Ezekiel's last minutes went.

Timothy swallowed. "That's awful."

I blew out a breath. "I'd like to talk to Ellie before I head back into town."

Timothy twisted his mouth. "Maybe you should wait until after the funeral."

"That might be too late. Whoever is doing this may strike again."

"I'll see if Ellie can see us. If she says no, we have to respect her wishes."

"Okay." I forked the last piece of meat loaf, and it melted in my mouth. My diet was a complete disaster at this point.

"Did you find out who sent the flowers?" There was a forced casualness in his tone.

I swallowed and the tiny piece of meat loaf felt more like a baseball in my throat. "The flowers?"

"Yes." He watched me.

I guzzled my Coke. "Actually, I did. I forgot to tell you about the float the college is putting on for the Holiday Parade." I grimaced. "Dean Klink drafted me to be a snowman."

A smile spread across Timothy's face. "That will be a sight."

"You have no idea. There was a fitting this morning and Dylan was there."

His smile disappeared.

I scraped my fork on my nearly empty plate. "He told me that he sent the flowers as an apology for Monday."

"That's an expensive apology. Couldn't he have just given you a note?"

"If he had, the student would have lost it," I said, trying to turn it into a joke.

Timothy didn't even crack a smile. "I was afraid of something like this."

"Afraid of flowers?"

"I don't like it. It's too personal." He flattened his hands on the tabletop. "I don't like the idea of that guy having a key to your house."

"We can't really change the locks on him. He owns the place." I pushed my plate away.

Timothy's jaw twitched.

I stood. "I think we should spend less time worrying about Dylan and the flowers and more time worrying about the deacon and whoever killed Ezekiel. I told the chief we were looking into it."

Timothy remained in his seat. "How'd she take that?"

"She didn't say no."

Timothy sighed and pushed his chair back. "I'm happier knowing she knows what you're up to." He stood. "I'll go find Ellie."

"Thank you."

Timothy piled the plates back onto the serving tray. "Promise me you won't push her too hard."

"I promise."

Chapter Twenty-One

T imothy kept his promise, and Ellie agreed to meet with me. In the late afternoon, we walked together toward her home. Although the air was cool, the sun's rays warmed my face. Timothy laughed. "Enjoy the sun while you can, because bad weather is headed our way. The weatherman predicts snow. We haven't had a white Thanksgiving in more than ten years. If there is enough snow, maybe we can talk *Grossdaddi* into hooking Sparky up to his sleigh."

"Grandfather Zook has a sleigh?"

Timothy nodded. "He's almost as proud of it as he is of his buggy."

That was saying a lot.

As we got closer to the house, I notice two houses in the back of the property. The large white two-story home with gray shutters could be seen from the pavilions, but beyond that a smaller one-story ranch-style home stood behind it painted the same colors.

"The first house belongs to the twins," Timothy explained as we passed the larger home. "Ellie and her husband lived there, but after her husband passed on, the family built the small home, leaving the big house for her sons."

"Neither of the twins married?"

He shook his head.

Clearly Timothy didn't know about Sadie and Ezekiel's relationship. I wondered who did. It was a miracle the couple kept the secret in such a close-knit community. Did the bishop know about it? Did he approve or disapprove? Could I find out from Ellie if she knew without breaking Sadie's trust?

Timothy squeezed my hand. "You look nervous."

Several Amish men stood outside Ellie's house, drinking coffee from metal thermoses. Remembering what the deacon said about my influence on the Troyer family, I removed my hand from Timothy's grasp.

Timothy's expression fell. He recovered, then approached the men, speaking to them in Pennsylvania Dutch.

A man who was a good foot taller than me stepped over to us. I got a crick in my neck looking up at him. "She's grieving," he said in English.

"I know," Timothy said.

The man was stone-faced. "You will have to come another time."

I stepped back, ready to go. The front door to Ellie's home opened, and Uri poked his head out. "It's okay, Levi. I knew they were coming. My mother is expecting them."

Levi cracked his knuckles and stepped away from the door. I suspected he was the Amish equivalent of a bouncer. In the English world such a man would be outside of a bar. In the Amish world he was posted outside of a home in mourning.

Uri held the door open so that Timothy and I could enter. We stepped into the living room, its furniture simple except for a large china cabinet against one wall containing a collection of beautiful hand-painted dishes. Three women sat in the room, working on needlepoint projects. They didn't look up from their work when we entered.

The house smelled like cookies. "*Maam* is in the kitchen." Uri's eyes were bloodshot and no remnant of his teasing nature remained. Despite everyone saying the twins were not close, the death of Ezekiel had obviously come as a blow to his brother. He nodded toward the kitchen. "It's the place she feels the most comfortable."

We followed Uri through the shotgun-style house with the kitchen in the back. The restaurant's kitchen had all the modern conveniences: stainless steel appliances, blenders, food processors, and electricity. Electricity was allowed in the family place of business. Their home was a different story. The kitchen was much like the one in the Troyer farm. It had running water, but the white appliances ran on propane, even the refrigerator, which hummed in the corner. A lit kerosene lamp hung low over the kitchen table causing me to wonder if anyone had ever knocked it with their head and caught their hair on fire.

"*Maam*," Uri said. "Timothy and Chloe are here."

Ellie pulled a cookie sheet out of the oven and placed it on the stovetop. She placed another sheet in the oven. "Have a seat and a cookie."

The kitchen table was piled high with cookies: chocolate chip, peanut butter, shortbread, and the list went on. Each one perfectly baked. There wasn't a burnt or misshapen cookie in the lot. "Wow, that's a lot of cookies."

She grunted as she straightened up. "I have to be ready for the viewing."

Uri leaned against the wall. "*Maam*, you know every lady in the district would make the cookies for you."

She eyed him. "They wouldn't be half as good. I won't have mediocre cookies at my son's wake."

I studied Ellie. Outwardly she appeared fine. Is this how the Amish women grieve? Through baking? More likely this reaction was specific to Ellie. Timothy and I sat at the table in front of a pile of white cookies that resembled coconut macaroons. They smelled like cinnamon. Despite having just eaten a full meat loaf dinner, my mouth watered.

"Go ahead and have one," Ellie said. "Those are my sour cream cookies."

Sour cream in a cookie? What did I know? I only baked those break-apart premade cookies from the supermarket. All you had to do was slap them on the tray and pop them in the oven. Still, half came out burned to a crisp and the remainder raw.

I selected the smallest of the sour cream cookies. Timothy reached across the table and took the largest one. It was light and fluffy, somewhere between a cookie and cake. "This is the best cookie ever."

Ellie moved perfectly round shortbread from a cool cookie sheet to the wax paper lying across the table. "I'm glad you like it. I'll give you the recipe."

I smiled, knowing my cookies would never come out like these. However, I'd happily share the recipe with Becky. Sigh. My diet was suffering a long and painful death. My wayward thought startled me and I cleared my throat. "When is the viewing?"

She sat at the head of kitchen table and selected a peanut butter cookie from the pile in front of her. "The police chief said his body will be released to the funeral home at four o'clock today. Uri, with the help of the men, will bring him here from the funeral home."

My brow shot up. "The Amish use a funeral home?" I clamped my mouth shut, feeling crass for asking such a question.

Ellie broke a cookie in half. "Yes, we do for the embalming part of death. We don't have anyone to do that, and it is the law. We don't have services there as the *Englischers* do. Instead, we hold our own services on the third day after death." She broke the cookie into quarters. "Because of the violent nature of my son's death, we have had to delay it. The body will be displayed in my home for two days and friends and family will visit. The funeral is on the third day."

"I'm sorry for your loss," I said.

"Death is unavoidable." Her expression fell. "No mother wants to outlive her child, but I have to accept this as the will of *Gott*."

I wasn't as sure about that. I still couldn't find God's will in my mother's death nearly eleven years before.

Timothy swallowed another sour cream cookie. "*Grossdaddi* sends his condolences."

Ellie smiled at that. "He's a *gut* friend. I hope he will be well enough to attend the funeral."

"I know that he will want to," Timothy said. "But the bishop has instructed the district to avoid him and the rest of the family for a time. *Grossdaddi* would not want his appearance to disrupt such a solemn day."

Ellie stacked peanut butter cookies five high. "I don't much care what the bishop and deacon want right now. If I want you and your family to be there, you should come. Chloe, I would like you to come too."

Uri cleared his throat. "*Maam*, this isn't a *gut* time to irritate the bishop."

"There's never a gut time for that. I hope he will respect my wishes."

"He's not the one I'm worried about," Uri muttered.

A timer dinged, and Ellie bustled to the oven. She pulled out the cookie sheet and slipped a new one inside. The baked cookies were just as perfect as every previous batch. "I know you and Timothy aren't here to talk about the bishop and deacon." Ellie returned to her seat and started stacking cookies.

I glanced at Timothy and he told Ellie about the attack on his grandfather.

Ellie dropped a cookie on the floor. "That's horrible. He could have been killed. Do the police think it's the same person who killed my son?"

Uri picked up the fallen cookie and tossed it into the sink.

"That's one possibility." I stacked a few cookies.

"It is hard to believe there would be two monsters like this in the district."

Uri plucked a sour cream cookie from the table. "Do you really think they are monsters, *Maam*? They may only be desperate men who made poor decisions."

She held her son's gaze. "Whoever would consider murder an option is a monster in my thinking."

Uri grabbed two more cookies and leaned against the wall.

She glanced back and forth between Timothy and me. "The police must catch this person."

"That's why we're here. We're helping the police in a . . . um . . . unofficial way." I resisted the urge to pick up another cookie.

Uri leaned against the wall again. "What does *unofficial* mean?"

"It means we are concerned citizens."

He didn't seem satisfied with that answer. Even to my own ears it sounded weak.

"I know *Gott* has a reason for all this, but I don't want it to happen again or to someone else's child." Ellie nudged her cookie stacks away from the table's edge. "How can I help you?"

"Can you answer a few questions?" I asked.

She snapped a cookie in half. "Go ahead."

I took a deep breath. "Do you know if anyone was angry with Ezekiel?"

"Chief Rose asked me the same thing. Ezekiel rubbed lots of folks the wrong way. A vendor or supplier always seemed to be mad at him. I don't know how many times I heard my son arguing with someone over the phone about the cost of something. He was a shrewd businessman and felt we deserved the best price and terms on everything. But we've worked with all of those vendors and suppliers for over twenty years. I cannot see why any of them would hurt my son now after all this time."

Ellie had a point. After twenty years, it seemed like a waste of time for those vendors and suppliers to kill Ezekiel now.

"My son was *gut* at his job. Without him the business would have failed when my husband died." She sighed.

Against the wall, Uri flinched.

"Was he close to anyone outside of the family?" Timothy asked.

Sadie's round face came to my mind.

Uri shifted in his place against the wall. "I loved my twin, but he didn't have many friends. He was prickly. Even so like *Maam*, it's hard for me to imagine anyone would want to kill him. Most people were irritated by him."

"It's hard to imagine the business without him." Ellie removed another cookie from the pile and placed it in front of her. "I know how to cook and run a kitchen, but I have no head for figures. Ezekiel took over managing the business, and it's tripled in size in the ten years since my husband's death." She sighed. "It will be up to Uri now to keep the business running."

Uri pushed away from the wall and scowled. "I'll be in the barn." He stomped out of the room.

Ellie sighed. "Uri's never had much interest in the business. He's let his brother do most of the work for years. He must realize that it's on his shoulders now."

I began stacking chocolate chip cookies. "And if Uri can't manage the business?"

She frowned and moved cookies crumbs around on her placemat. "Then I will have to reconsider what I want for the restaurant and flea market. My eldest daughter, Bridget, and her husband James have already hinted to me that they are willing to help." She frowned. "James has had his eye on the flea market since the day he showed up in his courting buggy."

Mentally, I added James to my list of people to talk to. "Do Bridget and James live in the district?"

She nodded. "They have a sheep farm down the road. It's been in James's family for generations."

I knocked over a stack of cookies and quickly restacked them. *Sheep farm? Didn't Chief Rose say the killer stabbed Ezekiel with sheep shears?*

"Are Bridget and James here today?" I asked, hoping my voice didn't sound as eager as I felt.

"They were, but they had to go home to tend the flock. They will be here as much as possible," Ellie said.

"Uri will rise to the challenge," Timothy said, "in time."

She smiled. "You might be right. You know it was his idea to enclose the pavilions, which despite everything, will be a great improvement for our family. Perhaps he will pull through." She sighed. "Time is what he needs. He's taking it hard. I know everyone thought the twins spent most of their time fighting, but they were close. They have lived together their whole lives. I worry about Uri. I hope he knows he can go on without Ezekiel."

I leaned forward. "Was Ezekiel acting strangely before he died? Anything out of the ordinary?"

She thought for a minute. "He was his typical grouchy self, but somehow he seemed less so. I even caught him smiling to himself once. I asked him what he was smiling about, and he snapped at me. That was his way. He didn't have time for frivolity."

Sadie. She was the one who'd managed to bring a smile to Ezekiel's face. I twisted my mouth. "Was there anyone else Ezekiel talked about outside of the family?"

She snapped a butter cookie in half. "You mean in business. He spoke of many people. You wouldn't believe the number of vendors, suppliers, farmers, and merchants we deal with on a daily basis to keep the restaurant and flea market running. Also, now with the construction, the number of folks Ezekiel dealt with had doubled."

"Any . . . um . . . friends?"

Timothy stared at me.

Ellie frowned. "*Nee*, my Ezekiel was too busy for friends, and neither of my sons has shown much interest in marriage."

"How old are the twins?" I asked.

"They just turned thirty this past May."

"That's not too old."

"Maybe in the *Englisch* world, but for the Amish they should have two or three children by now."

Timothy, who was twenty-seven, shifted in his seat. Had he stayed Amish, he would certainly be married by now with children. The idea made me sick to my stomach.

The timer went off on the oven again. "Do you have any more questions?" Ellie asked.

I opened my mouth, but Timothy was faster. "Not right now. Thank you for speaking with us, Ellie."

She opened the oven door. "You're welcome. In return, I expect to see both of you at the funeral."

I opened my mouth again to make an excuse, but again Timothy spoke first. "We will be there."

Timothy and I walked back to the restaurant together. "Why did you tell her that we would attend the funeral? You know how the bishop feels about it."

He peered down at me. "If a grieving mother wants me to attend her son's funeral, I'm going to be there. It's as simple as that."

"Are you free now?"

"I can be," Timothy said with a smile.

"Good, because I need to meet some sheep."

Chapter Twenty-Two

As I expected, Timothy knew the location of the Zug Sheep Farm. Mabel barked in the backseat of his pickup as the vehicle jostled onto the Zug's private road. Timothy stared straight ahead and concentrated on driving because over the past week the snow and ice had added more ruts and dips to the road.

"So," he said as the truck leveled out on a fairly even piece of froze ground. "You think James Zug murdered his brother-in-law so that he could take over the Young family business."

"It's a possibility," I said, defensively.

Woof! Mabel agreed from the backseat. I scratched her under the chin to thank her for the support.

"If that's the case, why kill one twin? Why not kill them both? There's no guarantee that Uri's not up to the task of operating the business."

"Maybe he feels he knows Uri well enough to know he won't be able to handle all the responsibility."

"I'm not arguing with you." Timothy lightened his tone. "We have to check out every lead. I just wanted to warn you that this might not turn into anything. Besides, if I were a sheep farmer, I sure wouldn't use sheep shears to kill someone."

Grudgingly, I admitted to myself that he had a point.

Riding along the Zug's driveway, even more rut-covered than the road, felt like an amusement park ride as Timothy's pickup bumped and hopped up the incline. Fencing lined with chicken wire protected either side of the drive and more sheep than I could count. The sheep wore thick, off-white winter coats, their limbs and faces black. I didn't see any lambs, only adults and yearlings. A yearling leaped over a larger sheep sleeping just on the other side of the fence. He landed in white powder and rolled onto his back, as if making a sheep's version of a snow angel.

"They're cute."

Timothy gave me a sideways glance. "They're not super bright."

"What does brightness matter when compared to cute?"

He rolled his eyes and parked the truck about twenty yards from a large red sheep barn. Farther down the road, stood a one-story ranch-style home. "Most likely they are in the barn since Ellie said they left to care for the sheep. I imagine they will do everything they need to here, then head back to Young's."

Timothy and I hopped out of the truck, and Mabel jumped out too. Her tail went into overdrive when she saw the sheep.

Timothy eyed her. "Mabel, sit."

She sat by the truck. Her tail swept back and forth across the frozen ground like a broom, but her eyes never left the sheep.

An Amish man in muddy work boots and a black overcoat came out of the barn. His beard was sandy blond, and he wore a black stocking cap on his head.

"Timothy," the Amish man said. "What can I do for you?" He shot a curious glance in my direction.

Timothy stuck his hands in his jeans pockets. "We've just come from Ellie's and shared our condolences."

A strange look crossed James's face. "*Danki*. It's been a hard time for my wife and her family." He half turned and shouted something in Pennsylvania Dutch into the barn.

A woman and girl stepped out of the barn, their skirts mud-encrusted at the hemlines. The girl was sixteen or seventeen and had round cheeks, bright pink from the cold, and dark hair tucked under a bonnet. The woman was an older version of her daughter.

"This is my wife, Bridget, and my daughter Abby."

Abby Zug. She was one of Leah's two friends. Would James attack his own child like that? Why hadn't Ellie mentioned her granddaughter was one of the girls attacked?

I cleared my throat. "Nice to meet you."

Abby wouldn't meet my eyes.

James placed a hand on his wife's arm. "Timothy and . . ." He looked at me questioningly.

"Chloe," I supplied.

He nodded. " . . . Chloe are here to pay condolences for your brother."

"We are so sorry for your loss," Timothy said. "Ezekiel was a smart man, a great business man."

"*Danki*." Bridget lowered her head and removed a white handkerchief from her black apron pocket. As she pulled her hand from the pocket, I saw a flash of metal, shaped like a circle.

"Business is all Ezekiel Young cared about," James muttered.

"James," Bridget said. "My *bruder* was a fine man."

James snorted. "A fine man. His twin *bruder* could barely tolerate him." He grimaced. "I'm sorry for the family's loss. Ellie's been *gut* to us. I don't wish any of them any ill will, but let's not pretend that Ezekiel was a saint just because he is gone."

I stared at the circle of metal sticking out of her pocket. "Are those sheep shears?"

Bridget removed the shears from her pocket. "Yes. We were

trimming some of the yearlings just now. They won't really be sheared until spring, but Abby and I were cutting out the burrs and knots from their coats."

The seven-inch long shears were like two butcher knives facing each other, welded together by a compressed circle of metal. They had a medieval appearance. If I were a sheep, I certainly wouldn't want to see those prehistoric scissors coming at me. The tips were sharpened to a fine point.

James turned to his wife and daughter, speaking to them in their language. They nodded and went back to the barn. When they were inside the barn, he glared at Timothy and me. "What is this really about? You could have paid my wife condolences the next time we were at Young's. I know you are working for them, Timothy."

Timothy shifted from foot to foot. "Do you know why anyone would want to hurt your brother-in-law?"

His eyes narrowed. "*Nee.*"

"Where were you the night your brother-in-law was killed?" I asked. It was a simple question but held so much weight.

James turned his hazel eyes on mine for the first time. "I was at the auction house, bedding down my sheep for the night. I sold them next day. Do you doubt this?"

I swallowed. "No."

"Because if you do, you can talk to any number of livestock owners who were there." He turned to Timothy. "Do you think I killed my brother-in-law?"

"We heard you want to run Young's," Timothy said.

James's jaw twitched. "I've made no secret of that. Why shouldn't I be included in the business? It is part of my wife's heritage. I could contribute to it."

"Uri and Ezekiel didn't want your help."

"Of course, they don't. They want to keep all of it, including the money. Let's make no mistake, theirs is one of the wealthiest,

Amish or *Englisch*, families in the county." James's face turned red. "I will not let you insult me on my land. Please leave."

I shook my head. "We didn't mean . . .

"I know exactly what you meant. Please, go. I see now why the bishop advised us to stay away from the Troyers."

Timothy's jaw twitched. "We are sorry to have offended you." He turned to me. "Let's go, Chloe."

Inside the truck, I stopped just short of punching Timothy in the arm. "Why didn't you tell me Abby Zug was Ellie's granddaughter?"

He shrugged. "I guess I forgot."

"You *forgot*? How could you forget that?"

"Chloe, everyone in the Amish community is related to someone else in some way either by marriage or blood or both. Half the folks in the county are related to me. It's hard enough for me to keep all my own relatives straight."

I sat back. "It changes things."

"You're right about that. Are you sure you don't want me to come with you to meet with the girls?"

"I'm sure."

It was too narrow to turn around in the Zug's driveway, so Timothy backed all the way out. As he did, James, his sheep, and his barn, grew smaller and smaller. Halfway down the drive, a face, pale and still, peeked out of the barn, and watched us go. It could have been either of the women standing there, but I was betting on Abby.

Chapter Twenty-Three

Before I left Young's, I went looking for Becky to make sure she had a ride home. I found her standing next to Aaron at the hostess desk, laughing at something he said. Her eyes were bright. Nope, Becky wasn't upset by Isaac's upcoming wedding—not one bit.

"Chloe?" She blushed. "Aaron said you were here. Where have you been?"

"Timothy and I visited with Ellie." I didn't mention our trip to the sheep farm.

Becky frowned. "How is she? She hasn't been in the restaurant all day. I think this is the first day since I started working here that I haven't seen her."

"She's baking."

Becky nodded as if that made complete sense. For someone who loved to cook and bake as much as Becky, it probably did.

"I'm going to take off now. Do you have a ride?"

She nodded. "Timothy found a new chain for my bike and put it on this morning."

As I drove out of Young's parking lot, a small red coupe cruised in. I blinked. The driver was Collette Williams. What was Harshberger's marketing director doing at Young's? Young's was one of the best restaurants in the county, so Collette might just be having dinner there. At least this is what I would have thought if I hadn't known about her interest in my connection to the Amish in Knox County.

I turned my thoughts from Collette to the Zug family. Was it a coincidence that two people from the same family, Abby and Ezekiel, were attacked? Did I believe James Zug's alibi? Timothy said he would call one of his friends, who worked at the auction barn, to see if James was really there the night Ezekiel was murdered. Perhaps Abby would speak to me away from the other girls.

I still had over an hour before my meeting with Leah and her friends at The Apple Core. I drove home and was relieved to find Gig the only one there.

At five o'clock on the dot, I stepped into The Apple Core. There were no customers and half of the shop's lights had been turned off. Leah locked the door after me. "Debbie and Abby are already here. They are stocking the shelves in the back of the store. We like to do this after the shop closes, so we don't bother any customers."

We wove through the aisles of gifts. On the back wall a tall girl in a plain, navy dress and white prayer cap, Debbie I assumed, handed Christmas-patterned tins to Abby who stood on a step ladder. The girls moved together in a comfortable rhythm. Pick up, hand, and place. Pick up, hand, and place. They didn't speak. I couldn't imagine Tanisha and I working together as quietly. Once we tried to paint the living room in our old apartment and got more paint on each other than on the wall. Mr. Green came over and finished the job in record time.

Leah said something to them in Pennsylvania Dutch.

A tin froze in Debbie's hand. She replaced it on the stack and turned to face me. She had dark, wide-set eyes, and a slight overbite.

"Chloe, this is Debbie, and Abby is on the ladder."

Abby shimmied down the ladder's rungs, giving no indication that we had met only two hours before. "I already told them about what happened to Grandfather Zook."

"And Abby's uncle?" I asked.

Abby kept her head down.

Debbie was breathless. "Ezekiel Young was a cranky man, but it's hard to believe that anyone would hurt him. We never—"

"We don't know anything about what happened to Grandfather Zook," Leah said. "Or Ezekiel."

I unzipped my coat. "You think it was the same person?"

"Maybe it was someone different." Debbie wrapped her arms around her waist. "Maybe over a bad business deal? My father said Ezekiel Young could talk a man out of his favorite horse and make him feel bad for not giving the horse up sooner."

Out of the corner of my eye, I saw Abby shuffle a few steps back.

Leah called over her shoulder. "You can talk to us as we stock. We all have to get home soon." She picked up a box of wooden dolls painted to resemble Amish people and set them delicately, one by one, on the wooden shelves across from the girls stocking tins.

"Can I help?" I asked. "It will make your work faster."

"There's a box by the door to the stock room that has Christmas ornaments. Hang them on the wire stand at the end of the row."

"Do you have a Christmas tree to hang them on?"

"Amish don't have Christmas trees."

No Christmas tree? "If you don't have a Christmas tree, why do you have the ornaments?"

"Because the *Englischers* buy them," she said.

"Right." I picked up the box and positioned it near the stand. I could see all three girls clearly from my spot.

Abby climbed back up the ladder. Debbie handed her a tin, her hand shaking.

"Debbie, can you tell me what happened to you?"

She shot a quick glance at Leah before she started talking. "I was on my way home from work. Most of the time, I work in the cheese shop next to the bakery, and I help out here when Leah needs me. I was just outside of Appleseed Creek when someone ran up from behind and cut my hair."

I had an ornament suspended in my hand. It spun on its plastic thread. "Someone ran up and cut your hair, just like that?"

"Yes."

"You didn't try to run away or fight back?"

She shook her head.

"Did you hear the person running toward you?"

She blushed. "No."

That was hard to believe. "Why not? They couldn't have been completely silent."

"I was listening to my MP3 player."

I blinked at her.

"I haven't been baptized yet," she said defensively. "I'm allowed to experiment." She straightened in her seat and removed the lime green device from her pocket. "One of my *Englisch* friends at the cheese shop gave it to me. I tell her what music I like and she loads it on my device from her computer. I don't use the computer myself." Her eyes widened. "You're not going to say anything, are you? My *daed* and the bishop wouldn't like it."

I held up a hand in mock Girl Scout salute, which was lost on the Amish girls. "I won't tell anyone."

"The music was loud, and I didn't hear the person until it was too late."

"Did you see the person?"

She shook her head.

"He threw a burlap bag over your head just like he did to me," Leah said.

Debbie shot a glance at Leah, who gave the faintest of nods. "That's right."

Was I wrong to think Leah was coaching her friends? "What about you, Abby?" My forehead creased. "How could someone cut off your hair if there's a bag over your head?"

Leah glared at me. "You don't believe us."

"I didn't say that." I spun a Christmas ornament in my hand. "I'm only trying to understand."

Debbie and Abby looked at Leah for the answer.

"The person surprised us from behind and threw the bag over our heads. While we struggled to get it off, he knocked us down to the ground. While we were pinned to the ground, he lifted the bag just enough to rip off our bonnets and cut off our hair." Tears gathered in her eyes. "We were taught not to fight back. Even if we'd wanted to, we were too scared to do it." Leah turned to her friends. "Isn't that what happened?"

They nodded.

I remembered the abrasion on Sadie's cheek from being thrown to the ground. There was no such mark on any of the girls.

"Where are the burlap bags that were over your heads?"

Leah slid a box of trinkets across the floor. "I told you I threw mine away. Debbie and Abby did the same thing. We don't want a reminder of such a horrible memory around us."

Abby dropped the tin and it rolled on its side across the pine plank floor.

Debbie chased after it and picked it up.

Leah placed four more figures on the shelf in a tight row. *Tap, tap, tap, tap.* "Abby, tell her what you told us."

She's definitely coaching them. Why?

"I was delivering eggs to my neighbor's house. They weren't home, so I left them on the front porch. I was writing a note to them when someone came up from behind me."

I hung two more ornaments on the display. "You didn't hear them either."

She shook her head.

"You had an MP3 player too?" I asked.

She shook her head.

"Who was the neighbor?"

"It was the Lambright family, but like I already said. No one was home."

Anna Lambright is Ruth's best friend.

"And your uncle?" I asked.

Abby climbed down the ladder. She was shivering so hard, she nearly missed a rung. "I don't know anything about my uncle or how he died." She glanced at Leah. "My mother and grandmother are heartbroken over his death."

Tears pooled in Debbie's eyes. "I can't believe this has happened. Nothing bad ever happens here."

"Have you told all of this to the police?" I asked.

Leah adjusted the Amish figures on the shelf. "The deacon advised us not to because this is a district problem."

"Now that there's been a murder, it's much more than a district problem." I hung another ornament and it spun from its wire.

Leah cleared her throat. "I spoke with the police because Darren asked me too. Abby and Debbie haven't."

Debbie clutched a tin to her chest. "We can't. The bishop wouldn't like it. Things are bad enough."

"Bad how?" I asked.

"We've been mutilated." Again, Leah answered for her friend.

"Because your hair was cut?"

Leah slammed a final wooden doll on the shelf. "It's so horrible. Everyone stares at us since it happened, and what man will want to marry a woman with short hair?"

"It's not your fault," I said. "And the hair will grow back."

"You don't understand," Debbie snapped. "We are forbidden from cutting our hair."

"It wasn't your decision to cut your hair, so how can anyone blame you?"

Leah flinched. "It doesn't have to be our fault for the bishop to blame us."

Debbie clutched a tin to her waist. "Everything in the district is different since Bishop Glick died. The deacon watches our every move and reports on what all the young people do at church." She stuck her MP3 player back into her apron pocket. "If the bishop knew about my music, he would tell my parents and ban me from Sunday services for two weeks. He's done it to others."

"Why do you have the MP3 player, then?"

"Bishop Glick allowed it as long as I was discreet, which I am. My family hasn't even seen it. Until I'm baptized, some rules about technology don't apply to me." Debbie handed a tin to Abby.

"Can't the bishop set the rules?" I hung an ornament from the highest part of the display.

Abby climbed off of the ladder. "He can, but he's not the one who is doing it. Deacon Sutter is."

If the girls were so unhappy, why'd didn't they leave the district? Not that it was easy. It had been difficult for Timothy and Becky, and they had an unusually supportive family—at least until the bishop reprimanded the Troyers.

Leah picked up her empty box and flattened it. "If you don't have any more questions, we need to finish our work so we can go home."

I had more questions for Abby and Debbie, but clearly I would not get honest answers while Leah was around.

"That's all," I said.

"*Gut.*" Leah took the ornament box from me. "*Danki* for your help."

I had been dismissed.

Chapter Twenty-Four

My cell phone vibrated on the nightstand. I squinted at it, stifling a yawn. Tanisha's face grinned back at me from the picture I took of her when her parents and I dropped her off at the airport for her flight to Italy over five months ago. Hard to believe I hadn't seen my best friend in such a long time. The screen went dark.

Almost immediately, the vibrating began again.

I snatched it up. "What time is it?"

"Noon here, which makes it six your time." Her voice was chipper, as usual.

I groaned.

"Sorry to call so early, but I couldn't wait another minute. Happy Thanksgiving!"

"Happy Thanksgiving," I mumbled, half into the phone, and half into my pillow.

"Anything new and exciting out in the country there?"

Her question made my eyes pop open. "You could say that."

"Ooh, that's sounds good. Does it have to do with dreamy

Timothy? I almost died when you e-mailed me his picture. He's *hot*."

Heat rose in my cheeks.

"Are you blushing?"

"How would you know that?"

"Because you sound like you're blushing."

"I sound like it? You can't sound like you're blushing." I flipped over onto my back.

"Trust me, you can. I always know when you are blushing. I wish I could find a boyfriend like Timothy."

"First of all, Timothy is not my boyfriend. At least we've never spoken about it."

She snorted. "From everything you've told me, you're dating him."

"We've never been on an actual date."

"Girl, you need to ask him, then."

"I can't do that. He's Amish . . . or used to be. He might be offended if a girl asked him out."

"I don't want to go all Women's Lib on you, but if he has a problem with that, there might be bigger issues down the road. You're not the type to sit home, have babies, and cook."

"Who said anything about babies?" I yelped. *Beth Hilty? Now, Tanisha?* "And cooking. He already knows I can't cook."

"See, and he still likes you. He's not as Old School as you think." She paused. "Maybe he thinks you're courting? How sweet is that? It's like you're living out a scene from *Pride and Prejudice*."

"More like *Little House on the Prairie*," I muttered. Desperate to change the subject, I ventured, "Speaking of guys, have you heard from Cole?" Cole was Tanisha's former fiancé. He broke off their engagement months ago when she refused to leave her teaching job in Milan to marry him earlier than planned. This was after Cole never voiced concern about Tee being away for two years of their engagement.

It was Tee's turn to groan. "Yes. I have ten e-mails from him in my inbox right now."

"What do they say?"

"I don't know. I haven't opened any of them."

"Tee . . ."

"I'm afraid to open them. What if he never wants to see me again?" She sighed. "What if he wants to get back together?"

"Which is worse?"

She groaned. "I don't know."

"Do you still love him?"

"I do, but there's another problem."

I didn't like the sound of this. "What?"

"You know how the dumpee keeps the engagement ring?"

"Uh-huh." I had a sneaking suspicion this story wouldn't end well. "You have the ring, then?"

"No."

"You gave it back to him?"

"No."

Uh-oh. "Tee, where is the ring?"

"Well . . ."

"*Tee?*"

She took a deep breath. "The weekend he dumped me was sweltering in the city. A group of teachers from school traveled to Lake Como to escape the heat. I went too."

I didn't like the sound of this. A lake was involved. I was afraid of what I would hear next.

"I kind of threw it into the lake."

"You . . . kind of?"

"Okay, I did. I threw the ring into the lake. It felt good." She paused. "At the time."

I closed my eyes and saw the pear-shaped, one-carat diamond ring that I'd spent hours helping Cole select. He wanted the perfect ring for Tanisha, and I knew what she liked better than anyone. I winced at the cost of the ring. It would pay six months of my rent.

"Are you still there?" Tee asked.

I rolled over to the other side on the bed. "I'm here."

"So, can't you see why I'm afraid to talk to him?"

"No kidding."

"And I don't want to hear a lecture about why I shouldn't have thrown the ring in the lake, okay?"

"I wasn't going to give any." I sighed. "Forward the e-mails to me. I'll read them for you. If they're bad I'll give you the *Cliff's Notes* version. If he wants to get back together, maybe he won't be that upset about the ring. Maybe he will understand."

"You think so?"

No. Not really. I wasn't going to tell her what I thought Cole's reaction would really be. Cole had expensive taste and appreciated money. He wouldn't want his ring to be at the bottom of Lake Como.

To get both of our minds off of our pathetic love lives, I said, "I have other news."

"What's that?"

"I found a dead body."

"What?!"

I had to hold the cell phone away from my ear.

"Tell me what happened. You let me go on and on about Cole and you are dealing with dead people. Spill."

"It was an Amish man."

Tanisha gave a sharp intake of breath. "What is it with you and dead Amish guys?"

I didn't have an answer for that. I proceeded to tell her about the haircutting and discovery of Ezekiel Young's body.

"How gruesome," Tanisha said, although the tone of her voice held a hint of morbid interest. After a moment, she said, "Do you think you're in any danger?"

"No, I don't think so."

I could smell bread baking. Becky must already be up.

The smile came back into her voice. "Timothy will protect you."

"What about Women's Lib?"

"I use it when convenient. Look, Chloe, I have to go. The American teachers at school are having a little Thanksgiving for all the school staff tonight. I'm making a pumpkin pie."

"Where did you find the pumpkin over there?"

"It wasn't easy." After a beat, she said, "I know this weekend must be weird since it's the first time you're not going to your dad's for Thanksgiving. Even though I'm not there, I want you to know how much I love you."

I released a deep sigh. "I love you too, friend."

After we hung up, I was unable to fall back asleep, so I threw my legs over the side of the bed. It didn't feel like Thanksgiving. Typically, on this morning, I was in California in my father's guest bedroom trying to talk myself into getting up and going downstairs to subject myself to my stepmother's criticism. Oddly, I missed it.

More than that, I missed the chance to see my half brother and half sister. I barely knew them, but each year they grew a little taller and a little more like mini-adults. I wondered if I would see them again. Would this be a standard thing? Sabrina talking my dad into a vacation each Thanksgiving? Maybe she planned it that way because it was the one holiday of the year that I spent with them. Almost ten years later, she had finally severed all contact between my father and me. Not that she was solely the blame. My father didn't try to stop her, and a small voice reminded me I gave up long ago. I had gotten burned too many times.

I followed the smell of baking bread and the drone of the television downstairs.

Becky hummed to herself as she removed sweet potatoes from the oven. A crust of lightly browned marshmallows lay over the top. On the small kitchen table sat an assortment of fresh baked breads and casserole dishes.

My mouth fell open. "What time did you get up?"

"I never went to sleep." She grinned. "I was up half the night looking for recipes on your computer. I found so many I liked, I had to make them all." She removed her oven mitt. "*Maam* said I could bring a few things for the meal today."

"A *few* things? It looks like you have the entire meal covered."

"Not even close. There's no turkey, and I could never make a pie crust like *Maam* can."

I pulled a kitchen chair out from under the table. "Can I help?"

"You can help pack everything in the car when the time comes."

"Deal."

"Do you want anything for breakfast?"

I shook my head. "By the looks of it, I'd better save my appetite."

"I can't wait to share all these recipes with my family." Her cheeks glowed from the heat of the oven.

When it was time to head to the farm, we carefully loaded the backseat and trunk of my Bug with all of Becky's dishes. She climbed into the passenger seat, and I handed her a casserole dish. "You'll have to hold the sweet potatoes. There's no room for them in the backseat."

"Too bad Gigabyte can't come," Becky said. "I don't like it he's alone on Thanksgiving."

"He doesn't like to ride in cars." I shivered at the memory of Gigabyte howling the entire way to Appleseed Creek the day we moved to town. "Plus Mabel will be there. They aren't exactly friends."

"We'll bring him some turkey."

"He'd like that."

As we turned out of town, Curt's green pickup approached from the other direction. He honked the horn as he passed me, and waved. I clutched the steering wheel and forced myself to stare straight ahead.

Chapter Twenty-Five

B ecky froze. After a long moment, she whispered, "I guess they really are back"

I loosened my hold on the steering wheel. "I've seen them a couple of times."

"You didn't tell me that." She gripped her casserole dish. "When?"

"I came across them in town yesterday."

Becky shifted in her seat, so that she faced me. "Did they say anything to you?"

"They know about Ezekiel's death and that I discovered his body."

"How would they know that?"

"Gossip, I'm sure. The whole town, both English and Amish, know by now." I checked my rearview mirror.

"Do you think they know because they did it?"

I shivered and wished I could reach into my coat pocket and grab my gloves, which were trapped by the seat-belt buckle. "I don't know."

Becky frowned. "Do you think they have somewhere to go this Thanksgiving?"

I pulled my eyes off the road to stare at her. "What? Why? You don't want to invite them to your parents' house, do you?"

"No," she said quickly. "Only, I feel bad for anyone that may have to be alone on the holiday."

"I'm pretty sure Curt's mother lives somewhere in the county, and besides they aren't alone. They have each other."

"I suppose."

I turned onto the Troyers' road, and a long line of buggies moved slowly up the street. Amish traffic jam. This was worse than the interstate during rush hour. "What's going on?"

"The Glicks live about a mile up the road."

The wedding. How could I forget?

I bit my lip and pulled in line with the Amish buggies. My little VW looked like an alien vessel fallen from the sky during the nineteenth century. "Good thing we left earlier. It might take us a little while to reach your house. We're not moving at all."

She wrapped her arms around the casserole dish like she was giving a teddy bear a good-night hug.

"You okay?"

The buggies inched forward two feet, and we did too. The Troyers' long gravel driveway came into view, but we were still too far away to turn in. A young Amish boy no more than six poked his head out of the back window of the buggy in front of us. He waved widely. The hand of an unseen adult reached out and pulled him back into the buggy.

"I think so. It feels strange to think Isaac's getting married. I don't love Isaac. I don't think I ever really did, but I thought for so long we would marry, if not for love, for companionship. It ties my stomach in knots to think about him marrying someone else, especially Esther Yoder." She gagged.

"I can see that."

"I do miss his friendship though. We had a lot of *gut*—I mean good—times together. Maybe someday he will forgive me." Her tone was sad. "The truth is, if roles were reversed, I don't know if I could forgive him. How can I expect him to forgive me?"

The buggies started moving again. Finally, we were even with the turnoff to the Troyers' drive. Behind us, a couple in the courting buggy watched Becky and I turn into the driveway.

Becky sighed. "The whole district will know we are at my parents' house before the first wedding sermon is over."

I thought about the warning Deacon Sutter gave me the day before. "Do you think we should leave?"

She poked her head out of the Bug's window. "It's too late for that now."

As I parked my car close to the house, I suspected she was right. We climbed out of the Bug and started to remove Becky's dishes from the trunk. The front screen door slammed against the house. Thomas flew down the steps, yanking his winter coat up onto his shoulders.

Becky handed him a casserole dish of sweet potatoes. "You're just in time to help us carry everything inside."

Ruth came more slowly down the steps. The hood of her shawl hid her face.

"Ruth, can you help too?" Becky called.

The thirteen-year-old ignored her older sister and sat on a bench overlooking her mother's vegetable garden on the opposite side of the house. The plants were long gone, plowed back down into the earth. A layer of dead leaves covered the vegetable patch to protect the rich topsoil. I removed the loaf of cranberry bread from the trunk, as snow began to fall in large, fluffy flakes. A white Thanksgiving, just as Timothy had predicted.

Timothy came out of the house then to help us carry in the

rest of the food, followed by his roommate, Danny Lapp. Danny was also formerly Amish. His family lived in western New York. Unfortunately, they were much stricter than the Troyers and had no interest in seeing their son after he left the order.

I nodded my head at Ruth. "What's going on with her?"

Danny's ever-ready dimple popped out. "Teenagers." He rolled his eyes.

Becky pulled a cake carrier from the backseat, a three-layer red velvet cake inside. My thick coat muffled my growling stomach. Maybe skipping breakfast was a mistake. "Is she upset about something?"

Danny took the cake from her hands. "Oh, yeah."

Before Becky could question him further, he spun on his heels and carried the cake into the house. Becky arched an eyebrow at Timothy.

Her brother pursed his lips. "She wanted to go to the wedding and was angry when *Daed* said no."

Becky's brow knit together. "Did he say no because of me? I don't mind if Ruth goes to the wedding."

Timothy shook his head. "The bishop said no one from our family was welcome. It must be related to the warning they gave our parents."

Becky's mouth formed a perfect "O" lined with her pearl-pink lipstick.

The deacon had told me the truth, as much as it hurt. The Troyers weren't excluded because of Becky or Timothy. Ultimately, they were excluded because of me. Guilt stabbed my heart. Silently, I promised myself that this would be my last visit to the Troyer farm.

I would make it count.

Chapter Twenty-Six

Mrs. Troyer's gaze took in the array of dishes we had brought in. "Becky, how can we possibly eat all of this?" She lifted the lid from one of the casseroles Becky had prepared. "What's this?"

"Manicotti." Becky removed the cornbread from the oven. "I got the recipe from television."

For the briefest moment, a pained look crossed her mother's face. Becky missed it, though, because she had closed her eyes to savor the warm cornbread smell. It did smell wonderful. Everything did. I groaned inwardly. My diet would resume after Thanksgiving, I promised myself. "Can I help?" I placed the red velvet cake on the maplewood hutch in the corner, piled high with desserts.

As expected, both Becky and Mrs. Troyer said in unison, "No, you're a guest."

Mrs. Troyer replaced the lid on the manicotti. "There is one thing, Chloe. Could you go outside and find Ruth? She should be in here to help her sister and me."

I supposed that since Ruth wasn't a guest that was allowed.

"Okay." I wrapped my scarf back around my neck. I hadn't yet removed my coat.

During the brief time I had been indoors, the snow had picked up considerably. As I slipped across the slick grass, I wished I'd worn practical snow boots instead of the stylish, calf-high pair with no tread. The boots were meant for walking the sidewalk of a city, not the fields of an Amish farm.

Ruth had not moved from the moment she stormed out of the house. She still sat on the bench, staring into the remnants of her mother's summer vegetable garden. Now a thin layer of snow lay over the leaves piled on the garden to protect the soil during the long winter. Snowflakes also gathered on the brim of Ruth's bonnet and her black apron.

"Ruth, are you ready to come back inside? Your mom sent me out here to look for you."

She shook her head.

"Mind if I sit?"

When she didn't react, I took that as a yes—or at least an *I don't care*.

As best I could, I brushed off the snow that had collected on the bench. The wet snow soaked the cotton fingers of my gloves, so I buried my hands deep into my coat pockets. "What are you doing out here in the cold?" I sat beside her on the bench. *Lord, give me the right words to say.*

She shrugged.

"You're not wearing your cloak. We should go inside. You'll freeze if you sit out here much longer."

"I don't care." Her voice was sullen. Spoken like a true teenager.

I suppressed a smile. Amish teens weren't that much different from English ones. Same attitude, just no Internet. "Why don't you care? Is it because you didn't go to the wedding?"

She gave a long, suffering sigh. "Yes, no, it's everything. I don't get to go anywhere anymore. I never see my friends, not even Anna."

I had the itchy feeling I wasn't the best person to have this conversation with Ruth, but I forged ahead. "I know rules in the district have gotten stricter."

She turned to me, her blue eyes accusing. "What would you know about it? You're an *Englischer*."

I swallowed. "I know what I've heard when your family has spoken about it." I wrapped my arms around myself for warmth. "But you're right, I don't really know about it. How has the district changed?"

Some of the anger died in her eyes. "The smallest step out of line is held up in front of the church during Sunday services."

"What do you mean by 'held up'?"

"Well, when one of Anna's brothers had his hair cut too short, the bishop mentioned it in church and asked us to pray for him. That way next time he would know the right way to style his hair. Anna's family was horrified. Her father was furious at Anna's brother."

"Maybe this is one reason they won't let Anna see you. They don't want that to happen again."

She folded her hands in her lap. "I know it is. No one wants to be embarrassed in front of the church." Her knuckles turned white. "Bishop Glick would never have reprimanded someone in front of the entire church for something so minor." She shivered, then continued, "The next week the bishop talked about our family. You should have seen *Daed's* face—I've never seen him so red." She paused. "The bishop spoke of you visiting us. Becky and Timothy, too. He warned how close friendships with *Englischers* can lead the community away from the church. Ever since then, we've been treated like lepers."

"When was that?"

"Two weeks ago."

And I'm just hearing about this now? Had I known all along, I would have stayed away from the Troyer home. I didn't want to be the reason for friction between them and their district.

"Yesterday, the deacon was here and told us not to go to the wedding. My parents weren't going to go, but Grandfather Zook promised to take me. I love weddings." Her eyes filled with tears. "At school, I told Anna I would be there. Now, she must think I forgot about her."

"You can tell her at school what happened."

"If she will talk to me."

"Sounds like she talks to you at school."

"Some. Not like before. She's afraid our teacher will tell her father. I only see her for a few minutes at recess."

"I'm sorry, Ruth." I didn't know what else to say.

"We aren't the only ones who have been singled out by the bishop. For the young people on *rumspringa*, the bishop and deacon have canceled all kinds of singing and social times. Many of the teenagers are angry. I saw a bunch of them standing outside church a few weeks ago, whispering together. The bishop canceled their fall social."

"Who were they?"

She thought a moment. "There must have been ten of them. I remember Leah Miller was there because she looked the angriest."

Leah again.

I kicked off the snow collecting on the top of my boots. "Isn't *rumspringa* free time for Amish youth?"

"It is, but the deacon and bishop don't care." She twisted her hands in her lap. She hadn't worn her cloak, but at least she'd had enough sense to wear her gloves. "Truth is they are going to drive more people away from the Amish."

For thirteen, Ruth was an astute observer of human nature. I stood. "Maybe the new bishop's adjusting. That's what your father thinks. It can't be easy being thrown in as leader. After some time, he will relax the rules, and I'm sure that Anna's family will let you see each other soon."

"You don't know how it works. The only way we can be *gut* friends again is if you, Timothy, and Becky stay away from us."

Her words stung. I suspected, though, that they were the truth.

She brushed snow from her lap and stood. "Sometimes I wish Becky and Timothy would come home, so we can be like we were before. Why can't they be happy with us being Amish?"

"It wasn't an easy decision for them."

She dropped her head. "I know."

"You think you will stay Amish when it's your time to decide?"

Her eyes widened. "Of course. I don't want to be anything else." She paused. I don't," she added, as if to convince us both.

I bumped her shoulder. "Not even for Danny Lapp?"

She turned bright red and covered her face with her hands. "I can't believe I behaved like this with Danny in the house. He must think I'm such a child."

"Ruth, he's at least ten years older than you."

"*Daed*'s eight years older than Maam. That's not much different." She looked wistful. "Do you think he will come back to the Amish?"

I doubted it, but I didn't tell her that. "Let's go inside."

The long dining table inside the kitchen was set. Becky and her mother bustled around the room with ease, Mrs. Troyer in her simple dress, apron, and prayer cap, Becky in her pink cable knit sweater, jeans, and makeup. I suspected that last Thanksgiving Mrs. Troyer had not thought that her daughter would be assisting a year later wearing American Eagle jeans.

Mrs. Troyer handed Ruth an oven mitt. "I'm glad you were able to make it inside, daughter."

Ruth bowed her head. "I'm sorry, *Maam.*"

Her mother nodded.

As the women worked in the kitchen, the men sat in the next room chatting in Pennsylvania Dutch. I smiled at the low-pitch rumble of their words punctuated by higher-pitched exclamations from Thomas and Naomi, who was too small to help her mother in the kitchen. I was not a man or a small child. I didn't fit in the living room.

Mrs. Troyer smiled and took pity on me. "Chloe, can you fill the water glasses on the table?"

I smiled. It was the first time Mrs. Troyer had asked me to help.

Finally, the meal was ready. Mrs. Troyer ventured into the living room to tell the men and Naomi that it was time for dinner. The family slid onto the bench seats with Grandfather Zook at one end, and Mr. Troyer at the other. As one we bowed our heads for the blessing. I waited to hear the Pennsylvania Dutch words.

Every Thanksgiving dish I could imagine, and some I didn't expect—like Becky's manicotti—covered the long oak table. The turkey, its tanned skin glistening and shining in the gaslight hanging overhead, had been placed near Mr. Troyer's plate. Mashed potatoes oozed butter next to a white, porcelain gravy boat. Amish noodles, green beans, corn, and relish all had their own serving dishes too. I didn't even look at the dozens of desserts on the hutch, waiting to be served.

"Dear Lord," Mr. Troyer began, his head bowed and eyes tightly closed. "Thank You for Your abundant blessing on this Thanksgiving Day."

My head snapped up. It was the first time he'd given the blessing in English, and it was for me. I was the only one in the room who couldn't understand Pennsylvania Dutch. Tears formed in the corners of my eyes. As I started to bow my head, I caught Timothy watching me. His smile showed me that he knew how I felt about the prayer. Mr. Troyer finished and the moment he said, "Amen," empty plates and full-serving dishes were being passed around the table.

Grandfather Zook took a sip of his water. "Chloe, did you see my beard? It grew at least an inch overnight. I have such a fine chin to grow a beard. That must be why the perp sought me out."

"*Daed*," Mrs. Troyer chided. "That sounds prideful."

Her father selected some dill pickles from a dish. "It's not prideful, just a statement of fact."

"It does look a little longer." I added relish onto my very full plate.

The old man grinned. "See? You don't notice, Martha, because you see me all day long, but those who are away notice more." He speared a pickle with a fork. "I'm looking forward to showing the boys at the general store come this spring."

"If they'll talk to you," Ruth muttered into her piece of manicotti.

A pained expression crossed her parents' faces.

Danny cocked his head. "Why wouldn't they? I imagine Grandfather Zook is the center of attention when he goes to the store."

Grandfather Zook pointed the pickle at Danny. "You're right about that."

Mr. Troyer spooned stuffing onto his plate. "Much in the district has changed in the last few months."

Thomas spoke up. "The bishop canceled the Thanksgiving play at the schoolhouse, even though we worked so hard on it." He created a small mountain of corn on his plate. "He said theatrics were sinful."

Grandfather Zook shook his head. "The Amish Bread Bakery

said they didn't need our milk or cheese anymore. They would get it from someplace else."

Mr. Troyer scowled at his father-in-law and said something in their language.

"*Daed*?" Timothy paled. "Is that true?"

"It is," his father answered.

"It won't be long before other Amish businesses fall in line. Everyone wants to stay out of the deacon's way." Grandfather Zook cut into his ham slice. "Becky, this is *gut*!"

She beamed.

"Don't you mean the bishop?" Danny asked.

"The deacon's the one who is really running the show. I'm sure he's happy to see our dairy struggle."

A knot formed in my stomach. *The dairy farm is struggling?*

Danny's dimple receded into his cheek. "Sounds an awful lot like my old district."

Becky sliced into the turkey breast on her plate. "What did you do about it?"

Danny cleared his throat. "I left."

Mr. Troyer set his mug of coffee on the table. "Most of our milk goes to the *Englischer* milkman. There is no need to worry. No more talk about the bishop or *Grossdaddi's* beard. This is Thanksgiving. We should be counting our many blessings from the Lord, not our challenges."

I cleared my throat. "I'm going to be in the holiday parade tomorrow."

Thomas bounced in his seat. "What? Really?"

I told them about the snowman costume. Even Mr. Troyer cracked a smile.

Thomas looked at his father. "Can we go? I want to see Chloe, the snowman."

Mr. Troyer considered this. "We'll see. It depends how you behave today. If you are *gut*, maybe *Grossdaddi* will take you."

Grandfather Zook chuckled. "That means eating all of your carrots."

Thomas's eyes widened. He looked at the carrots his mother had piled on his plate. With determination, he forked one and shoved it into his mouth.

The conversation shifted as Danny, who worked as a stable hand at a horse farm, told about the summer he worked as a rodeo clown. Everyone laughed at his story except Ruth.

Suddenly, the very real threat of tears caused me to duck my head. *This* was the Thanksgiving dinner I had always hoped for, and in a place I never expected. I composed myself and looked up. Ruth had barely touched her plate.

As much as I wanted to be with this family, though, I wouldn't be the cause of Mr. Troyer's farm failing—or the reason Ruth wouldn't eat.

Chapter Twenty-Seven

Unable to sleep because of worries about the Troyer family, I got up in the middle of the night. I pulled my iPad from my nightstand and logged onto my e-mail account. The box was full of notices about great Black Friday sales in stores I used to frequent when I lived in Cleveland. Not one of those stores existed in Knox County. I deleted them all. Following the ads were four forwarded message from Tanisha—all from Cole.

I opened the first one. *I'm sorry. Cole.*

My stomach constricted. The message was dated in October.

Next message, a few days later. *Baby, I'm sorry. Can you forgive me? C*

The next e-mail showed up two weeks after that. *I never expected you to be this cold. Please contact me. I love you. C*

I bit my lip. The final message was dated the Monday before Thanksgiving. *Tanisha, if you can't forgive me, I want my ring back. Cole.*

Uh-oh.

There was another e-mail from Tanisha. *Okay, give me the Cliff's Notes version. I can take it. Tee.*

I wasn't so sure about that. I sent a reply. *Umm . . . he's sorry, says he loves you, and asked about the ring.*

Instantly, her e-mail reply appeared. *First, what are you still doing up? It must be two in the morning there. He asked about the ring? Not good.*

I typed my reply. *Not good at all.*

We e-mailed back and forth until I was too tired to hold my iPad up.

The next morning you wouldn't know it was Black Friday in Appleseed Creek. The only open shops in town were Amish owned, and the grocery store didn't have the same draw that the large department stores in Columbus or even the English discount stores in Mount Vernon did.

I didn't miss the frenzied shopping. Typically, on this day I would be in the San Diego airport waiting for my flight back to Cleveland. As expected, I ate way too much at the Troyers' farm yesterday and felt queasy when my alarm went off at seven that morning. I groaned.

By the time I arrived at Harshberger's gymnasium I was more awake, but no less queasy. I hadn't even bothered entering the kitchen that morning because our refrigerator and counters were packed with leftovers from the day before.

I walked around the building and pulled up short. The float. Two days before it looked like a flatbed truck that had gone three rounds with an enormous cotton ball. Today, it looked like a winter wonderland. A large igloo with a pretend campfire in front of it sat on one side. Red and orange tissue paper agitated by a small fan underneath moved the flames back and forth. On the opposing end, a blue kidney-shaped platform represented a frozen pond. The largest stuffed animal polar bear I'd ever seen stood at the edge of the pond. It was taller than I was. In the middle of the float stood a red and white North Pole.

"Like it?" Billy asked. "I bought the bear on eBay. Thirty bucks."

"It's impressive." I peered into the igloo. "Can someone fit in there?"

"Sure. I fit, and three people your size would be comfortable." He pointed to the middle of the float. "That's where you're going to stand, right next to the North Pole. You will be the float's main attraction."

Great.

Collette stepped out of the gymnasium, her face pinched. "Chloe, please come inside and put on your costume. We have to join the parade line in twenty minutes."

Was it a bad sign that I may need the entire twenty minutes to don my snowman suit?

I wanted to ask Collette what she was doing at Young's on Wednesday afternoon, but she bustled around the gym with an irritated expression on her face. This wasn't the time.

Mary was waiting for me in her makeshift sewing studio in one corner of the gym. Next to her was the snowman suit.

She smiled shyly at me. "What do you think?"

What could I say? The snowman was cute. The first piece was the body and would fall to the middle of my calf. It had large black buttons running down the tummy and a red bow tie. The head had a felt carrot nose, eye holes, and a red fabric smile. Regardless of the costume's cuteness, I didn't want to wear it.

Collette strode by at a fast pace. "Stop staring at it and put it on."

Mary took a step back from her. While Collette moved on to the next victim, I rolled my eyes at Mary, and she smiled. She handed me a pair of white leggings and the body of the snowman suit. I stepped behind a Chinese screen in the corner of her work area. As I waddled out from behind the screen, I knew what a penguin felt like.

Mary adjusted the suit on my shoulders so that it hung straighter.

"How did the wedding go yesterday?" I ventured.

"*Gut*. I don't think I have ever seen Esther so happy." She took a lint brush to the back of the costume.

"I'm glad for her," I said, meaning it.

She put the lint brush away in her sewing box. "I'm sorry that none of the Troyers were there. I heard you were at their home yesterday."

I hadn't mentioned the Troyers when Mary and I met, but apparently she already knew my connection to the family. Becky had been right. Our presence at the Troyer home during Thanksgiving was known across the district. "I was. We had a nice Thanksgiving meal."

She picked up the snowman head from the floor. "The bishop wasn't pleased when he heard the news."

"What did he do?"

She wagged her chin and handed me the head. "Everyone else is outside."

I pressed her. "Did he say anything?"

She began to pack up her sewing kit. "I can't say."

I'd been dismissed. Reluctantly, I waddled out of the gym. Collette stood with Billy and Dylan next to the float. Billy had hitched it to a pickup truck and would be driving us through the parade. I blinked when I saw Dylan's costume. I'd seen Dylan's male figure skater getup on Wednesday, but apparently it hadn't yet received its full, bedazzled treatment by then. I hadn't seen so many sequins outside of Disney World. I muffled a giggle. A professor from the art department was his skating partner.

Looked like Dean Klink was unable to find any more recruits for the float.

The art professor ignored me. She was already on the "ice," practicing her moves. Dylan however made a beeline for me. "You look great, Chloe." His voice was muffled.

He had to be joking, right? I was a *snowman*. The costume's large head impaired my view, so I couldn't see his expression.

"All aboard," Billy cried.

Dylan hopped onto the float and took his place next to the art professor. I stared at the step up. It was two feet off the ground. Normally this would be a minor challenge at my height. In a snowman suit, it was impossible.

Billy chuckled. "Let me give you a boost." Despite the enormous suit, Billy picked me up and placed me on the float as if I weighed no more than a matchbook.

He climbed into the truck's cabin.

Collette pointed at each of us in turn. "Please don't embarrass the college. Chloe, we need to talk after the parade."

Talk? About what?

The truck fired up and Billy jerked the trailer along after him. I grabbed the North Pole to keep from toppling over. Billy waited for the high school marching band, the mayor in a convertible, and a flock of cheerleaders to pass before he turned the float into the line.

I kept my hand firmly placed on the North Pole as we made the turn. A block away from the college, the citizens of Appleseed Creek lined the tree lawns and sidewalks six deep. I hadn't ever realized there were that many people living in town. Most were English, but I saw several Amish faces in the crowd too. A little boy cried "Frosty!" when the float rocked by, and I found myself smiling. This wasn't so bad.

We crawled another block and turned onto the square. Chief Rose stood at the edge of the square with her hands on her hip, her sober, don't-mess-with-me face, firmly in place.

Sadie stood outside of the bakery. The smallest of smiles played on her face. I hoped the parade lifted her spirits. I waved at her. She waved back even though she couldn't possibly know who was behind the giant Frosty head.

I suspected she was alone at the bakery today. Esther would be at the Glick farm, cleaning up after the wedding. I decided to stop by the bakery after the parade. Collette and her talk would have to wait.

Curt and Brock stood a little farther down the sidewalk. The pair made wolf whistles at the art professor in her sequined outfit. I was never happier to be in the snowman suit. I didn't wave to them. Not that they noticed.

Through the open back window of the pickup, Billy called, "We go around the square twice. Be sure to hold on tight during the curves."

When we passed the place were Curt and Brock had been standing, another familiar pair stood in front of the cheese shop—Deacon Sutter and Collette. The odd duo stood inches apart. Collette waved her arms as she spoke, and the deacon, arms folded, glared back at her. My hand slid from the North Pole, and I righted myself so as not to fall off of the float. Appleseed Creek was tiny, but how did she get there so quickly from the college? What could they possibly have to say to each other? As the trailer pulled around the next curve, I pivoted so I could look at them. The stomachache I'd had earlier in the morning came back with a vengeance.

Billy turned down the next road off the square, keeping pace with the cheerleaders frolicking in front of him. As we turned the corner, Timothy, Becky, Grandfather Zook, Thomas, and Naomi waved widely at me. They knew who was hiding in that snowman suit. I waved back and grinned from ear to ear. I had family waiting for me. An unfamiliar sense of peace washed over me.

"Yea! Chloe, the snow lady!" Thomas cried in top voice over

the marching band and the cheerleaders. As we passed, I turned so I could wave to them until we were out of sight. As I did, I faced the art professor and Dylan, who stood as if frozen on the ice. He no longer twirled about the blue platform with his partner, but instead, stared at me and the way I gleefully waved at the Troyers. His partner continued to twirl and leap as if she were giving a private performance for the Olympic trials.

I dropped my hand.

Back at the college, Billy lifted me off of the float. I removed the snowman head.

The art professor leaped off the float. "That was wonderful." Then she danced away.

Dylan walked over to me. "Chloe, I hope you didn't forget I planned to work on the house today."

I chewed the corner of my lip. I *had* forgotten.

Irritation crossed Dylan's face. "You forgot."

"It's fine if you come over. I have to run an errand now, but Becky should be there if I'm not home by the time you get there. She doesn't have to work until late this afternoon."

He nodded and turned away.

I waddled back into the gym. Mary and her makeshift studio were gone. She had left a note asking me to leave the costume in the corner of the gym and someone would collect it. I stepped behind the Chinese screen and changed back into my jeans and sweater.

I placed the snowman suit in the place directed. I was the only person in the gym. Apparently, Dylan and the art professor had somewhere else to change. *Unless the outfits were part of their private collections.* I could believe it about the art professor.

Collette was missing too, for which I was grateful. Guess our talk would have to wait. Her conversation with the Amish deacon may have been completely innocent, but something in my gut fluttered.

Behind me, footsteps echoed through the gymnasium. My chest tightened. I had thought I was alone in the building. The steps quickened. I glanced behind me as a looming figure stepped out from behind the folded bleachers, and poised myself to run.

Chapter Twenty-Eight

I picked up the snowman head, ready to hurl it at the approaching figure.

"Whoa, Chloe!" A campus security guard stepped up to the bleachers. "What are you doing with that snowman?"

My face burned. "I . . . um . . . I was on the float." I let the snowman head drop to the ground.

He eyed it as if he knew there was more to it than that. "Are you done here? I need to lock up the building."

I replaced the head in its designated spot. "I'm done. Have a nice weekend." Then, I fled.

From Harshberger's gym I walked straight to the Amish Bread Bakery. The bell on the bakery door rang as I entered. Sadie worked alone in the front of the shop, business brisk as parade watchers came in for a sweet treat and something warm to drink. A lock of hair fell from Sadie's prayer cap. This time, no one made any comment as she tucked the jagged, stray hair behind her ear.

A woman in a neon orange winter coat stepped to the front of the line. "Five donuts," she said.

Sadie lifted a piece of waxed tissue paper from the box on the counter and selected the donuts. The line grew longer as she moved to the cash register to ring up the woman's purchase.

A large man stepped into the store, surveyed the line, then let out an irritated sigh and left. I wove through the crowd. At the cash register, Sadie looked close to tears.

"Do you need any help?" I asked.

She blinked at me. "I—"

"Miss, miss," the English woman waiting to pay for her donuts said. "I don't have all day. My daughter and I want to get to Columbus to shop before all the deals are over."

Sadie seemed confused by this comment. I slid behind the counter, washed my hands in the small sink, and donned a white apron that hung from a peg by the kitchen door. "Sadie, you run the cash register, and I will help customers with their selection."

I turned to the next customer. "What would you like?"

"Three blueberry muffins, please."

I removed the wax tissue paper from the box and selected three muffins from the large, domed-glass counter case. My movement spurred Sadie into action. She rang up the impatient shopper.

After the last customer left, I removed the apron and hung it back on the peg.

"*Danki* for your help." She opened the cash register and counted out some bills. Sadie held some out to me.

I waved the money away. "No."

Her shoulders relaxed, and she returned the money to the drawer. "Would you like some *kaffi*?"

"I'd love some."

She took two large, white mugs from the shelf from behind the counter and filled both with black coffee. She set a cream pitcher and sugar dish on the small table in the coffee nook. "Why don't you pick out a couple of donuts for us?"

My stomachache was completely gone, and I realized I was hungry. I selected two chocolate cake donuts. My diet would start *the day after* the day after Thanksgiving.

I sat with Sadie at the table, each of us doctoring our coffee to our liking.

The cake donut melted in my mouth.

"*Danki* again. Esther's not here today because of the wedding."

I warmed my hands around the coffee mug. "Did you attend? How did it go?"

"*Gut.* I think they are a match for each other. Both Isaac and Esther were happy."

"I'm glad." Isaac deserved some happiness after the year he'd had.

Her eyes dimmed. "Yesterday I couldn't help but think of my wedding, the one that is not to be." She touched a paper napkin to the corner of her eye.

"Are you okay?"

"I am. This must all be part of *Gott*'s plan for me and for Ezekiel. The hardest part is no one knows about our understanding. You are the only one I've told."

"You didn't tell any of your friends?"

"Ezekiel was my only friend. Everyone else turned away from me when my father became the bishop. They blame me for his rules, as if I can change his mind. I can't. The only time anyone speaks to me is here at the bakery. That is, except for you."

I thought for a minute. Sadie's situation wasn't much different from the Troyers' and it circled back to the rules imposed by the bishop and deacon.

"Do you know why your father has become so strict?"

She was quiet for a moment, and I wondered if she would answer at all. "He never wanted this. He didn't even want to be a preacher. Being the bishop is so much more. He was heartbroken when he found the verse in his songbook."

"Sadie, did Ezekiel have a dispute with anyone?"

The chocolate donut stopped halfway to her mouth. She set it back on the plate. "What do you mean?"

"Could there be anyone that may have wanted to hurt him or his family?"

"I thought the person who cut my hair killed him. Isn't that what the police think?"

To be honest, I didn't know what the police thought. Chief Rose hadn't shared her theories with me, although she had certainly expected me to share my ideas on the crime with her.

"I can't think of anyone." She grimaced. "Ezekiel wasn't well liked. He could be prickly. He was a shrewd businessman and didn't show many people his softer side. I may be the only one who saw it."

What was it about Sadie that made Ezekiel lower his guard?

"Did he ever talk about his brother-in-law, James Zug?"

"Maybe once or twice."

"What did he say?"

She moved the donut crumbs around her plate with the tip her finger. "James wanted to be part of the business. Ezekiel and Uri didn't want him to be."

"Why not . . . he's family?"

She blinked at me from behind her glasses. "Because it's owned by the Young family and should stay in the Young family."

"Bridget is a Young. She's still part of the family."

"She's married. It is different."

Primogeniture was alive and well in Amish world.

"And James is Abby's father, which makes Ezekiel her uncle. Don't you think it odd that two people in the same family were so brutally attacked?"

"I—I don't know. Everyone is related to everyone else in the district," she said, basically giving me the same explanation that Timothy had.

"How did he get along with his brother?"

Sadie's eyes darted all over the bakery. "His brother?"

I nodded. "I know they were twins, but they seemed distant."

She laughed, but the mirth didn't reach her eyes. "Different temperaments."

"Is that all?" I reduced my donut to crumbs and stopped myself from licking the plate clean.

"Ezekiel was angry at Uri about something."

I leaned forward. "What?"

"I don't know. Ezekiel wasn't one to talk about how he felt. Most Amish men don't. I knew he was angry about it because Ezekiel and I went on a walk right after he fought with Uri. I've seen him upset at Uri many times but never this angry."

"What did he say? Do you remember anything specific?"

"He said if he wanted something done right, he would have to do it himself."

"Was he angry enough to confront his brother? Maybe the two got into a fight?"

"Ezekiel wasn't afraid to confront anyone. That's what I loved about him. I'm afraid of my own shadow, but Ezekiel's fearless." She twisted her paper napkin on the tabletop. "He'd protect me."

"Can you show me the alley?" I asked.

"The alley?"

"The back entrance of the bakery where you were attacked."

She shivered, and after a long minute she nodded. She led me behind the counter and through the kitchen. Huge mixers and convection ovens stood quietly, waiting until the early morning when they would be used again. In the back of the kitchen, Sadie opened a heavy metal door, and propped it open with a chair.

Even in the middle of the day, the light in the alley was dim, blocked by the shops facing the square, such as the bakery and cheese shop next door, and the one-hundred-year-old bank building that soared above us. Two cement steps led to the gravel-speckled blacktop. I imagined Sadie standing on the steps in the early morning darkness, trying to unlock the door. A faceless man comes up behind her, throws the burlap bag over her head, and knocks her to the ground. I swallowed.

The alley was wide enough for one car to drive through, or perhaps a delivery truck, although it would be a tight fit. A green Dumpster sat between the bakery and cheese shop back doors. Sadie had said she heard a vehicle drive down the alley after her assailant left. Could it have been Curt and Brock?

Sadie pointed to a spot to the left of the door on the blacktop. "This is where I was held on the ground." Tears gathered in her eyes.

"I'm sorry, Sadie."

Through the open back door, we heard the front door bell ring. She exhaled a breath, as if in relief. "I must go."

I touched her arm. "Can I pray for you?"

Tears gathered in her eyes. "*Ya.*"

Sadie and I returned to the front of the store to find an English customer examining the bakery's cake selection. I thanked Sadie for the donut and left the shop. A conversation with Uri Young was in order, but I would wait until Timothy was able to join me. The next stop I could make on my own.

Chapter Twenty-Nine

L ike in the bakery, locals and visitors in downtown Appleseed
Creek for the morning's parade crowded the small cheese
shop. Three women worked at the deli counter cutting Swiss,
Muenster, Colby, and other cheeses to their customers' specifications.

Long, open-air refrigerator cases lined the two walls and
another case ran down the middle of the room. What looked like
Astroturf surrounded large hunks of cheese and their handwritten
name cards. A white container of toothpicks sat beside each card
with quarter-inch cubes of free cheese samples.

A line wrapped around the store as visitors wanted to taste
every cheese. Debbie was halfway up the first chill counter, refilling
the containers of samples. I stepped into line. Two middle school
boys were in front of me in droopy jeans and coats three times too
large for them. They whispered together as they skewered cheese.
"You ask her," one snickered.

"No way? You ask," the friend whispered back.

We inched forward. The boys stuffed their mouths with cheese.
Finally, they were right next to Debbie. They jostled each other.
The larger of the two asked, "Hey, do you have an outhouse?"

Debbie blinked at them.

His friend laughed. "She can't answer you because she doesn't speak English."

The larger kid asked more slowly, "Do. You. Have. An. Outhouse?"

Debbie concentrated on her work of refilling the cheese tubs.

I stepped between the boys and Debbie, and arched an eyebrow at them. "Do you have a belt?"

The kid straightened his shoulders. "I wasn't talking to you, Red."

I'd met a mini-Brock. I gave them my best responsible adult glare. "I know you weren't talking to me, and she wasn't talking to you either. Why don't you pull up your pants and get out of here."

Mini-Brock, who was almost as tall as me, got in my face. "Are you gonna make me?"

"No, but that guy will." I pointed to a large Amish man who had just stepped into the store with a milk delivery.

The smaller of the two pulled on his friend's sleeve. "This is lame. Let's go."

"Yeah. We weren't going to buy anything anyway."

Like that's a surprise.

"Are you okay?" I asked Debbie when mini-Curt and Brock were out the door. The milk delivery man left the store not knowing the role he'd played.

"I'm sorry. Usually kids like that don't bother me."

"Does that happen a lot?"

She shook her head. "Not every day." Her wide-set brown eyes brimmed with tears. "Today, I'm afraid of my own shadow."

"After what has happened to you, I can see why."

She began refilling the peppercorn cheese.

"Did I say something wrong?"

"No. I'm sorry." She cleared her throat. "Can I help you make a selection?"

"Of cheese?"

"That's why you're here, isn't it? That's what we sell."

"I know that. I'd like to talk to you about—"

"I can't," she whispered. "I've already told you everything I know."

A woman elbowed between us. "Sue! Sue!" she cried to a friend. "They have peppercorn. Isn't that your husband's favorite?" She stuck her toothpick into the largest piece. "Oh my, it melts in your mouth, but there's a kick." She stepped out of line and joined her friend at the deli counter.

"What kind of cheese do you want?" Debbie asked.

How could I possibly take more food into the house with Thanksgiving already overloading our kitchen? "Did Abby say anything about her uncle?"

Debbie moved to the next cheese container. *Onion cheese.* "You will have to ask her."

I plan to.

"I can't talk to you about this. Leah said not to talk to you." She replaced the lid on the onion cheese container.

"Do you do everything Leah says?"

She glared at me through watery eyes. "Do you plan to buy something? Now, what kind of cheese would you like?"

I sighed. "Cheddar."

She stepped away from the counter. "Follow me." I wove around guests to the end of the opposing counter where she gestured to its contents. "We have fourteen kinds." Then she walked away.

In the end, I bought a half pound of yellow cheddar. I knew Becky could use it for something.

Chapter Thirty

I parked on the street in front of my house and stared at the all-too-familiar green pickup truck in my driveway. A shiver traveled down my spine. Should I call Chief Rose? Timothy? Both?

Before I could make up my mind, the front door opened. Dylan stepped onto the front porch followed by Curt and Brock. I jumped out of the Bug. "Dylan! What's going on here?"

A slow smile moved across Curt's face. "What's the matter, Red?"

Dylan walked down the porch steps. "What's wrong? I told you I'd be working on the house today."

"I knew you were, but you didn't tell me that they'd be here," I hissed.

"They are helping me with the restoration. I told you I might have some workers with me."

"Yes." I didn't want to get into my history with Curt and Brock. "Please, ask them to leave."

Snow fell onto Dylan's dark head, like dandruff. He brushed the snow away. "I can't ask them to leave now. We just started."

"I'm sorry, Dylan, but you will."

Curt and Brock poked at each other on my front porch, reminding me of the two boys at the cheese shop.

"Where's Becky? Is she here?" It made me queasy to think of Becky being in the same house with Curt and Brock.

"She left for work a half hour ago." Dylan's voice sounded close to a whine.

"She let them inside our house?"

"No, Curt and Brock were late." He flushed slightly. "She left before they got here."

"I want them out, Dylan. *Now.* They aren't welcome in my house."

He glared at me. "It's not your house. You sound like my wife. I can make decisions too."

I stepped back. "I'm sure you can, but if they are going to be on the property, Becky and I are moving out."

"You can't do that—you have a lease." He gave me a lopsided smile. "Besides, they said they were friends of yours."

"Do they *look* like my friends?"

Brock lumbered down the steps. "Aw, Red, that hurts. It really does."

"You two have to leave." My voice shook.

Curt moseyed over. "Why's that? We're working."

"If you don't leave right now, I'll call the police." I pulled my cell from my coat pocket.

"No reason to get your dander up, Red." Brock held up his hands in mock surrender. The snow crunched under his feet as he took a step back.

Curt turned to Dylan. "If you have another job, give us a call. This one's not going to work out for us."

Dylan's mouth fell open. "But . . ."

Tobacco juice flecked onto Curt's cheek. "See you around, Red."

He and Brock sauntered to their pickup. Seeing the two of them around was becoming more frequent by the day.

After the green truck roared down the street, Dylan threw up his hands. "Now, I have to find someone else for the job."

I tried to keep my voice level, but I heard it shake. "Curt and Brock aren't welcome here. The Troyer family and I have a history with them. I don't want to talk about it. If you want to know what it is, read last summer's edition of the Mount Vernon newspaper."

"This is my investment. I can't tiptoe around when I have progress to make."

"I live here, and you should respect my wishes," I snapped. "Timothy offered to help you."

"I don't want any Amish help," he said through gritted teeth. "And I most certainly don't want Timothy's help."

"Timothy's a professional."

"Are you saying I'm not?" he asked. "Kara, you don't trust me at all."

I froze. "Who's Kara?"

He blinked at me as if waking up from a dream.

"Kara is your wife, isn't she?" I whispered.

He turned and stalked to his car in the driveway. "Next time I show up with a work crew, we are going to work. I don't care if you approve or not." He slammed his car door.

I stood on the frozen lawn in stunned silence. Timothy's truck came up the street from the opposite direction. He turned into my driveway and hopped out, holding a small brown sack in his hand. "It's freezing. What are you doing outside?" He stepped closer to me. "Chloe, what's wrong?"

I told him.

Timothy clenched the fist holding the paper sack. The brown

paper crunched under the pressure. "I think you and Becky may need to find another place to live."

I silently agreed. It no longer felt like home. It no longer felt safe.

"You're going to catch a chill. Let's go inside." He steered me in the direction of the house.

Gigabyte crawled out from under the sofa when we stepped through the front door. He yowled.

I scooped up the cat. "Oh, Gig. Are you okay? They didn't hurt you, did they?"

He yowled again.

Timothy placed the sack on the coffee table and removed his coat. "I'm going to take a look around."

I perched on the edge of the armchair with Gig in my lap and listened as Timothy moved from room to room.

He was back within minutes. "I didn't notice anything out of the ordinary . . ." He stared at the wall that separated the living room from the mudroom and kitchen.

"What is it?"

Timothy traced his finger along the wall.

I stood up, still carrying my cat, and stood by him. There was a faint penciled *X* on the wall.

Timothy knocked on the wall there. "This is hollow." He peered up. "See at the ceiling line the plaster is a lighter color? This wall was added after the original construction of the house."

I pointed at the *X*. "Becky and I didn't do that."

He shook his head. "I didn't think you did. Dylan drew this line. He's going to knock down this wall."

"What?" I squeezed Gigabyte to my chest. He kicked at me with his back claws, and I dropped him to the floor. "He can't do that."

"We need to talk to Chief Rose about this and maybe Becky's lawyer too." Timothy dropped his hand from the wall.

"I don't think they were here very long." I crossed my arms. "Dylan said they came after Becky left for work, so they were here all of twenty minutes before I arrived."

"Good thing. You might have returned to find a hole in your wall." He sighed. "I wish I'd been here sooner."

"Why are you here?" I paused. "Not that I don't appreciate it."

Timothy walked over to the brown bag on the coffee table. "To bring you this." He handed it to me.

I opened the bag and saw a delicate African violet inside. The leaves were velvety and deep jungle green, the petals soft and almost black purple. "It's beautiful."

"I know it's not very big, but I saw it at Young's gift shop today and thought of you."

Unwittingly, my eyes glanced at Dylan's mum arrangement by the front window. It was lavish, bright, and over the top. In comparison, the violet was small, understated, and alive. I bit my lip, hoping that my black thumb would keep it that way.

Timothy misread my expression. "I know it's not as big as Dylan's flowers."

I placed a hand on his arm. "It's perfect. I love it. Thank you."

A smile broke on his face. "Ellie thought you'd like it too. She wrapped it up for me." He reached into his jeans pocket and handed me a folded piece of loose-leaf paper. "She wrote down the directions on how to care for it too."

"These will help." I took the paper. "Is Ellie back at work?"

"No, she just happened to be in the shop when I made the purchase."

"When is the funeral?" I placed the violet on an end table by the front window. It was a miniature next to Dylan's mums.

"Tomorrow."

"I'd like to talk to Uri about his brother."

Timothy sat on the couch. Gig jumped into his lap, turned

twice, and lay down. Timothy stroked Gig's back. "That makes sense. Uri knew his brother best."

"Do you think I can talk to him today?"

Timothy's brows knit together. "I don't know. I suppose we can go over to Young's and see if he's in the office. He planned to be there most of the day. Really, he should be sitting at home with his mother."

I told him about my visit with Sadie Hooley and Debbie Stutzman. "I can't help but think Leah, Debbie, and Abby know more than they are telling. Sadie too, but I think she knows something different from the other three girls."

"I could see Abby knowing something because Ezekiel is her uncle. And yes, now that I've thought about it, I do think it's strange that two members of the same family were attacked."

"Thank you."

"But what would Sadie Hooley know about any of it? She was an innocent victim as far as I could tell."

I sat back in my chair. "She knows more than you think. She and Ezekiel were secretly engaged."

"What? Sadie Hooley and Ezekiel Young? I don't believe it! She's so quiet and sweet, and he was . . . well . . . not."

"It's true. She's brokenhearted by his death. She says I'm the only one who knows about it. Now, you know too. You can't tell anyone. From what she says, her father would not approve of the match."

"I'm not surprised. The Youngs are one of the more liberal families in the district. How did she keep it a secret?"

"The question isn't how they did it—it's whether they were able to do it. I think there might be a connection between the engagement and the murder and haircutting."

"That may be true, but it still doesn't account for what happened to *Grossdaddi* or those three girls."

I frowned. "You're right." I paused. "What about James Zug?"

"No luck. I talked to my friend who works at the auction stables. James was there until after ten bedding down his sheep for the night. My friend saw him when he did his rounds at three, five, seven, and nine. James was with his sheep each time. When did you find Ezekiel?"

"Six thirty."

"That ends it, then. The auction barn is twenty miles from Young's. There's no way he could have been gone for a long period of time without someone noticing, and it would have taken almost an hour to get to Young's from the barn by buggy. That's one way."

"That leaves us with Uri," I said.

He removed his cell from his pocket. "Let me call Uri's office. If he's there, we can head over now." Timothy punched a number into his cell phone. When the person on the other end of the line answered, he hung up. "He's there."

"You hung up on him. He's going to know it was you who called and try to phone you back."

He laughed. "Chloe, the Amish don't have caller ID, even for their businesses."

He held out his hand and helped me out of the chair. Spontaneously, he pulled me into a hug and whispered into my hair. "Please be careful." After a beat, he added, "For me."

I swallowed hard and promised him I would.

Chapter Thirty-One

The back quarter of Young's parking lot closest to the family homes was filled with Amish buggies. Timothy nodded at them as he parked his car near the back entrance to the restaurant. "They're here for the viewing."

"Ezekiel's body is in the house?"

Timothy nodded. "Been there since yesterday afternoon."

I grimaced.

As Timothy and I walked to the front door, I asked, "Where's his office?"

"It's in the back of the restaurant. He shared it with his brother."

Despite the wake happening a building away, the energy in the restaurant was festive. The buffet was set up for a second go at Thanksgiving dinner, and English guests loaded their plates. I didn't know how they could eat a meal like that two days in a row. However, I doubted their Thanksgiving menu had been as extensive as mine.

Aaron waved at us as we passed the host stand, but we didn't stop to chat. Instead we continued down a long hallway to the left.

Uri approached us from the opposite direction. "Timothy, how is everything in the pavilion?"

"Fine," Timothy said. "Can we talk to you?"

His head turned back and forth between us. "This is about my brother, right? I don't know what more I can add to what my mother told you." His brow furrowed. "I've spoken with the police already. Twice. Chief Rose is relentless."

"I can vouch for that," I said. "I was surprised to learn Abby Zug was your niece."

Uri's head jerked back. "Why's that?"

"Her hair was cut too."

"I know that, but it can't be related to my *bruder*."

"Why not?" Timothy asked.

"It doesn't make any sense. It's too random. You and the police have this all wrong. What if the person who cut off the girl's hair wasn't the same person who killed my brother?"

"But the haircutting . . ."

Uri shrugged. A waitress walked by and slipped into the restroom.

Timothy nodded in her direction. "I don't think we should talk about it out here."

"This is not a good time," Uri said. "I need to get home for the viewing. If I'm away much longer, James will have my mother convinced to sign the flea market over to him."

"Do you think James could have done this?" I asked even though I knew the sheep farmer had an alibi.

"*Nee*," Uri said.

My cell phone rang. I reached a hand into my pocket to silence it.

"You should answer that." Uri moved to step around me. "I have to go."

I held up my hand. "What did you fight with Ezekiel about a week before he died?"

Uri sucked in air. "How would you know about that?"

Timothy watched Uri. "So, you did fight with him."

Uri glared at him. "We had an argument about the business. Timothy, I suggest you stop this *Englisch* girl's questions or you will be out of a job, and I will make sure your fledgling contracting career never starts." He stomped away.

My cell rang again. This time, I removed it from my pocket and checked the read out. "It's Miller." I placed the device next to my ear.

"Chloe?"

"Hi, Miller. Did you have a nice Thanksgiving?"

Miller breathed heavily. "Leah tells me you are pestering her and her friends."

I spotted a white bench outside of the restroom and sat. "I talked to them, yes. I told you I wanted to do that."

"I know that. When I said you could talk to them, I didn't think you would bother them."

"I thought you wanted to find out who hurt them too."

"Leah's very upset by all your questions. I should have known better than tell you where to find her. The best thing for you to do is leave this to the police."

"Miller, I didn't mean any harm. I want to help."

"The police don't need any help. I'll see you Monday." He hung up.

Timothy arched an eyebrow. "That didn't sound like it went well."

"It didn't. Leah told Miller I pestered her and her friends. He told me to stop investigating."

"Will you?" he asked with a knowing smile.

"No. However, it does make me even more suspicious of Leah and her friends. When I spoke to Debbie this morning, she was scared, but she still wouldn't tell me anything. Leah trained her well. If anyone in that trio will talk, it will be Abby."

"You can play up her uncle's death."

I frowned. "That's what I was thinking. Do you think she's at the wake?"

"If James and Bridget are here, she is too."

I bit my lip. "Do you think Uri will fire you?"

"I don't know," Timothy said.

"I don't want that to happen."

"Neither do I, but if he killed his brother, I don't want to work for him."

He had a point.

Chapter Thirty-Two

Halfway through the night I lay awake going over in my mind everything that I had learned. How could all the people from the victims of the haircutting be related? Grandfather Zook, Leah and her two friends, Sadie, and Ezekiel. The only things that they all had in common was they were Amish and had their hair or beard cut by some unknown assailant. Other than that there wasn't any known connection. However, I was able to group them.

Sadie and Ezekiel were together because of their secret, possibly not so secret, engagement.

Abby and Ezekiel were family.

The three Amish best friends were together.

Then there was Grandfather Zook. He didn't fit into any group. Perhaps because he was the one who stuck out, then he was the key to the case. If I fit Grandfather Zook's puzzle piece into place, maybe the rest would fall in line too.

I sighed. To see Grandfather Zook I would have to visit the Troyer's farm. I didn't want to get the Troyers in any more trouble with the bishop than they already were. Thinking of the bishop turned my thoughts to the deacon. What was he doing talking to Collette today? He didn't seem to be enjoying the conversation, but they were an odd pair. Curt and Brock standing a few feet away making catcalls to the cheerleaders made the scene even more peculiar.

Of all the people Dylan could hire to work on the house, why Curt and Brock? Was he really going to knock down that wall in the living room? I pulled the covers up over my head as when I was frightened at night as a child. Timothy and I agreed not to tell Becky that Curt and Brock were inside the house. She was making great progress getting over the trauma of the summer, and we didn't want anything or anyone to upset that.

Dylan's charm came off phony to me. I didn't trust him. I thought a distant landlord was bad, but I have since discovered that one living down the street was much worse. I needed to get out of this rental, which was a shame because I loved the house. It had so much character.

My thoughts were muddled. Silently, I prayed for clarity and for sleep.

A scream from the next bedroom shook me from my thoughts. Fully awake, the sound was even more eerie than when it woke me from a deep sleep. Becky's nightmares were back. Gigabyte slipped under the blanket as I found my slippers. He wasn't going to risk me stomping on his tail again.

I stepped into Becky's room. Outside the window, the streetlight reflected off the falling snowflakes. We'd wake up to several inches of snow the next morning.

"Ah!" Becky sat up straight in bed, her eye clenched shut and fists shaped into tiny, pale balls.

Remembering my chin knock the last time, I touched her shoulder from an arm's length away. "Becky? Becky! Wake up!"

Her eyes snapped open, and she panted, holding her chest.

I took a step closer. "Lay back down." I pressed down on her shoulder until she reclined. "You had another nightmare." I patted her hand.

"I-I'm . . . sorry." Her breathing was heavy.

"It's fine. Take a deep breath."

She lay there just breathing for a full minute. Then, she said, "I'm better."

"Maybe we should talk to someone about your nightmares."

She blinked at me. "Who?" Her eyes reflected the ambient night-light, like Gigabyte's.

"A counselor. A pastor. This is a deeper problem and these episodes are happening more often." I almost added "psychiatrist," but thought that would be pushing it.

"I don't want anyone to know. They will tell."

"A counselor or pastor can't tell anyone anything you say in confidence. It's part of their job."

She licked her chapped lips. "I don't know."

"Think about it." I tucked the sheet and blankets over her again and started to leave.

She grabbed my arm. "Chloe, wait."

I sat back down on the bed.

"I've been thinking about something."

"What is it?"

"I do want to go to college. Will you help me study for the GED?"

I smiled. "Of course. I'll help you any way I can."

Her shoulders relaxed. "I'm glad."

I started to stand, and she grabbed my arm again. "And I want to cut my hair."

"Your hair?"

"I'm not Amish anymore. It's a heavy weight pulling on the back of my head. It gives me headaches. I think if I cut it, the nightmares will stop."

"Becky, your nightmares aren't related to the length of your hair."

"I·know that, but then, they kind of are."

Her parents wouldn't like this. I knew it. Her jeans and makeup were one thing: the jeans could be replaced by plain clothes, and the makeup could be washed away by soap. Her uncut hair would never be uncut again. Even if it grew back to its impressive length, it had still been cut.

I thought of Sadie and the other girls. Their hair had been cut when they didn't want it to be. Someone else made the choice for them in a brutal fashion. I winced. Maybe I had been pressuring the girls too much. I was engrossed in the facts instead of considering their loss.

Becky cutting her hair would be the final statement that she was no longer Amish and wouldn't be going back. Aaron came to mind. I knew Becky cared for him, but he was baptized. If he left the Amish to be with her, he would be shunned. It would not be the awkward tightrope Becky and Timothy walk. For Aaron, it would be complete exile, as if he never existed. The Troyers would have to shun him too.

Would she be Amish again for Aaron?

I sighed. Becky's hair wasn't my decision. I squeezed her hand. "Whatever you decide about your hair is fine with me. Long, short, buzz cut—it doesn't matter."

"Thank you, Chloe."

"Promise me something. Before you cut it off, pray about it."

"I promise."

I finished tucking her in and left the room.

Chapter Thirty-Three

Good morning, Chloe." Tyler Hart, Becky's lawyer, answered his phone on the first ring. "Is everything okay with Becky?"

"Everything is fine. Officer Fisher is going to recommend Becky's probation be reduced as soon as she finishes her community service hours."

"That's great news. She should be able to place the entire accident behind her by springtime."

Thinking of Becky's nightmares, I wasn't so sure.

"So what's up, if it's not related to Becky?"

"This time it's about me."

"I hope you don't need a criminal lawyer." His voice was teasing.

"No, I don't, but I do think I need a lawyer or at least legal counsel. I don't know who else to ask."

"What's the problem?"

I told him about Dylan purchasing the house and insisting to remodel it while Becky and I still lived there.

"I can see why you would want to move." His tone was thoughtful. "I'll tell you what. E-mail me a copy of the lease and I will take a look at it today and let you know what I think. I'll give Greta a call too about this. You said she met the guy."

"Yes."

"I'll get Greta's take. If she doesn't trust him, I wouldn't either. She's a good judge of character." He cleared his throat. "I don't believe he can knock down walls while you are living there."

"He wants to restore the house to its original form. Everything must be historically accurate. He flipped out on Timothy for using the wrong latch on the window."

"Maybe I can get a blueprint of the house from when it was originally built. The historical society should have one. Those ladies would love it if I dropped in for a visit." He chuckled. "When was it built?"

"1909. 1910. I'm not sure."

"That gives me a ballpark at least."

I thanked Tyler and went straight to my laptop and e-mailed him the lease.

Becky walked into the living room rubbing her eyes. "You're awake before I am. What's going on?"

"Dylan was here yesterday."

She flopped on her dog pillow. "I know. I let him in, remember?"

"Check out that wall." I point to the one with the penciled X on it.

"What about—did you draw on it?"

"I didn't. Dylan did. Timothy thinks he wants to knock it down because it's not an original part of the house."

She sat up. "While we live here?"

I nodded. "This place will be unlivable with debris floating around, not to mention the noise. I just got off the phone with Tyler, and he's going to read the lease to see if there is a way out of it."

Her eyebrows shot up. "Where would we go?"

"I'm sure we can find another house to rent somewhere in town."

She frowned. "I like this house."

"I do too, but I don't like someone we don't really know going in and out of it all the time."

She stuck out her lip. "I guess." She stood. "I'd better get ready for work."

After Becky left, I found myself torn between whether or not to pay a visit to Grandfather Zook to ask him again about the attack. This was one of those times I wished the Troyers had a house phone. I could call him with my questions and the deacon would never know.

Instead I called Timothy's cell. "I want to visit Grandfather Zook and talk to him again about the attack."

"Okay," he said, the tone of his voice confused, as if he didn't understand my hesitation. "I'm sure he'd love to see you."

I bit my lip before speaking. "I know he would, but I'm worried about causing more trouble for the family."

"Chloe, we can't be afraid to visit my family."

"I know you're right, but Ruth was so upset. If we stay away, maybe Anna's parents will change their minds and let the girls see each other."

"Ruth's thirteen. Waking up in the morning upsets her." He paused. "And Anna's parents base their decisions on what the bishop says. A quick visit to see my *grossdaddi* is not going to worsen the bishop's opinion of us." He sighed. "You know what? I have an even better idea. We can talk to Grandfather Zook, but there's a stop I'd like to make first. Be there in ten minutes. Wear old boots with a good tread, not the ones with the heels."

As promised, Timothy arrived on my doorstep ten minutes later. I held up my foot, so that he could get a clear view of my old, ugly but practical, winter boots. "These babies were made for the Iditarod trail."

Timothy's expression was total bafflement. "What's that?"

I laughed. It wasn't the first time I made a reference to something from the "outside world" that Timothy knew nothing about. "I'll tell you in the truck."

The truck bounced along new potholes in the road that snow and ice had left behind. "So where are we going?" I stroked Mabel's head as it lolled over the front seat.

"Bishop Hooley's."

I searched his face. "Are you joking?" Mabel's head popped up, giving him a good once-over too.

"Nope. It's time to go to the source of all the changes in the district. Maybe he can explain some of them."

"Timothy," I began as gently as I could. "Do you really think he will listen to you? You're not a member of the district anymore."

He tapped the steering wheel. "That's true, but my family is. I need to know what is really going on and what needs to be done to get him to leave them alone."

"Aren't you afraid this will make it worse?" I didn't want to voice that concern, but I thought that I must.

"I am, but I have to try."

Another concern came to mind. "Won't my being there make it worse?"

"I don't think so. The bishop and deacon may say they have a problem with you, but their real problem is with Becky and me. We are the ones who left *before* we even knew you."

"Won't he be at the funeral?"

"He will be, but it won't start for a few more hours. Since he will have to speak there, I know where to find him. That is if he hasn't changed his habits since he was a preacher."

Timothy pulled the truck up alongside a frozen pasture peppered by the occasional tree. That was it. No houses, no barns, not even any outbuildings.

"Where are we?"

"A field."

I eyed him. "I know that, but I thought you were taking me to the bishop's house."

"I said I was taking you to the bishop. I never said his house. He's in the pasture with his sheep."

"His sheep?"

Timothy smiled. "You'll see. Mabel, stay in the truck."

The black and brown dog settled in the backseat for a nap.

I followed Timothy along a well-worn path through the pasture. The crunch of frozen ground under our sturdy boots was somehow comforting. I watched Timothy's gloved hand as we walked, wishing that I had the courage to reach out and grab it. I frowned. As much as I wanted to do that, I didn't believe that walking hand in hand with their oldest son would help our case that I wasn't corrupting the Troyers with my English ways.

The phrase, "Are we there yet?" was on the tip of my tongue when we went over a rise. Ten yards in front of us was an Amish man. He wore a calf-length, black wool coat, and black stocking cap instead of the usual felt hat.

He faced a flock of thirty or so sheep. Most of them stood on the snowy ground staring at him. A handful found patches of earth where the snow had melted away and lay down with their hooves tucked under their wool coats.

The bishop held a crook in his hand as he spoke to the sheep. He spoke Pennsylvania Dutch, so I didn't understand a word. Despite not knowing the language, I heard a hesitation in his voice. Every so often he stamped the end of his crook into the ground to make a point.

"He's practicing his sermon for Ezekiel's funeral."

"To the sheep?" I whispered.

The bishop spun around and found us standing there. His dark brown eyes glared at us, but something else registered in his gaze. Fear.

Chapter Thirty-Four

Bishop Hooley said something in Pennsylvania Dutch. His tone was sharp, but the hesitation was there.

Timothy stepped forward. "Please speak English, Bishop. Chloe doesn't understand our language."

The bishop's dark gaze turned to me. "V-very well. Wh-what are you doing here? This is my pasture land. Y-you have no business here."

No wonder the bishop was uncomfortable speaking. He had a stutter.

"We came to talk to you," Timothy replied, his tone respectful. "May we?"

"What about?" the bishop asked. He fumbled over the two simple words.

"About my family."

The bishop stood a little straighter and grasped his crook as if it were the support holding up his confidence. "I have no r-reason to talk to you about them. You are no longer Amish."

"You're right. I'm not."

Timothy's straight answer gave the bishop pause.

"But I do have a right to talk about them. I'm their son. They are my family. My being Amish or not Amish doesn't change that."

One of the sheep ambled over to the bishop and bumped his hand with her head. The bishop's sheep were a different variety than James's. They were larger, and their faces and limbs were a tan shade. The bishop sunk his fingers into her wool as if the sheep's touch offered him comfort. "I see. Nothing you can say to me w-will change how I manage the district. Only *Gott* can influence me there."

"Only *Gott*?" Timothy asked. "What about Deacon Sutter?"

The bishop's eyes flashed. "The deacon has been a trusted advisor, but I make all the decisions about what happens in the district."

Sure, you do.

"If you make all of the decisions, then you're the right person for us to talk to about my family."

"Fine, you may talk. I don't have much time. Ezekiel Young's funeral is this afternoon. Since your family is so close with the Youngs, I trust you will allow me to go."

"Of course," Timothy agreed. "What has my family done to make you single them out in the community?"

"What does single them out mean? I don't understand your *Englisch* expressions."

"Why did you say before church that the community should keep their distance from my family? Why are parents not allowing their children to play with my younger siblings?"

The sheep lay at the bishop's feet, and a second one joined the first. Bishop Hooley gripped his crook. "If parents in the district choose not to allow their children to socialize with a particular a child, that is the parents' choice, not mine."

Timothy blew out a long breath. "You advised them to do it."

"I advised them to be wary of the *Englischer* influence that seems to have overtaken your family." He pointed at me. "You are the *Englischer* who has caused all this trouble."

"What are you talking about?" I asked, speaking for the first time.

"The deacon has told me what you have done."

"Can you tell me? Because I honestly don't know what I did that was so horrible to offend him."

"The entire district is talking about it. You are leading the Troyers astray from the community. You may have tricked Timothy and Rebecca, but I won't allow anyone else to fall under your spell."

Timothy's face turned bright red. "I left years before Chloe ever moved to Appleseed Creek. Becky left before too. Chloe living here had no influence on our decisions about being Amish. They were ours and ours alone."

"Y-you say that, but isn't it true she is holding you there in the *Englisch* world? Isn't it true you care for her when you could have affection for an Amish girl and join the church?"

"Yes, I could love an Amish girl and be very happy."

Timothy words cut into my heart like a paring knife, nicking off the corner.

Timothy continued. "Many are happy in the Amish. Many can feel close to *Gott* in the Amish way. I cannot, and there's nothing wrong with that."

The bishop took a step forward. "You deny how you feel about her? She has no power over you?"

They spoke as if I wasn't even there. Part of me wanted to turn and flee, but I feared my practical boots were frozen to the ground both figuratively and physically.

Another sheep stood, this one smaller than the others, perhaps even a yearling. Instead of going to her master as the first sheep had, she sauntered in my direction. She lay on my boot-clad feet. Instantly, her heavy warmth sunk into my frigid toes.

Timothy's voice was low. "I would never deny how I feel about Chloe. No more than I would deny how I feel about *Gott*."

What does that mean?

Timothy took my hand. "If I had to choose between her and being Amish again, I'd choose *her*."

The bishop seemed taken aback by Timothy's response.

A smile formed on my lips.

The bishop glared at me as he took in my expression. "You've made your choice, then. Now, I must go." He turned and started walking away from us, across the field. The sheep followed without being asked. Even my foot warmer stood up. The moment she moved, my toes curled in against the cold. The sheep *baaed* and joined her flock.

Timothy's chest was moving up and down as if he couldn't catch his breath.

"Timothy, are you all right?"

He nodded, but I had my doubts. I wanted to talk to him about what he'd said to the bishop, about how he felt about me. I had a million questions. I wanted to tell him I felt the same.

Instead I squeezed his hand. "Let's go talk to your grandfather now."

Walking back to the truck, I held his hand the entire way.

Chapter Thirty-Five

As Timothy turned on the road that held his family's farm, a realization struck me. I grabbed his forearm. "Timothy!"

He shook off my grasp. "Chloe, don't grab my arm like that when I'm driving. We could get into an accident."

I retracted my hand as if burnt. "I'm sorry." The warmth I felt walking hand in hand back to the truck evaporated like mist on a pond.

He flashed a quick smile. "It's okay. I'm sorry I snapped at you like that. What is it?"

"I just realized Bishop Hooley is a shepherd."

"So?"

I turned in my seat, so he could see my face. "Timothy, Ezekiel Young was stabbed with sheep shears."

I watched as that news sunk in. "You don't think the bishop . . . he wouldn't . . . what motive would he have?"

I frowned. "I don't know, but he would have shears."

"Every Amish barn in the county has a pair of sheep shears."

The memory of standing in the cloakroom at church came back to me. "When I was in the cloakroom at church and heard those two ladies gossiping, one suggested the haircutting was a message to the bishop about his rules imposed on the district. Maybe because the bishop was a shepherd, sheep shears were used to drive the point home?"

Timothy glanced at me. "Was that a pun?"

"No, I'm serious. Whoever is doing this wants the bishop to notice."

"How could he miss it?" He turned to me again. "I'm not shooting down your ideas. You may be right. Let's see what *Grossdaddi* has to say." Timothy parked the truck by the Troyer home and got out. Mabel jumped out after him with a joyful *woof*. My hand hovered over the door handle of the passenger side. I'd broken my promise to myself. I was at the Troyer farm two days after I thought I would never be back. My fingers touched the handle. What if this visit was the final act to make the bishop decide to shun the Troyer family? I felt sick.

Through the windshield I saw Timothy frown. He walked to my side of the truck and opened the door. "What's wrong?"

"I don't want your family to be shunned," I whispered.

"Neither do I," Timothy said again as more snow began to fall.

"Then we shouldn't be here, especially after the argument with the bishop."

"It will be all right, Chloe." He reached across my body and unbuckled my seat belt. His arm brushed my waist. "Let's go inside."

I climbed out of the truck, knowing it was a mistake.

When Timothy and I walked into the kitchen, Ruth was at the ironing board, pressing laundry with an old-fashioned iron that needed to be heated on the stovetop. "What are you doing here? You promised to stay away."

"Watch your tongue, Ruth. I'm still your eldest *bruder.*"

She lifted her hand from the iron's handle, leaving it on the white shirt in front of her. "I know that."

Timothy hung his coat over a kitchen chair. "Where is *Grossdaddi?*"

Ruth didn't look up. "In his room. He hasn't been feeling well."

Timothy left the room.

Ruth yelped and removed the iron from the shirt. A brownish burn mark marred the front of her father's white dress shirt. "Now, look what you made me do. *Maam* is going to be furious. This is *Daed*'s new shirt too. He's never even worn it."

"Maybe she can fix it," I said.

She gaped at me. "You don't know anything about laundry." She added under her breath, "Or our ways."

I bit the inside of my lip. "Ruth, I'm sorry you haven't seen Anna and you missed the wedding because of me. Can you forgive me?"

She looked up from her father's ruined shirt. Tears were in her eyes. "If you were sorry, you'd stop coming here, but here you are." She stormed out of the room.

Ruth's words stung.

I should have followed my instincts and avoided the Troyer home. *Lord, please give me the strength to stay away from this family I've grown to love.*

Grandfather Zook stepped into the kitchen, leaning heavily on his crutches. Timothy followed him with his hands out poised and ready to catch his grandfather if he stumbled. Grandfather Zook took his place at the kitchen table with a groan. It was the first time I'd seen the older man show a visible sign of physical pain. He'd seemed better at the hospital right after his beard was cut.

"These old bones don't work as well as they used to," he lamented. "It's like the cold weather freezes my joints. The winter can't pass fast enough in my opinion."

"Mine too," I sat on the bench. "I much prefer summer. It's been snowing here, but I don't think you get as much snow as I'm used to in Cleveland." I shivered. "And the cold wind coming off Lake Erie is enough to blow you flat on your back."

Grandfather Zook grinned as if he liked the image of someone being blown over by a cold wind gust. "I shouldn't complain. *Gott* created winter, so that we have a better appreciation for summers."

"You might be right." I squeezed his papery wrist.

Timothy sat across from me.

"Ruth stormed past us and up the stairs as we entered the kitchen." Grandfather Zook rubbed his short beard. "She reminds me of Martha when she was that age. My, she was a hot potato. Just about anything would set her off."

I arched an eyebrow. "Hot potato. Isn't that an English phrase?"

Grandfather Zook grinned. "I heard an *Englischer* say it at the grocery store when talking about his wife a few weeks ago, and I liked it very much."

Between "hot potato" and "perp," Grandfather Zook was becoming fluent in American slang. I tried to imagine Mrs. Troyer as the moody "hot potato" that Grandfather Zook described. It didn't fit.

"Where are *Maam* and *Daed*?" Timothy asked.

"They went to the funeral." He frowned. "I wanted to go myself, but my legs are acting up, and I don't have the strength to climb into the buggy."

"The bishop won't complain that they are there?' Timothy asked.

Grandfather Zook pulled at his short beard. "He will, but no one will make a scene at the funeral."

Timothy and I shared a look. I prayed that was true. And I hoped the bishop wasn't too upset by our confrontation with him in the pasture that he would take it out on the Troyers. Grandfather

Zook folded his hands on the table. "I hope Ellie's not too upset with me for missing it."

I patted his hand. "She will understand."

He twisted his mouth in uncertainty. "What brings you two here? Not that I'm not happy to see you."

I cleared my throat. "We want to talk to you again about the night you were attacked."

Grandfather Zook nodded. "I thought you would come back to that. Ask away. I've been thinking about it a lot. I knew you were investigating."

I grinned. "You were hitching Sparky, and the person came up from behind you."

"That's right."

"You said it was a man."

"Yes."

"Are you sure?"

His white bushy eyebrows shot up. "Yes. I heard him cry out when Sparky bit him. You think whoever cut my beard killed Ezekiel."

"Yes," I said.

"Ezekiel Young was a strong man. How could a woman stab him in the back like that?"

Rage, I thought. Complete and full-blown rage. The only problem was I couldn't find anyone with rage against the flea market owner. Annoyance, disdain, jealousy, yes, but no rage.

Grandfather Zook propped his chin on his fist. "I guess the only one who really knows the killer's identity, is Old Spark. He bit a chunk out of the perp after all."

I smiled when he used the word "perp" again. I suspected it would be a permanent fixture in his working vocabulary.

"If you find that coat, you find the killer," Grandfather Zook said after a long moment.

How could we find a black wool coat in a sea of black wool coats? It was like being in the church cloakroom all over again.

He stood on shaky feet. "You know, I don't feel much better, but if you wouldn't mind, I would love a ride out to Young's. Pain or no pain, I have to pay my respects."

Minutes later, I slid into the tiny backseat of the truck cabin with Mabel. Timothy helped his grandfather into the front passenger seat with care.

"Fire up your horses," Grandfather Zook said after he was buckled in.

Timothy revved the engine, and the old man laughed.

Chapter Thirty-Six

At Ellie Young's house, Timothy helped his grandfather out of the truck and walked him over to the group of mourners.

Ellie broke away from the others. "You shouldn't be here," she chided him. "Martha and Simon told me you were too ill to come."

"I'm not tip-top, but I will get by." He adjusted his crutches on his elbows.

Ellie squeezed my arm. "Chloe and Timothy, I'm happy to see you. Thank you for bringing Joseph."

The bishop and deacon were watching. I caught Timothy's eye and nodded in their direction. "We're just here to drop off Grandfather Zook."

Ellie shook her head. "You're staying. I insist."

The deacon and bishop weren't the only ones who were watching us. Uri glared at us too.

Ellie took Timothy and me by the hand and led us into her house. In the living room all of Ellie's furniture was removed. Bishop Hooley, Deacon Sutter, and two other Amish I didn't know stood at the front of the room beside Ezekiel's open casket. I looked away as Ellie pointed to two seats for Timothy and me. His seat was on one side of the room, and mine was on the other. I gave a sigh of relief when I saw it was next to Becky. She wore her plain dress, which was her uniform at the restaurant. I slipped into the seat, feeling conspicuous in my jeans and pea coat and aware I was being watched by nearly everyone in the room. Was the bishop right? Was everyone in the district talking about my friendship with the Troyers and my relationship with Timothy? If the hairs standing up on the back of my neck were any indication, he was.

The room was dark and tightly packed, hot even. I would have removed my coat if I didn't think I would elbow someone in the head during the process.

Bishop Hooley opened a large black tome, the German Bible, and read from it. Each of the four men spoke in turn, some read and some spoke from memory. Ellie sat at the front of the room with her head bowed. There were no wails or outward demonstrations of grief. No flowers, eulogies, or songs.

My mother's funeral took place in a large church in downtown Cleveland I had never been in, nor been back to since. Family and friends came from all over the country. My father's wealthy clients and business associates were there, everyone dressed like they were ready to walk the streets of New York. Paid singers from Severance Hall and members of the Cleveland Orchestra, who never met my mother, provided the music. Famous preachers spoke about dying young, but not about the woman my mother had been, because they didn't know. There had been so many flowers my father paid the funeral home to dispose of them. He didn't want them in the house.

How was that better than this?

The bishop closed the Bible. He and the four men closed the casket. Several young men from the community stood and lifted the simple pine box onto their sturdy shoulders.

Men and women filed out of the house. "Where are they going?" I whispered to Becky.

"To the cemetery. It's about a mile away at the back of the Young's land," she whispered back. "Don't worry. We don't have to go. I need to get back to the restaurant. Come with me."

I followed Becky out through Ellie's kitchen. On the way to the restaurant, I scanned the crowd climbing into their buggies to ride to the Amish cemetery.

Becky quickened her pace. "Don't worry. I texted Timothy and told him you were with me. He'll meet us inside."

I blinked at her. Now, why did she think of doing that before I did?

Becky and I entered Young's through the side door. I sighed when I saw the other *Englischers* in their blue jeans and bright-colored parkas. Here, I blended in with the crowd. My cell rang as Becky waved to me as she ran to the kitchen.

"Chloe, it's Tyler."

I walked through the restaurant and sat on a bench near the entrance to the bustling pie shop.

A *binging* sound came over the phone like Tyler knocked his pen on a coffee mug. "I've looked over your lease."

"And?"

"It's with the company in Cincinnati. There is no mention of Dylan at all, and no mention the lease can be transferred upon the sale. I can get you out of it. No problem."

Relief washed over me. "Now, I have to find a new place to live."

"I might have a solution for you there too. I have a client who spends the winter in Florida. He's looking for someone to watch his house during the winter months. That will give you until spring to find the place you really want."

"That might work. I'll have to talk to Becky."

"It's a big house. Has a huge kitchen."

I smiled. Even Tyler knew Becky loved to cook. "Becky will love the kitchen."

"I did some digging on Dylan Tanner too."

"What did you learn?"

"He doesn't have a criminal record or anything like that."

"How do you know that?"

"Greta checked him out the day you thought he broke into your house."

I wasn't surprised.

Tyler continued. "He's worked at the college for the last four years in the biology department. His wife recently left him."

"Was her name Kara?"

"That's it."

The name Dylan called me.

"I happened to talk to a friend of Kara's. Her father died about a year ago and left her a substantial inheritance. Not like millions or anything, but somewhere between twenty and thirty grand."

"That would be a lot of money to Dylan." I knew how much Harshberger's faculty made.

"Right. Anyway, Dylan invested the money into a new business and lost it all."

"I assume that didn't go over well with Kara."

"You got it. She left him over it."

"Where's Kara now?"

"She moved to Oregon."

"Trying to get as far away from Dylan as possible?"

"I think that's the idea." Tyler made a humming sound. "Here's where it gets really strange. I told you I would talk to the ladies at the historical society about your house."

"Yes."

"They found the original blueprints right away. Dylan was there just three weeks ago looking for them."

"That makes sense if he wants to restore the house."

"The strange part is the name of the original owner of the house. Gerald Tanner."

"Tanner? That's Dylan's last name."

"Exactly." He paused. "I figured you'd want to talk to the ladies at the historical society. I told them you would stop by. They close at three today, so you'd better get over there right now."

I thanked him.

"Don't mention it." A phone rang on the other side of the line. "I gotta go. Unfortunately, I can't do anything about the lease until Monday since it's the weekend."

"I understand. Thanks for your help." I hung up as Timothy walked through Young's front door.

I jumped up, and a smile spread across his face. "Let's go." I linked my arm through his.

"Where to?" He tightened our arm link.

"To learn some local history."

His brow shot up as I pulled him through the front door.

Chapter Thirty-Seven

The Appleseed Creek Historical Society was in a centennial home close to the square, much like the house in which Becky and I lived. The home was a narrow mint green Queen Anne with a tower and wide front porch. Bungee cords held forest green tarps over the wicker furniture.

Timothy rapped the horse-shaped knocker. The door flew open a half second later and a five-foot-nothing elderly women peered up at us. She wore a blue and white Scandinavian print sweater that hung to her denim-clad knees, and her hair was set in white pin curls. A smile broke across her face. "She's here!" The woman called over her shoulder. "I told you if Tyler said she'd come, she'd come. Tyler is a good boy and hasn't let me down yet." Her head swung back toward us. "Don't stand there and let all of the heat out."

The front door of the Victorian led into an arched foyer, which opened into a large sitting room. Antique chairs and waist-high display cases dotted the space, and floor-to-ceiling bookcases circled the room. An elderly man with a white handlebar mustache peered at a yellowed document with a magnifying glass. He had white gloves on his hands that reminded me of the ones the bell choir at my small home church in Cleveland wore when playing the bells. "Tyler's a lawyer," he said without looking up. "How can he be a good boy?"

"You used to be a banker," she shot back. "You have no room to talk." She walked into the room with the man. "Max, this is Chloe Humphrey. She's the girl Tyler was telling us about, who lives in the old Tanner place on Grover Lane."

"I know who she is." Max straightened his back with a groan. "Tyler left no more than a half hour ago. You think I forgot what he said?"

"Your memory isn't as reliable as it used to be. You forgot what year Appleseed Creek was established." She whispered to Timothy and me. "It's 1808. Max said 1807."

Max glared at her. "You always throw that back in my face." He eyed Timothy. "Who's the Ken doll?"

Timothy's brow wrinkled, which made me smile. I suspected he had no idea who Ken, not to mention Barbie, was.

The older man pointed his magnifying glass at me. "If he's Ken, I guess that makes you Skipper."

I frowned, no longer finding the comparison amusing.

Still looking confused, he said, "I'm Timothy."

"Silly me! I forgot to introduce myself. I'm Minerva Hammer, the president of the Appleseed Creek Historical Society." She stood a little straighter as she recited her title, then she pointed a thumb in Max's direction. "Max Dudley's the secretary-treasurer."

Max's mustache shook. "The secretary-treasurer is an important job."

"Did I say it wasn't?"

"You implied it." He chewed on his mustache.

She waved a dismissive hand at her cohort. "Sit, sit, you two."

Timothy and I each sat in a flower-patterned wingback chair.

"We haven't had this many visitors in years. The Tanner boy, Tyler, and now you two. We are going to be spoiled by all the attention." She perched on a blue velvet settee.

I folded my scarf in my lap. "When was Dylan here?"

Max tucked the magnifying glass in the breast pocket of his button-down shirt. "About three weeks ago."

"He was here about the house on Grover?" I unzipped my coat. The home was unbearably warm. Both Minerva and Max wore short sleeves.

Minerva nodded. "He said he bought the Old Tanner place on Grover and planned to restore it. He wanted blueprints of the house's original plans."

He bought it over three weeks ago and never thought to mention it to me. We work at the same college. Our offices are in the same building.

Timothy removed his winter coat and a sheen of sweat gathered on his forehead.

"Are you hot?" Minerva asked. "Max, go turn on the floor fan."

A stand-up fan was in the corner of the room. Max grumbled under his breath but followed her directions. The oscillated air came as a relief.

"Our thermostat is stuck at eighty. It's been broken all weekend. We haven't been able to get the furnace man out because of Thanksgiving. He was supposed to be here this morning but hasn't shown up. We've called four times."

Max's mustache wiggled like a caterpillar. "It wouldn't be that way if you hadn't cranked it up in the first place."

She glared at him. "It was so cold in here, it felt like a tomb. I had to take the chill off."

Max moved the fan as close to us as the cord would allow.

"I can take a look at it if you want," Timothy said.

Minerva brightened. "Would you?"

Max wasn't nearly as thrilled. "Are you licensed in HVAC repair?"

"No," Timothy admitted. "But I'm a contractor and have worked on heating and cooling before. I still recommend that you have your regular guy out, but at least I can stop the furnace. Your heating bill will be astronomical."

"I say we do it, Max, and since I'm the president, what I say goes. We'll show you where everything is right after we finish our little visit."

Max's white eyebrows knit together. "As I was saying, Dylan Tanner visited three weeks ago. I was mighty impressed with his knowledge of local history. It's nice to see young people taking an interest."

Timothy pushed the sleeves up on his flannel shirt. "What is the history on the house?" Minerva opened her mouth, but Max was faster. "Gerald Tanner, Dylan's great-great grandfather, built the house in 1910. He lived there until he died in 1945. He was seventy-five when he passed. He was a local boy and by the time he retired was a vice president of the largest bank in the county. Really, though, he was a frustrated architect. He designed and drew up the plans of the house himself." Max tapped the document on the glass top with his white-gloved finger. "Come take a look. I have the original drawing right here."

Timothy and I walked across the room. Max stood closer to the fan and it ruffled his mustache. The paper, yellowed with age, had an ink drawing of the interior of my rented house. The plan was rough, however, it did show the location of the walls. The wall in the living room that Dylan marked with an X wasn't in the rendering.

Timothy leaned over the drawings. "Those don't look like any blueprints I've ever seen. It's not even to scale."

"This was Gerald's first rough sketch of the plans. The real one, the one the workmen and contractor must have used to build the home, is lost. It's possible the village was never given a copy."

"It could have been misplaced too," Minerva chimed in. "The historical society wasn't formed until 1940. Before that no one really kept track of these pieces of history."

"This is all you have? You didn't give Dylan the blueprint?" I asked.

Max's eyebrow shot way up. "Certainly not. Nothing in the historical society is available to loan. Artifacts may only be viewed in house under the supervision of a board member."

"So Dylan doesn't have a copy?" Timothy asked.

"He does," Max said. "He took a picture with his camera."

"May I take a photograph with my phone?" I asked.

"Yes," Max said. "But no flash."

I retrieved my smartphone from my purse, turned off the flash, and snapped two photos of the blueprint. Within seconds I e-mailed them to my personal and work accounts.

I slipped the phone into my pocket. "When Dylan saw the blueprints of the house, did he know that his great-great grandfather once owned the house?"

"Oh yes." Minerva nodded. "He knew and asked us to find whatever we had on Gerald. We were more than happy to help."

"Did you find anything else?" I asked.

"Not much. If the family doesn't donate to us, we don't have much record other than what we found in the village newspapers— Appleseed Creek used to have two papers, one English and one Amish—and town photos."

"Anything in the newspaper?"

"His retirement was announced from the bank in 1928. Close call for him. Had he stayed one year longer he would have lost everything in the crash."

Timothy's brows knit together. "The crash?"

"The Great Depression. The stock market crashed in 1929," I said, surprised Timothy didn't know about it.

Max gave Timothy a skeptical look. "They aren't covering the Great Depression in school anymore? This is a travesty. How is the country supposed to move forward if we don't learn from our mistakes?"

"They didn't cover it in my school," Timothy said, leaving it at that.

I tried to steer the conversation back to Gerald. "Wasn't Gerald's money in the bank? Wouldn't he still lose money even if he didn't work there?"

"He would have if his money was in the bank. Look at these photos." He pulled three black-and-white photographs from a white acid-free envelope and lined them up on the glass top.

Timothy traced a finger along one of the pictures. Max slapped Timothy's hand away with his white-gloved hand. "Don't touch that! You'll ruin it."

Timothy retracted his hand. "I wasn't going to rip it or anything."

"The oils from your hand will get on the photograph and make it degenerate faster. Only the person with the white gloves can touch the artifacts." Max held up his hands to show us. "I'm the only one with white gloves. I'm the only one who can touch."

Minerva rolled her eyes. "Max, don't be such a fussbudget."

Timothy glanced at me as if wanting me to translate "fussbudget." I shook my head.

Max gave us each a beady look. "Now that we have set the ground rules. Look at the second photograph." He handed me the magnifying glass because the picture was tiny. It was about six inches tall and four inches across. I leaned over the photo holding the glass, taking care not to touch it. The image was grainy but

showed an elderly man in a bow tie and full beard looking down
at something on a tabletop. I leaned closer. A cloth-padded tray of
coins sat in the foreground of the picture. Understanding settled
over me. "This was how he preserved his money. Coins."

I straightened up and felt a twinge in my back. If he leaned over
tiny pictures like this all day every day, I could see why Max had a
slight arch to his back.

Minerva beamed at me. "That's right. She's a bright one." She
winked at Timothy. "I'd keep her if I were you."

My cheeks flushed. If anyone asked, I planned to blame it on
oppressive heat.

"Was he a collector?" I asked.

Max nodded. "Yes. The money he didn't spend building his
home, he spent on coins." He walked across the room and removed
a file from the small writing desk in the corner. He opened the
folder on the glass-topped case to an old newspaper clipping inside.
"The English paper wrote a feature on the coin collection. The date
on this is March 1, 1931."

The clipping had a photograph of Gerald in front of the
house on Grover. It looked much the same from the outside, but
clearly the one in the picture was in much better repair than the
house falling down around Becky and me. "That date is right in
the middle of the Depression," I said. "Can I take a photo of this
too?"

Max nodded, and I snapped another picture. In addition to the
photograph of Gerald Tanner and the house, there were three close-
ups of coins.

"Look at all those old coins." Timothy's finger hovered over the
picture. He was careful not to touch it so he wouldn't get smacked
by Max a second time.

"They're from the Civil War." Minerva squeezed in between
Timothy and me. "Some are Northern and some are Southern."

"Did he specialize in Civil War coins?" I asked.

Max stepped back. "No. He was an equal opportunity collector. The only criterion was that the coin was valuable. He didn't waste his time on pennies. His collection would be worth a bundle nowadays, especially with the dollar going into the tanker."

Timothy rocked back onto his heels. "Dylan knew about the coin collection before he came here."

"Oh, yes," Minerva said. "He said the family frequently talked about Gerald and his coins." She clapped her hands. "Max, take this handsome man downstairs to take a look at Big Bertha."

Timothy squinted. "Big Bertha?"

"That's what we named the furnace."

Max smoothed his mustache with a white-gloved hand. "That's what Minerva named the furnace."

Minerva sniffed. "I figured with all the trouble she's causing, she earned a name."

It was Max's turn to roll his eyes. "Come on, Ken. I'll show you where the furnace is."

"My name is Timothy." He sounded confused again. I would have to explain Ken and Barbie to Timothy later, but I would leave Skipper out of it.

Max shook a wrinkled finger at Timothy. "And know that I'll be watching you like a hawk every minute to make sure you don't break anything."

Timothy glanced over his shoulder and gave me a pleading look as Max led him from the room.

I mouthed, *You'll be fine.*

While Timothy and Max went to see about Big Bertha, I scanned the books on the shelves. Most were local and Ohio history. *Did Dylan want to restore the house in memory of his great grandfather? Then, why didn't he just say that? Why give me the story about wanting to restore the house to flip it?*

Minerva sat in the wingback chair Timothy had abandoned.
"You might as well take a seat. They're not coming back any time
soon."

I sat on the matching chair.

Her eyes sparkled. "So tell me about that delicious man."

My face flushed.

A knowing smiled crossed her face.

I scooted as far away from Minerva as I could without actually
standing up and leaving my chair. "He's a friend."

She *tsked*. "What a waste. I can tell by the way he watched you
that he doesn't want to be just a friend." She wiggled in her seat.
"He's a keeper. I can always tell. Good man stock comes from the
farm. He's a farm boy, isn't he?"

I nodded.

She tapped her teeth with a hot pink fingernail. "And you're
a city girl. There lies the issue. You think the two of you are too
different."

We were different. And there was the whole Amish thing, but I
wasn't going to explain that to Minerva.

"How are you going to snatch him up? Do you have a plan?"

"A plan?"

"Oh yes," she said seriously. "I'm positive you aren't the only
girl with your eye on him."

I grimaced, thinking of Hannah. Tomorrow was Sunday, which
meant I would see her at church again.

"I see from your sourpuss face, I'm right. You need to tell that
boy how you feel before he thinks you don't care and looks else-
where. I bet your competition doesn't have any reservations about
making her feelings known."

Hannah certainly didn't have any qualms about that. Everyone
knew how she felt about Timothy—even Timothy. I wished he'd
discourage her more.

Suddenly, there was silence. The constant hum of the furnace, which I hadn't noticed before, had stopped.

Minerva clapped her hands. "He did it. We are saved." She winked at me. "Told you, he's a keeper. If you can find a man who can fix things, string a complete sentence together, and is as easy on the eyes as your Timothy, I say snap that boy up." A small smile curled her lips. "Trust me, if I was forty years younger, I'd give you some competition."

Much to my relief, Timothy and Max reentered the room. "Call the furnace man as soon as you can," Timothy told Max. "He still needs to come and look at it. All I did was turn it off. If you turn the furnace on, it might jump to eighty once again."

Max nodded. "I will." Then, grudgingly, he added, "Thank you."

Timothy smiled.

I jumped out of my chair. "Are you ready to go?"

Timothy's eyebrows shot up. "I guess you are."

I nodded and grabbed our coats from the chairs. We thanked Max and Minerva for their time.

"Remember what I said," Minerva called out the front door behind us.

The cold wind felt good on my overheated skin, so I left my coat off and enjoyed the cool air while we walked to the truck.

Timothy tossed his coat into the back of the pickup, waking Mabel in the process. She opened one eye and closed it again. "What did Minerva mean by that last comment?"

I climbed into the truck. "Nothing important," I mumbled, even though the opposite was true.

Chapter Thirty-Eight

A s Timothy drove the truck around the town square, I asked, "Why didn't Dylan tell me the house belonged to his family?"

Timothy shook his head. "I knew there was something off about that guy the moment I met him."

I frowned. *Why hadn't I known?*

"Those old photographs made me think."

"About the coins?"

He shook his head. "I don't have any pictures of my great-grandparents, my parents, or my younger siblings. Seeing those pictures, I could see how looking at them could bring someone comfort. I see how the picture of your mother brings you comfort. Is that why you keep it?"

"Yes, and I'm afraid I will forget what she looks like." I scratched Mabel's head hanging over the front seat.

As Timothy's truck rolled down our street, I saw a buggy in front of the house. Timothy slowed. "That's not *Daed* or *Grossdaddi's* buggy."

I sat up straighter. "Who else would it be? We aren't particularly popular among the Amish right now."

Timothy pursed his lips. "That's why they're here."

"They?"

Before he could reply, I saw who he meant. Both Deacon Sutter and Bishop Hooley stood in the middle of my front lawn watching the house.

"It's probably best if you wait in the truck," Timothy said.

"But—"

He squeezed my hand. "Chloe, please." Timothy stepped out of the truck and walked over to the two men. I rolled down the window, but the trio spoke in Pennsylvania Dutch. Their words were meaningless to me.

Deacon Sutter pointed his gloved index finger at the truck, but more specifically at me. Mabel whimpered in the backseat. "I know, Mabel. I don't like them either."

Guilt twisted in my gut. I knew going to the Troyer farm had been a mistake and attending the funeral had been a worse one. What would this mean for the Troyer family?

The conversation became more heated. The deacon threw up his hands and shook his fist at Timothy. The bishop said nothing and didn't move. Timothy listened to the deacon with his arms folded across his chest.

"Mabel, you stay here."

I stepped out of the pickup. The cold air, welcome after being inside the historical society's house, chilled me to the bone. I walked to the back of the truck to stay out of the men's way while fumbling with the zipper of my coat.

"Psst, Chloe!" Aaron waved from the backseat of the buggy.

I hurried around to the other side of the buggy so that the deacon and bishop couldn't see me. "What are you doing here?"

He arched an eyebrow at me. "Paying a call to you, I guess. I thought I was headed home after another day at Young's, but *Daed* decided on the detour."

"The bishop came with you."

"I should have realized we weren't going straight home since the bishop was riding along."

"What are they saying to Timothy? What's going on?"

"They are yelling at him for attending the funeral today."

"Did Ellie get in trouble?"

Aaron shook his head. "The bishop believes she was misguided by grief."

"What else are they saying to Timothy?"

Aaron shrugged. "The usual. The deacon tells him to stay away from the Troyer family because his presence, oh, and yours and Becky's too, are leading them from the Amish way. He says this is the final warning. The next time you all are seen with the family, they will be shunned."

I bit my lip.

Aaron frowned. "I feel so useless. I'm stuck up here. I can't even climb out of the buggy to defend my best friend to my father."

"It's not your fault."

Aaron shooed me. "They are coming back to the buggy."

I waved and hurried around the back of the buggy only to run smack into Deacon Sutter. We both stumbled back after the impact.

"You need to watch where you're going," the Amish leader hissed, reminding me of a snake.

I straightened my shoulders. "What are you doing here?"

Timothy stepped around the deacon's horse and stood beside me. "Come on, Chloe. They both said everything they needed to say."

The deacon glared at me. "Not everything." He pointed a finger at me. "I don't know how you've been able to worm your way into the affections of the Troyer family, but rest assured that's the only family you will lead from the Amish way."

"I didn't . . ."

Timothy squeezed my elbow as if telling me to stop, but I couldn't. A question which had been plaguing me popped into my head. "Deacon, what were you doing Friday talking to Collette Williams?"

The deacon glowered. "What are you talking about?"

"When I was on the float, I saw you speaking with Collette from the college. I want to know why."

Deacon Sutter clenched his jaw. "You mean the *Englisch* woman who wanted me to tell her how wonderful the college is to my community. The college does nothing for my district. We do not want or need *Englischer* help. I'm offended by the idea of it. You were the one who put her up to it, then?"

I felt my cheeks grow hot. "No."

His glare darkened. "I don't believe you. The college has had no interest in us before you moved here."

"I—"

Ding, ding! The bell on Becky's bicycle announced her arrival. She cruised down the street and slowed as she saw Timothy and me squaring off against the deacon and the bishop on the road side of the buggy.

It was dusk. The temperature seemed to fall with each inch of sun that disappeared behind the houses to the west. Becky jumped off her bike while it was still in motion and dropped it in the middle of the driveway. Seeing how she treated it, I knew why her chain broke so often.

She hurried over. "What's going on?"

Timothy glanced at his sister. "Bishop Hooley and Deacon Sutter were just leaving."

Becky chewed her lip and glanced up into the buggy. Her eyes lit up when she saw Aaron. He grinned back at her and cleared his throat. "You need to be careful, Becky. It's not safe for you to ride your bicycle home this late. You could have been struck on the road."

"I was careful." She gave him a high-wattage smile.

The deacon watched their exchange. A red stain crept up Deacon Sutter's neck and onto his wind-blown cheeks. He balled his leather-gloved hands into a tight fist as a knowing expression crossed his stern face followed by one of resolve. He snapped at his son in their language.

Aaron responded in English. "Becky is my friend. If I want to talk to her, I will."

The deacon turned a peculiar shade of purple. He turned to Becky. "Stay away from my son." His voice shook. "You will not lead him away."

Becky glared at the deacon but did not reply. She wore her own look of resolve that twisted my stomach up into knots.

The bishop and deacon climbed into the buggy, and the Troyer siblings and I stepped back onto the front lawn of the house. As the buggy drove away, Aaron waved at us. Becky waved wildly back, with the deacon watching her in the buggy's side mirror.

Timothy sighed when they were out of sight. "I need to get back to Young's to make sure the job site is shut down for the night. Are you girls going to be okay?"

I nodded.

Becky picked up her bike and walked it to the garage.

Timothy touched my arm. "Before you go to bed tonight, take one of your kitchen chairs and shove it under the doorknob of the front door. That will make it more difficult for anyone to get inside the house."

"Like the deacon?"

"Like Dylan."

I stuck my hands in pockets. "I don't think he'd bother us at night."

Timothy didn't appear convinced. "Maybe I should spend the night on the couch."

I shook my head. "You need your rest, and that couch wasn't made for sleeping on. We'll be fine. I'll use the kitchen chair."

He smiled. "Thank you. Call me if you feel uncomfortable."

"I will."

When Becky and I were safely inside the house, I said, "I thought of another good reason to move." I locked and bolted the front door.

"What's that?" Becky asked.

I shoved the kitchen chair under the doorknob just as Timothy had told me to. "Deacon Sutter won't know where we live."

That night, I sat up in bed looking at that rough printout of Gerald Tanner's original plans for the house on my iPad. I enlarged the space in the living room that was missing a wall. Then, I scanned the plans for the second floor. Another wall was missing between mine and Becky's bedrooms. Instead of three small bedrooms on the second floor, there had been one large room and a smaller one. In the house now, the extra bedroom was empty. Becky and I didn't have enough furniture to fill it.

I grimaced. Would Dylan want to knock down the wall between our bedrooms? I prayed Tyler was right and that getting out of the lease would be as easy as he thought.

Chapter Thirty-Nine

Becky and I walked to church on Sunday morning. "Can we please avoid Hannah as much as possible?" she said. "I don't want to hear how wonderful Esther's wedding was."

Fine by me.

I stepped over a pile of gray snow. "I thought you were over the fact that Isaac is married."

"I am, but I still don't want to hear about it." She slid along the icy sidewalk like a child pretending to skate. I was only five years older than Becky, but sometimes I forgot how young she was. Having grown up Amish, she was much more naïve than other nineteen-year-olds I knew.

"I spoke with Tyler yesterday."

"What did he say?"

"He will start working on the lease problem tomorrow."

She looked crestfallen. "I'm still going to miss that house."

"Me too."

The church came into view. Because of the freezing temperature, no one stood outside waiting for the service to begin. The church's snow-covered steeple appeared as if it had been cut from a postcard and carefully placed against the bright blue sky. Despite the cold, the sun shone. The bright winter sun and blue sky misled people into believing that nothing bad could happen in a place like Appleseed Creek. I knew better.

Becky slid to a stop. "Have you heard from your dad or Sabrina? Are they back from their trip?"

Her question made me stumble on the edge of the sidewalk. She put out a hand to steady me. The peace of the wintry scene vanished. "I haven't heard from them and don't expect to. I'm not sure when they are getting back. Sabrina doesn't give me a detailed itinerary of their plans."

"Do you think that they will ever visit you here?" She began skating again. "Will I meet them?"

I barked a laugh. "Not likely."

She slid to a stop again. "Did I say something wrong?"

I forced a smile. "No."

She frowned. "You never talk about them, and they're your family. Don't you miss them?"

"I do."

"Then invite them to come here. I'm sure the children would love Ohio at Christmas. They will see snow."

"Becky, it's too complicated." I shivered, imagining what my stepmother would think and say about Appleseed Creek. Surely, she would offend the entire town within the first fifteen minutes of her visit. "You have to understand that your family couldn't be more different from mine."

I hurried up the church's steps speckled with rock salt, hoping that was the end of the conversation. A greeter opened the church door for us. "Good morning, ladies."

We smiled and replied with our own *good mornings*.

Timothy and Danny sat in a pew toward the back of the sanctuary, and—surprise, surprise—Hannah and her minions sat in the pew behind them. As the opening music played, Hannah leaned over the pew, patting Timothy on the arm.

Becky pulled back and hissed. "We can't sit over there. Hannah will talk about the wedding. It will be excruciating. She'll tell me about every bite of food and what everyone wore. She'll be sure to tell me what they said about *me*."

I watched Hannah laugh at something Timothy said as if it were the funniest comment she'd ever heard. I took a step in that direction. What had Minerva said? I'd better make my feelings to Timothy known or someone else would snap him up. Hannah looked like she could snap really well—like an alligator.

Becky pulled my arm. "Chloe, please. I can't bear to hear her go on and on about it." Her large blue eyes were the size of ping-pong balls.

"Okay." I followed Becky to the other side of the room. We sat next to an elderly man who was already asleep even though the sermon hadn't begun.

Hannah tossed her dark hair over one shoulder and caught my eye. A catlike smile curled on her lips as she whispered to her two friends.

"It's like watching church leaders huddle together before they shun someone," Becky whispered.

I was thinking it was more like watching the three witches of *Hamlet*, but I suspected either of our cultural references would be appropriate.

Hannah tossed her hair again. If she weren't careful, she'd hit the parishioner behind her in the eye. She, Kim, and Emily stood and moved to Timothy's pew. Timothy shook his head and pointed to the seat next to him. Hannah pouted and shook her head. She scooted an inch closer to him. Timothy scooted away and bumped into Danny. Hannah pouted more and pointed at me. Timothy turned and we made eye contact. His eyes drooped, as if hurt. I opened my mouth, but he wouldn't hear me unless I shouted across the sanctuary. Not a good idea.

Hannah turned Timothy's head back to face her.

My stomach dropped. Maybe Minerva was right.

A few rows up from Timothy and Hannah, Beth Hilty, Hannah's mother, turned all the way around in her pew to watch the exchange between her daughter and Timothy. A catlike smile, identical to her daughter's, curled her mouth. As if she sensed my gaze, her head snapped in my direction, and her eyes narrowed.

"I don't think she likes you," Becky said under her breath.

The pastor began morning announcements, sparing me from a reply.

After church, Timothy and Becky had choir practice. They both signed up to sing in the Christmas cantata in a few weeks. I couldn't hum a tune, so I walked home alone.

I kicked a pile of snow as I walked. Hannah was also in the choir, and no doubt she'd stay as close to Timothy as possible during practice.

As I climbed my porch steps, I heard a scraping sound. Startled, I dropped my house key on the porch. When I scooped it up, I found Abby standing in front of me. I gasped. "What are you doing here?"

"I need to talk to you." She inched away from me to the far corner of the front porch.

I clutched the keys in my hand. "Okay."

"Not now. I have to get back home. I was able to sneak away from services for a few minutes."

I glanced up the street. No buggy. "How did you get here?"

"Don't worry about that. I have to go. Will you meet me?"

"Why can't you talk to me now?"

Her eyes skittered back and forth. "I can't. I've been gone far too long already."

I pursed my chapped lips. "Where and when would you like me to meet you?"

"Later today. Meet me at Appleseed Pond at one o'clock." She retreated farther away to the side of the house.

I took a few steps after her. "Where is that?"

She held up her hand to stop me. "Not far. It's a mile past Young's on the same road. It's in between my farm and the flea market. I'll tell my parents I don't feel well enough for afternoon church and meet you." She disappeared around the side of the porch. I waited half a second and ran around to see where she had gone. I leaned over the porch railing and looked into the backyard, but I couldn't see her. I blinked. *Where did she go?*

I reached into my pocket for my cell phone and called Timothy. Voice-mail. I called Becky next. That call went to voice-mail too. Practice wouldn't be over until three. I sent them both text messages and hoped they would get them in time.

Chapter Forty

I wouldn't call the place in front of Appleseed Pond a parking lot. More like a muddy field. The Bug bumped along the uneven, half-frozen ground. I gripped the steering wheel a little tighter with each thump. The little car wasn't built for this type of terrain. As I climbed out of the car, there wasn't a soul around.

A twig snapped to my left and Abby stepped out from behind a tree. "I'm glad you came."

"Why couldn't you talk to me back at my house?"

"No one can see us together," she whispered. "It could be dangerous."

"Dangerous? Why?"

She didn't answer.

"Does this have something to do with the haircutting? With your uncle Ezekiel?"

Her eyes brimmed with tears. "I don't know anything about Ezekiel," she said in a rush. "I don't."

I opened my mouth again.

"Follow me. The pond is only a half mile in. It's beautiful this time of year and frozen over. We are too close to the road here. Someone will see."

I waved my hand. "Lead the way."

We walked for several yards in silence. Only the crunching sounds of our boots on the ground and the twittering of birds that didn't bother to fly south for the winter disturbed the quiet.

"I'm sorry we had to meet like this. Between the farm and stocking at The Apple Core, I have very little time to myself."

"Are you still stocking for Christmas at the shop?"

"Yes. Leah expects better sales this year and ordered extra of everything. She, Debbie, and I will finish tomorrow morning before the shop opens. I'll be happy when it's done. I'm more comfortable on the farm."

I cleared my throat. "Abby, why did you want to talk to me?"

"I don't want anyone else to get hurt." She stopped in the middle of the path. "Can you stop it?"

"Can you tell me something that will help me stop it?" I plucked a dead leaf from a tree.

She turned away from me, her face hidden by the edge of her bonnet. I wondered if Amish women really wore bonnets for modesty or as a way to conceal their feelings from the rest of the world. "Things went too far. This wasn't what we wanted."

"Things? What things? What do you mean 'we'? You, Leah, and Debbie?

Before she answered, Appleseed Pond came into view at four times the size of Archer Pond on Harshberger's campus, which was inappropriately named Archer Lake. About a quarter mile across, it appeared frozen solid. Instead of floating in its chilly water, Canadian geese waddled across its glassy surface, squawking at each other as they went. The dead stems of reeds and cattails circumnavigated the edge. Leafless willow tree branches dipped into the pond and froze into their prayerful positions.

A doe ate grass poking up through the snow on the other side of the pond. Her head popped up as we drew closer to the water. She turned and fled into the woods with her white tail upright in retreat, and I turned to Abby. "How did I not know this was here? It's beautiful."

For the first time since I'd met her, Abby gave me the smallest of smiles. "It's one of the best kept secrets in the county. Most *Englischers* don't know about it because it's on Amish land, and they don't pay attention to anything they can't see from their cars. Courting couples in the district have skating parties here in the winter and picnics in the summer. At least they did before."

"Before what?"

She raised the hood of her cloak over her bonnet. "Before we got a new bishop."

"It seems like few in the community are happy with Bishop Hooley." I dropped my leaf and it slid onto the frozen ground. A chickadee clung to one of the willow branches with his talons, choosing to hop up its length rather than fly.

"Why would they be happy with him? He's a tyrant. Everything's different now. I never before thought about leaving the Amish, but now I don't know if I can stay."

"Before you said it's gone too far. What did you mean?"

"Th-the district. The bishop holds us back." She walked around the edge of the pond.

I watched my footing. The pond was frozen, but on closer inspection, the ice wasn't as thick as it appeared from farther away. "What went too far?"

She looked at me as if seeing me for the first time. "I can't."

"Can't what."

She shook her head. "I can't do this. Everything will be fine," she said more to herself than to me. "I know it." She stopped in front of another trailhead. "You should stop meddling in Amish matters. We will solve this in our own way and in our own *gut* time."

I blinked. Her demeanor had completely changed. Gone was the frightened young girl. A new assertive person, one with resolve, had taken her place.

What wasn't she telling me? She asked me to meet her at the pond as some sort of confession but couldn't bring herself to actually do it.

"Abby, what did you want to tell me?" I said in a hushed voice.

Some of her strong façade cracked. "I can't do this. I can't tell you."

"I'm only trying to help."

She wrapped her arms about her waist. "I can't."

"I thought you didn't want anyone else to get hurt."

She glared at me. "You cannot understand. You're *Englisch*."

"Did Leah tell you not to talk to me?"

"Leah is my friend."

"I know that."

"She protects us."

"Who? You and Debbie? She didn't protect you from getting your hair cut off."

Abby blinked away tears. "I must go." She pointed down the trail. "It's faster for me to walk home this way. Follow the trail back the way we came and you will reach your car."

Before she disappeared into the trees, I said, "If you ever change your mind, you know where to find me."

She didn't reply. Instead she just kept walking.

I stood on the edge of the pond and watched the geese squawk at each other as they slipped across the ice. Maybe I would ask

Timothy if he'd like to go ice skating here. Tanisha was right. I
shouldn't be afraid to ask him out on a date. If he were truly part
of the English world now, he should know how it works. I doubted
Hannah was as discreet.

I turned my thoughts from Timothy and Hannah and back to
Abby. She and her two friends, Leah and Debbie, knew much more
about the haircutting than they were telling Chief Rose or me. How
would I convince one of the girls to talk? Abby seemed like the
weakest link, yet just now, she had not cracked. I frowned. I should
tell Chief Rose and let her try. I bet she was pretty good at getting
a confession when she needed one.

A twig snapped. I turned expecting to see Abby returning on
the trail or another deer rushing through the thicket. Instead I saw
the two people I least wanted to come across while alone in the
woods.

Chapter Forty-One

Mrs. Green always said that some people were like a bad penny—they kept turning up. As Brock and Curt smirked at me, I finally understood that expression.

Brock stood in the trailhead that Abby had walked down, and Curt blocked the one that led to my car. The only other option was to walk across the pond. The ice might be firm enough to hold the geese, but that didn't mean it could hold me.

In a moment of panic I wondered if Abby had set me up.

"Did Abby tell you I would be here?"

"Who's Abby?" Brock asked. "That Amish girl you were talking to? You spend too much time with the buggy riders, Red."

Curt nodded. "Brock's right. You don't need those Amish wimps. Come with Brock and me. We'll show you a good time that will calm you right down." He took a step forward.

I took a step back toward the ice. *Maybe if I can get them to follow me onto the ice, I can circle back around and run to my car.* My cell phone felt heavy in the inside pocket of my coat. The phone's plastic body sat on my chest, but it might as well have been in my office at Harshberger—it was buried under too many layers in my coat to grab easily.

Brock walked to the edge of the pond. "You aren't thinking of going ice skating now, are you?"

"You know how to ice skate?" I snapped.

A lazy smile crossed his face. "I might be willing to learn for the right person."

My stomach curdled. "Can't you leave me alone? Don't you realize Chief Rose wants an excuse to throw you back in jail?"

Brock straightened to his full height. "That hurts, Red, that really hurts."

Curt pulled at his goatee. "I don't care what the lady cop wants. I only care about what we want. Right now, it's you."

My heart pounded so hard in my chest, I wondered if the geese could hear the thumping. Without a thought about the thinness of the ice, I raced for the frozen pond. My boot, sturdy or not, slipped on the glassy surface. When I was on the ice, I saw the movement of water. My stomach dropped. The pond was melting.

Brock took advantage of my hesitation and stepped on the ice. I held out my hand. "Don't come any closer!"

He rushed ahead.

"No! The ice will break."

As I yelled the last word, a deafening crack shook the ground beneath my feet. I turned and ran full tilt to the opposing shore. The cracking sound followed me. Behind me I heard a cry and a splash. I didn't look back until safely on firm ground. Grasping my knees, I gulped air.

Brock's head bobbed over the edge of the ice.

"Dude, stand up!" Curt's voice was three octaves higher than normal.

"I can't." Brock was already turning a bluish gray color. "The water is too deep. I can't touch."

Brock was over six feet tall. The water had to be eight or more feet at that point for him not to be able to touch the muddy bottom.

Curt took a step onto the ice. A crack raced across the surface, and he jumped back. His eyes, wide with fear, locked with mine across the ice. "You have to help. I'm too heavy. I'll break the ice."

Brock's eyes were the size of softballs.

I could easily get away now. They would have no way to stop me. I could be in my car within five minutes, but I knew I could never leave them like that. "Is your truck here?"

"Yea. So?" Curt said. Even with his best friend in danger he had attitude to spare.

I ignored his tone. "We need some rope. Do you have any rope in your truck?"

He nodded.

"Go get it."

Curt didn't move.

"Go!"

Curt turned and ran. I heard him stomp through the forest breaking branches and leveling saplings in his wake. While Curt got the rope, I fumbled with my coat and pulled out my cell phone.

"911. What's your emergency?"

"This is Chloe Humphrey. I'm at Appleseed Pond. Someone fell through the ice."

The operator voice was sharp. "How long as the person been in the water?"

"Maybe three minutes," I guessed. It seemed longer than that.

"I'll send a squad right away. What's the name of person in the water?"

"Brock Buckley."

I looked out over the ice, no longer able to see Brock's head.

"Brock! Brock!"

"Miss, what's going on?"

"I can't see his head. I have to go look."

"Miss, stay on the phone . . ."

I tucked the phone back into my inner coat pocket but didn't hang up.

"Brock! Wave a hand if you hear me."

The tip of his fingers appeared and relief rushed through my body. I took a tentative step out onto the ice. The cracking started again. It wasn't as loud as when Curt stepped onto the pond. I crouched on all fours and slid onto my stomach to distribute my weight more evenly across the ice. The ice would be less likely to crack that way—at least I hoped so.

"Lord, please don't let the ice break," I whispered.

Cold seeped in through my jeans and coat. My legs were soaked to the skin. I slid. Brock was twenty yards away from me.

I inched closer and reached the edge of the hole Brock bobbed in. His face was blue. Ice crystals gathered across his eyebrows and eyelashes.

I lowered my right hand into the hole in the ice. Freezing water slashed my exposed wrist, sending chills through every nerve in my body. "Give me your hand."

His teeth chattered, and eyes stared at me as if he didn't understand the words coming out of my mouth.

"Give. Me. Your. Hand."

He did, his fingers so blue they reminded me of the blue raspberry popsicles Mrs. Green gave Tanisha and me in the summers. I shook the childhood image from my mind and concentrated on Brock.

Curt crashed his way back through the forest. "I got the rope!"

I gripped Brock's hand, my fingers already numbed by his frigid touch. The cotton glove I wore was no help. I cranked my neck in an awkward angle to see Curt. "Make a loop with the rope that's big enough to fit over his head and shoulder. Can you do that?"

Curt nodded.

"Then do it," Brock snapped. It was the first time he had spoken in a long while.

Curt fumbled with the rope. Finally he was able to tie it into a loop.

I was eye to eye with Brock now, closer than I ever wanted to be. I could make out the individual shapes in the tobacco stains on his teeth. I saw the hair inside of his nose and the bloodshot veins in his eyes.

"Throw it to me!" I yelled.

Curt threw the rope, but it landed way off the mark to my right. I would have to let go of Brock's hand in order to reach it. My hand was so cold, I knew if I let go I wouldn't be able to grip his palm again.

"Try again."

"He can't throw a rope." His teeth chattered. "C-Curt's never done that. He's not a c-cowboy," Brock said.

"Be quiet," I snapped. "You're not helping."

Despite the blue look to his face, he glared at me. The fear I saw earlier was gone. Now, he was angry.

The rope hit me in the side, and I grabbed it with my free hand. It's roughness scratched the surface of my palm. I hadn't realized I'd lost my left glove sometime during the rescue.

While I tried to maneuver the rope into place, I felt Brock's fingers slip from mine. I gripped them. "Don't let go of my hand."

His eyes were closed and his head lolled to the side. Thankfully, it rested on the edge of the ice, so it wasn't under water where he could drown. I let go of the rope and slapped him across the face.

His eyes snapped open. They were glassy, but fury resided there too. I felt the strength come back into his hand as he held onto mine. A half hour before, he could have crushed my small hand in his. Now my hand was keeping him alive. I reached again for the rope and slipped it over his head and under his left armpit, pulling it tight. To do that, I had to put my arm up to the elbow in the icy water. It felt like a thousand syringes stabbing my hand and arm all at the same time.

I angled my body, so that I could see Curt. "I got him. Pull on the rope." I slid back on the ice to make room. Brock held onto my hand with renewed strength. "W-Where are you going?"

I pulled my hand from his. "I have to go to the pond's edge to help Curt pull you out."

Tears sprang to his eyes and he placed his large head back on the side of the ice. A stab of guilt hit me.

"I need help!" Curt cried, spurring me into action. I belly-crawled in his direction.

"He's too heavy," Curt said. "Or he's caught on something. I can't pull him out."

Thrashing and cries came from the direction of the parking lot in the woods—like Big Foot himself was headed our way.

The first one to pop into the clearing was Chief Rose. She took in the scene.

"We're holding him up by a rope but can't pull him out." A full body shiver shook my being. I wrapped my arms around myself.

EMTs crashed through the woods. One took the rope from Curt's hand, while a second EMT tethered yellow nylon to the harness around his waist. He wore a wetsuit. Something told me this was not the first time someone had been fished out of Appleseed Pond.

Someone wrapped an aluminum blanket around my shoulders. It helped, but I wondered if the shivering would ever end.

The EMT wrapped another rope around Brock and spoke with him. He held up his thumb, and three large EMTs yanked on both of the ropes. Nothing. The EMT on the frozen pond used an ice pick from his tool belt to free the parts of Brock's clothing that had stuck to the edge. He gave the thumbs-up sign again.

They yanked and Brock popped out of the hole like a penguin from the ocean.

The EMT on the ice wrapped an aluminum blanket as best as he could around Brock, and they pulled him the rest of the way to safety. Suddenly he was surrounded by EMTs.

Curt crowded them. "What's going on? Is he okay?"

One of the EMTs elbowed him away. "We need room to work."

Curt jumped back like a puppy that had been struck on the head.

Chief Rose sidled up to me. "How are you?"

My teeth chattered. "Fine, I think."

Those ever-present aviator sunglasses sat on the top of the police chief's head, tucked in between her brown curls. "What on earth were you doing out here with these two? More than once I thought I told you to stay away from them."

"I wasn't here with them. We ran into each other."

"You seem to run into them a lot." She removed her leather gloves and tucked them under her arm. "Give me your hands." She sounded so much like I had just moments before when I asked Brock to give me his hand. She removed the soaked-through cotton glove from my right hand and stuck it into her leather coat pocket, then she put her gloves on my hands.

Her gloves were a touch too large. My fingers didn't reach all the way to the tip, but they were warming up. "Thank you," I murmured.

"How did you run into them?"

My teeth chattered again. "I was here talking to Abby. There was something about the haircutting she wanted to tell me."

"What was it?" Her tone was sharp.

My shoulders drooped. "I don't know. She chickened out and wouldn't tell me. In the end, all she told me was to stop investigating and leave the Amish alone."

The chief looked disappointed. "I hear that all the time myself."

"My gut tells me Abby and her friends are more involved in this than we were first led to believe."

"You might be right. I will take a look at them again, but I don't believe any of them were strong enough to stab Young like that."

An EMT walked up to us. It was Nate, the same one who took me to the hospital the night I found Ezekiel's body. "Chief, we need to take Miss Humphrey to the hospital to check her out."

I grimaced. "I feel fine. It's nothing a hot cup of coffee and a warm bath can't fix."

Nate shook his head. "We either check you out at the hospital or you sign a form that says if you die from hypothermia it's not our fault."

Excellent bedside manner. Grudgingly, I said, "I'll go."

"This conversation is not over," Chief Rose said. Her curls bounced as she moved, giving her a girlish air. However, one look into her eyes told you she was no girl. She placed a hand on my shoulder. "You know, if you hadn't been here, he might have drowned. You saved his life."

The weight of her comment sunk in. I watched as a group of EMTs hoisted Brock onto their shoulders on an emergency plank. Curt followed at a distance. He seemed to have shrunk in the last hour. Uncertainty ruled his expression, and his hands were clamped together as if he didn't trust their movement.

"Will Brock be okay?" I asked the EMT.

"He should make a full recovery. He won't even lose any fingers or toes."

Really, the guy should go into grief counseling.

The EMT cleared his throat. "You are going to have to call someone from the hospital to drive you home."

I dreaded that call to Timothy. He wasn't going to be happy about it. Neither was Becky. They already thought I was fragile from my spill after finding Ezekiel's body. This incident, because it involved Curt and Brock, almost felt worse than finding a dead body.

"What about my car? Should I just leave it here?"

Chief Rose held out her hand. "Give me your keys. I will have one of my officers drop it off in front of your house."

I reached into my pocket and dropped the keys into her gloveless hands.

She clasped her fingers around them. "I'll be seeing you later at your house—not at the hospital." She smiled. "You keep going to the hospital like this, Humphrey, they will have to name a ward after you."

I rolled my eyes.

"Ah." She snapped her fingers. "I got a smile out of you. That's what I wanted."

I knew she wanted a lot more than that.

Chapter Forty-Two

I couldn't believe I was in the emergency room again. I was even on the same examining table, surrounded by a pink curtain. A nurse slid a protective covering on an ear thermometer. "I didn't expect to see you back here so soon." She checked my temperature. "Ninety-seven point nine. Low, but nothing a hot mug of cocoa can't cure." She made a note on my chart and slipped behind the curtain.

I let my feet dangle from the hospital bed as they did on doctor's visits as a child. *Thump, thump, thump.* My heels hit the drawers under the bed. In a rush, I remembered being at the doctor with my mother and her telling me not to kick the hospital bed. In my mind, I heard her voice and saw her annoyed expression. It took my breath away.

The nurse pulled back the curtain. "We have a couple of guests that insist on seeing you."

Timothy and Becky rushed toward me.

Becky threw her arms around my neck. "Chloe, what happened? Timothy said you fell into the ice and almost drowned."

I hadn't much time to explain to Timothy what had happened. I'd told him over the phone that someone had fallen into the Appleseed Pond. I hadn't meant to imply it was me. I figured it was better to tell him about Curt and Brock in person. "No, I'm fine. I wasn't in the water."

The nurse made another note on her chart. "She saved the guy who fell in. She's a hero."

"You saved someone." Becky squeezed my hand. "Tell us everything."

Timothy frowned and watched me closely, as if he knew he wouldn't like what I was about to say.

I swallowed. "It was Brock."

Becky dropped my hand. I doubted she could be more surprised if I had told her I'd flown to the moon and back while they attended choir practice.

Timothy became extremely still. "How is Brock?" He directed his question to the nurse.

"He'll be fine. We're keeping him in the hospital overnight for observation. His temperature dropped dangerously low, but I expect he'll be discharged by early afternoon tomorrow." She patted my shoulder. "You're free to go now, Chloe. Do me a favor. Don't show up here for a while. This is turning into a weekly occurrence." The nurse slipped by the curtain and on to the next patient.

I climbed off of the examining table. "I'll need to grab my coat and we can head home. The nurse said it was at the front desk. I left it in the ambulance."

"Becky, can you find her coat?" Timothy asked.

Becky's face fell into a slight pout. "I want to hear about what happened."

"You will." His tone was firm. "I want to talk to Chloe alone for a moment."

I sat back down on the table.

Annoyance flashed across Becky's heart-shaped face, but she did as she was told.

When she disappeared behind the curtain, Timothy glared at me. "What were you doing alone with Brock?"

"Curt was there too."

His eye twitched. "Does that make it better?"

I folded my arms across my chest. "I tried to call you twice. I sent you a text message."

"What did it say? I'm going into the woods with Brock and Curt. See you later."

"No. If you'd ever look at your messages, you'd know I was meeting Abby there. There was something she wanted to tell me about the haircutting."

He glared down at me. "What was that?"

My face flamed. "I-I don't know. She changed her mind. She's afraid of something or someone."

"Okay, so you were in the woods with Abby. First of all, why didn't you meet her in town? How stupid it is to go into the woods alone with someone you hardly know. I thought you were from the city. Don't you have street smarts?" His voice shook.

"She wouldn't talk to me otherwise. She was scared someone would see us, and furthermore, she's an Amish girl. What harm could she do to me?"

"Plenty. What happened after she didn't tell you whatever she had to say?"

"She left and I was about to walk back to my car when Curt and Brock showed up."

"How did they know you were there?"

"They saw my car from the road. I ran away from them across the pond. Brock followed me, but he was too heavy. The ice broke and he fell in. Since I'm lighter than Curt, it made sense that I hold onto Brock until the EMTs and police arrive. Did you want me to leave him there to drown?"

Timothy's chest heaved up and down. "No. I wouldn't want that."

I threw up my hands. "So then what's the problem?"

He took one long stride and was right in front of the examining table. Our legs touched. He grabbed me by the shoulders and pulled me up until I was right in front of him. Without ceremony, he lifted my chin and kissed me full on the mouth. My body went rigid, and against my own will, relaxed into his embrace. When he finally released me, his voice was an octave lower than before. "Please, don't run off like that again without telling me."

A smiled curved on my lips. I couldn't help it. It was as if my muscles had turned against me. My mind told me to be upset by his behavior, but my body had no qualms with it at all.

The nurse peeked through the curtain and found us standing there toe to toe. "Everything okay in here?"

Heat rushed up from the bottom of my feet to the top of my head.

"Everything's fine," Timothy said.

She looked at me.

I nodded. "We're fine. Thank you for checking."

She nodded and disappeared behind the curtain again.

Timothy took my hand. "Let's get you home."

My fingers laced with his. I was calling Tanisha tonight. I didn't care if I woke her up.

Chapter Forty-Three

Becky stood in the ER waiting room a room I was a little too familiar with having only lived in Knox County for four months. She held up my coat, and her eyes fell to my hand interlaced with Timothy's.

I took the coat with my free hand, reluctant to release myself from Timothy's grasp. It was as if holding onto his hand made the kiss more real, and less a figment of my imagination. Timothy squeezed my hand reassuringly, as if he understood my hesitation.

I was about to let go when someone from behind me cleared his throat.

Becky took a step back. Timothy and I turned around and came face to face with Curt Fanning, the last person I wanted to see when so happy. He was the sewing needle to my happiness balloon.

His eyes fell on my hands intertwined with Timothy's, and his lip curled. Timothy held my hand a little more tightly.

Curt fondled the dog tag hanging from his neck. "I want to talk to you."

"Why?" the question popped out of my mouth.

"This isn't easy for me to say," he said, his voice barely above a growl. "But thank you."

My mouth fell open. Curt might as well have tap danced in the middle of the waiting room.

His Adam's apple bobbed. "If it hadn't been for you, Brock would have died. I can hardly stand him most of the time, but he's my best friend. I don't know what I would do if I'd lost him."

My mouth felt dry. "You're welcome," I managed.

"There's something else," he said, sounding more like himself.

Of course there was. Who was I to think that Curt would say thank you and let that be the end of it?

He sucked on his teeth. "I think I know why that Amish girl, the one you were with in the woods, wanted to talk to you."

I went very still. "Why?"

"To confess."

"To what?"

"The haircutting."

I took in a sharp of breath. "What are you talking about?"

"Two weeks ago, Brock and I got back into town from . . . being away." He gave me a level stare when he said this. "It was late, like four in the morning."

A light went off. Was Curt and Brock's green truck the vehicle Sadie had heard that morning?

"Don't you mean early then?" Becky asked.

His eyes cut in her direction. "It would if we'd gone to sleep that night."

Becky inched toward her brother. "Oh."

"What did you see?" I asked.

"I took a shortcut down the alley behind the bakery. That Amish girl that works in the bakery, not the cute one, but the one with glasses, she was being held on the ground by another Amish girl wearing men's clothes. A potato bag was over her face. A third girl used some type of old fashioned scissors to cut off her hair."

"There were only three girls there?" Timothy asked.

Curt cracked his knuckles. "No, there was a fourth. She was watching the alley."

"Other than Sadie, who works at the bakery, what did the girls look like?"

He squinted at me. "I don't know. They were Amish."

"Why would an Amish girl cut off another Amish girl's hair? I've never heard of such a thing," Becky argued.

"I don't know," Curt growled. "I just know what Brock and I saw."

"Why didn't you stop them?" Becky pressed.

Curt's eyes narrowed. "It's not my job to interfere with the Amish."

Timothy jaw twitched. "That must be a new policy for you."

"So what if it is, buggy rider?" Curt's lips curled back. "You don't believe me?"

"It's hard to believe," Timothy said.

"Brock and I saw them. They cut off that girl's hair."

"You can't be serious," Becky blurted out. "Maybe you are the ones who did it, and you're making up this story."

He glared at her. "I'm telling the truth."

"It would be the first time." Timothy gripped my hand so tightly my knuckles hurt.

I pulled my hand from Timothy's grasp. "Curt, I believe you."

Timothy's face was incredulous, but I did believe Curt. "The chief is going to want to talk to you," I said.

His expression became hooded again. "I'm not talking to the cops."

The receptionist leaned over the counter. "Mr. Fanning? The doctor said Mr. Buckley has been moved to his room on the third floor. You can visit him there now. Visiting hours end at seven."

Mr. Fanning? Mr. Buckley? The receptionist's formal address of Curt and Brock didn't fit them.

He turned to go.

"Curt," I called.

He pivoted on the linoleum floor, the rubber soles of his boots squeaking.

"Thank you for telling me this."

"You're welcome." He said the words as if they caused a strange taste in his mouth, then continued down the hallway.

Timothy was gaping at me. "You believe him?"

"Yes, I think this is what Abby wanted to tell me today, and she lost her nerve." I ignored the No Cell Phone sign and called the chief. The receptionist glared at me but didn't tell me to put the phone away.

"What is it, Humphrey? I told you I would see you later," Chief Rose said in my ear.

"Something new has come up." I repeated Curt's story.

"Huh."

"Huh? You don't sounds too surprised."

"I'm not. There was something about those girls' story that didn't sit well with me. I need to talk to Curt."

"I told him that. He's not eager to talk to you."

She chuckled. "I'm not surprised. Typically we start a conversation with me Mirandarizing him. Is he still there?"

"As far as I know. The hospital is keeping Brock overnight. Curt was just told he could go up and see his friend."

"All right." She clicked her tongue. "I'll head to the hospital."

"Do you want us to wait for you?"

"Nah. I'll swing by your house after I talk to Curt. Do not

talk to the girls. I don't want them to get spooked that we know something."

I hung up.

"Where do we go now?" Becky asked.

"Home," I said.

I just prayed Dylan wouldn't be there.

Chapter Forty-Four

Timothy threw a pillow into the corner of the couch. "This will work for me."

Becky removed her coat and hung it in the hall closet. "The pillow?"

Gigabyte yowled at her first, and then at me. He was tired of being alone so much.

"The couch," Timothy said. "I'm staying the night. I'll sleep right here."

I slipped off my boots and eased myself into the armchair. The aches and pains of pulling Brock from the icy water were beginning to set in. My right bicep was sore. If rescuing people was going to become a regular thing with me, I should start lifting weights. I glanced at Timothy. "You don't have to do that."

He set his jaw. "Yes, I do."

Becky flopped onto her dog pillow on the floor. "Why? Do you think Curt and Brock will come here?"

"Brock's not going much of anywhere until the hospital releases him, and I think Curt will be at his side until that happens." I rubbed my arm.

Becky shook her head. "Who would have thought Curt cared so much about Brock?" She stood up. "I'll pull some leftovers together for dinner."

Becky made up hodgepodge plates of leftover manicotti, turkey, mashed potatoes, sweet potatoes, ham, homemade cranberry relish, and green beans. Despite the strange assortment, my mouth watered. Saving someone's life had made me work up an appetite.

"Can we eat in front of the TV?" Becky asked. "Paula Deen is coming on."

"Sure." I went to the hall closet and pulled out folding TV trays.

Timothy set up the trays, and we ate in the living room watching one of Becky's favorite cooking shows. I laughed as I watched Timothy and Becky chew with their eyes glued to the TV.

Timothy swallowed. "What?"

I grinned. "I was just thinking you two are eating dinner in front of the television. You really are English now."

The doorbell rang, and Timothy hopped up to answer it. "Come on in, Greta. We were having dinner. Would you like to join us?"

Her peridot eyes sparkled. "I would."

Timothy grabbed a kitchen chair and a fourth TV tray while Becky went to the kitchen to fix a plate for the chief.

She handed me her coat and I hung it in the closet. Then I moved myself and my tray to the front of the couch, next to Timothy's spot. "You can sit in the armchair."

"What service," Chief Rose said as she sat down. Timothy set the tray in front her.

Becky appeared with a plate. "I brought you a little of everything."

"Looks good to me." The chief placed her paper napkin on her lap.

We sat back in our places, and Becky reluctantly turned off the TV. One of these days I was going to have to show her how to use the DVR.

The police chief bowed her head before she started eating. She picked up her fork, then caught me gawking at her. "Does it come as a surprise to you, Humphrey, that I pray?"

Embarrassment washed over me. "Uh, yes . . ." I flushed. "I mean no."

"Are you a Christian, too?" Becky asked the chief.

The side of Chief Rose's mouth tipped up. "I am. I don't think I could be a police officer without my faith. I see the worst of what people can do to each other. If I didn't know God, that's all I would see." She cleared her throat. "So I talked to Curt."

Relief washed over me when she let me off the hook.

"What did he say?" Timothy picked up his water glass.

She cut a small bite of ham. "Same thing that he told all of you."

"Do you think he's telling the truth?" Becky sounded unconvinced.

"I do. I spoke to Brock, too, separately. He was irritated that Curt told us about what they saw, but he corroborated the story."

"But why did he tell us?" Becky asked. "I feel like he must have some type of motive."

The chief was thoughtful, her fork poised over her plate. "It's always possible Curt had an ulterior motive. That is his method of operation. However, right now, as far as we know, he didn't really have any reason except to show Humphrey his gratitude."

"Gratitude?" Becky murmured. "*That* must have been different for him."

"Do you think the girls killed Ezekiel Young?" I asked.

Timothy tapped his fork on the side of his plate. "Ezekiel was Abby's uncle. It's so hard to believe."

The police chief shook her head. "No. Whoever did that was

much taller than any of the girls. I got the autopsy report back today. The coroner said the person was either Young's height or taller. Since Young was six feet tall, I can only assume I'm looking for a man. Not many Amazons strutting around Appleseed Creek."

"There are two groups cutting off Amish hair?" I asked.

"That's my thought. I believe the murder was a copycat crime. The haircutting is well-known in the county. Whoever wanted to kill Young used that to his advantage and made it look like it was related to the other crimes against the Amish." She diced her sweet potato. "I'm not sure where the attack on Grandfather Zook falls in all of this."

"*Grossdaddi* did say he was certain that whoever cut off his beard was a man," Timothy said.

"Are you going to arrest the girls?" I asked.

"I could, but like Becky, most people wouldn't think much of a story like that from an ex-con. Who are they going to believe? Three innocent-looking Amish girls . . . or Curt? Don't answer that. I know the answer." She paused for a sip of water. "Also, if I arrest the girls outright or even question them about their whereabouts, it will cause hard feelings between the English and Amish in town. I would like to keep the peace. There is enough division between our two worlds as it is."

Becky's fork stopped halfway to her mouth. "So you're going to do nothing?"

The chief's eyes narrowed into heavily made up slits. "No. Here's the deal. The Amish don't want me to come knocking on their door, but they might talk to you, Humphrey. I don't know what it is about you. You're like the Amish whisperer or something."

Becky rolled her eyes.

"What do you want me to do?" I asked.

"I need you to talk to the three girls together."

I moved my water glass onto the other side of my TV tray. "Abby told me she, Leah, and Debbie were going to finish stocking The Apple Core for Christmas tomorrow morning before the store opens."

The chief clapped her hands. "Perfect. Tomorrow, I want you to stop by The Apple Core and talk to them. Tell them that you discovered something about the haircutting they need to know."

"I have to work tomorrow. It's the last full week of the semester, and the office is going to be busy with student computer meltdowns."

She shrugged. "Your staff can handle it."

I opened my mouth to dispute that.

"Besides," she waved her hand, "I already called Dean Klink and got you off the hook. I told him you were in the hospital today because you saved someone's life. I promised him the Mount Vernon newspaper would include that you worked at the college when they write it up. He was very enthused about the life-saving piece."

"Gee thanks," I muttered.

"You're welcome." She ignored the sarcasm in my tone. "At the meeting, get them to confess. I will have you wear a mic. I've been dying to try out the hand-me-down wire I got from the sheriff's department."

Becky's nose wrinkled. "What's does 'wear a mic' mean?"

The chief sipped her water. "We are going to bug Humphrey."

Becky scrunched her forehead, looking even more confused.

"It means Chief Rose will record my conversation on a microphone."

"Oh." Becky nodded, as if that made sense.

Chief Rose arched an eyebrow at Becky. "You need to watch more cop shows."

"And how do I get them to confess?" I asked, hoping to get the conversation back on track.

"That's up to you. Like I told you, you're the Amish whisperer." The police chief stood. "Thanks for dinner. Humphrey, I'll be here at nine a.m. tomorrow to pick you up."

"What about us?" Becky asked.

The chief arched an eyebrow again. "You can go about your day as normal."

"I'm going with Chloe," Timothy said.

"The girls are more likely to talk to Chloe alone, but if you want to sit in my cruiser and listen to her wire, you're welcome to do so."

"Can you get me out of work tomorrow?" Becky sounded hopeful. "I want to listen to the wire too."

"Sorry." The chief collected her leather coat. "You're on your own there."

After Chief Rose left, Timothy folded his arms across his chest. "Are you sure you want to do this?"

"What choice do I have? If the girls attacked Sadie, we need to know why. They may lead us to whoever attacked Grandfather Zook and killed Ezekiel."

Timothy nodded, his expression sobering.

Becky started clearing the TV trays. "How cool is it that you will wear a wire like a spy or something?"

I admitted, if only to myself, that yes, it was kind of cool.

Chapter Forty-Five

Unable to sleep, I called Tanisha. It was early morning in Milan, and I knew she would already be up. Tee was one of those irritating people who woke up cheerful in the morning. Her entire family was like that.

When I lived with them, the Greens knew I wasn't fully awake until ten a.m. or after an extra strength dose of coffee. I smiled while listening to the phone ring, waiting for Tee to pick up. Christmas morning was the worst. The Greens unwrapped gifts at four a.m. Since Tee would be in Italy for Christmas, I wondered what I would do this year. I'm sure the Greens would be happy to have me. I hadn't been back to Cleveland since I moved to Appleseed Creek, but a larger part of me wanted to spend the holiday with Timothy.

"Wow, what time is it there?" Tanisha asked, fully awake.

"Midnight."

"What are you still doing up?"

"Remember those two guys I told you about? Curt and Brock?"

"Yeah. I thought they were in jail."

"Not any more." I told her about my day.

"Chloe, I can't even believe this. How's it possible you're having a more adventurous life in Amish Country than I am in Italy?"

"I have no idea. I didn't move here looking for adventure. Have you heard anything more from Cole?"

Her sigh was so exaggerated it sounded like a wind tunnel in my ear. "I sent him an e-mail and told him about the ring."

"How'd that go over?"

"About as well as you'd expect." She groaned. "I don't want to talk about Cole anymore. How's Timothy?"

"Well . . ." I told her about the kiss. Good thing the room was dark. Not that she'd be able to see my red cheeks or the stupid smile on my face.

She squealed. "What?"

"Sheesh, keep it down. You're going to wake up your roommates."

"They won't care. I've told them all about you and Buggy Boy, and they are in love. I can't wait to tell them the latest installment."

I rolled my eyes and said good-night.

THE NEXT MORNING, CHIEF Rose showed up at nine o'clock on the dot. She rubbed her hands together. Her peridot eyes, outlined in forest green, which made them appear even more catlike than usual, sparkled. "Let's get to work."

In my opinion, the chief was far too excited about the wire I had to wear.

She eyed the sheets and blankets folded in the corner of the sofa.

"Timothy spent the night," I said.

The chief removed her stocking cap. Her brown curls flew in all directions. "Ah."

Timothy's jaw twitched. "I slept on the couch."

"Relax, Troyer. I wasn't thinking anything tawdry." She patted the black case, roughly the size of a toaster. "I brought everything with me." She set the case on the coffee table and opened it up. It contained a tiny microphone and a receiver, not much different than the wireless lapel mics we used at the college.

She held up the microphone. "I'm going to have to tape this to your breastbone to conceal it. Lift your sweater up."

Timothy's cheeks reddened. He turned his back, and she affixed the tiny microphone just below my clavicle with cloth tape. "There." She clicked on the receiver and a screeching sound broke the silence of the room. Gigabyte jumped three feet in the air before streaking out of the room.

Timothy held his hand over his ears. "Turn it off."

The chief moved the switch to the off position.

"Let me give it a try," I said.

She stepped back and cocked her head. "You think you can make it work?" she asked, her tone dubious.

"I do this kind of stuff for a living, remember?"

"Fine. Knock yourself out." She gave me some room.

I made some adjustments to the frequency and volume. "That should do it." I turned the mic back on. Nothing.

"It's not doing anything," Timothy said.

"That's a good thing," I said. "I'll go upstairs and see if you two can hear me."

In my room, I whispered, "Testing. One. Two. Three."

"We can hear you!" the chief called up the stairs.

When I got back downstairs, the chief's eyes glowed. "We're good to go. I'll have my officers stationed near the front and the back of the store in case the girls make a run for it."

I arched an eyebrow. "Do you really think that will happen?"

"No, but it's good practice for the team. They're getting lazy. We don't see much action." She zipped the case closed and looked me in the eyes. "At least we didn't until you moved here, Humphrey."

Somehow, that didn't bring me comfort.

Slipping the strap over her arm, she said, "You know what to do. Timothy and I will be in earshot."

I nodded.

"You have nothing to be afraid of."

"I'm not afraid." I wasn't. Maybe I was a little afraid I wouldn't be able to get the confession, but that was it.

Becky laced up her boots to bicycle to work. "I wish I could go too."

The chief shook her head. "It's for the best. Can't have too many cooks in the kitchen, you know."

"Shouldn't you have a code word if something goes wrong?" Becky asked. "That's what they always do on TV."

Chief Rose dug one hand into her hip. "How much television do you actually watch?"

I could answer that. "A lot."

Chapter Forty-Six

The apple-shaped bell over the glass door of The Apple Core rang. I wasn't afraid. Leah and her friends may have been able to jump Sadie when she was caught off guard, but I knew what they were capable of. What bothered me was the *why*. I believed Curt's story about what he saw, but why would the girls do that to Sadie, and presumably to themselves too?

Did they do it out of spite, like some Amish version of a high school clique? Apparently, American high school wasn't as far from the Amish as I'd thought.

"May I help you?" Leah asked from her post behind the counter. Her face fell. "It's you."

"Good morning, Leah. I was wondering if I could talk to you and Abby and Debbie. They're here, aren't they?" I removed my coat and hung it over my arm. I was afraid that the wool would muffle the microphone too much. "It's about the haircutting. There's been a development in the case you should know about."

She paled. "Debbie and Abby are in the back putting up the rest of the holiday stock."

Debbie appeared from around a display shelf. "Leah . . ." she paused. "Oh, I didn't hear the bell."

"Can you go get Abby?" Leah's voice was tight. "She has something to tell us about the haircutting."

Debbie swallowed and disappeared behind the display. She and Abby, her face pale, reappeared a minute later. "What are you doing here?" Abby asked.

"I need to talk to all three of you."

Leah folded her arms on the counter. "What about?"

"Don't you find it odd that of the four girls whose hair was cut, only Sadie is missing from this tight little circle?"

Debbie walked behind the counter and stood next to Leah. "So? What about Grandfather Zook?"

I wondered how far to take this. Chief Rose should have given me confession extracting tips before I talked to the girls. I squared my shoulders, keeping my eyes on Abby. "I don't think Grandfather Zook or the death of Abby's uncle is related to what happened to you."

Abby concentrated on the tops of her black sneakers.

Debbie nudged Leah, their ringleader since the very beginning, in my estimation.

"Just because you think something doesn't make it true," Leah said.

"A man didn't cut your hair, did he Abby?" I said. "It was a girl your own age. Wasn't it."

Debbie's mouth fell open. "Abby, what did you tell her?"

Abby shook her head. "N-nothing."

I continued. "Abby and I had a nice talk yesterday."

Leah glared at the pale girl. "What?"

Abby's head snapped up. "She's telling a falsehood."

I cocked my head. "Did you or did you not ask me to meet you at Appleseed Pond yesterday to talk about the haircutting?"

Perspiration gathered above Abby's brow. "Ye-yes."

Debbie cried out. "You told her!"

"Debbie, be quiet," Leah barked.

"N-no," Abby stuttered. "I didn't tell her. I didn't."

"But you wanted to," I said.

Abby gave the faintest of nods. A tear slid down her cheek. "I can't keep this awful secret anymore."

Leah ran around the counter and pinched her friend's arm. "Don't say a word."

Tears fell from Abby's eyes. "I have to. I have to. It's different for you and Debbie. My uncle is dead."

Debbie's hands were flat on the counter. "We had nothing to do with that."

"I know." Abby pulled her arm from Leah's grasp. She looked at me. "We did it," Abby whispered.

"What?" I stepped closer to her, wanting the microphone to pick up her words.

"We cut our own hair . . . and Sadie's."

Leah stepped away from her friend, her expression twisted, as if she didn't even know the person in front of her.

"Why?" I asked.

Debbie's face crumpled. "The bishop. He's ruined everything in the district. We had to show him that he wasn't in control. The haircutting embarrassed him."

Through gritted teeth, Leah said, "Stop talking."

Debbie's eyes filled with tears. "I cannot, Leah. I can't keep this secret anymore either. We did this to embarrass the bishop, but we are hurting each other more." Gruffly, she wiped a tear from her cheek with her hand, her gaze steady on me "You don't know what it's been like. The bishop and the deacon have been horrible. A half a step out of place and they punish you. Look at the Troyer family you love so much."

"Is Sadie involved? Is she part of your little group?" I asked.

"No." Abby held herself around the waist. "We were afraid the deacon or police would realize we cut our own hair because we were close friends, so we decided to cut the hair of someone we weren't friendly with."

I nodded. "The extra bonus was that she's the bishop's daughter."

Debbie hung her head in shame. "Yes."

"And Grandfather Zook? What about his beard?"

"We didn't do that," Abby spoke up. "We would never hurt an elderly man like that."

"You wouldn't hurt an old man, but what about Ezekiel Young. Did you kill him?"

Abby gasped, then covered her mouth and ran from the room. After a moment, we could hear the faint sound of retching from the back of the store.

Leah leveled her glare at me. "No. That is enough."

"I don't think so," I said. "I know you didn't kill Abby's uncle—the coroner already proved that. But someone has used your haircutting prank to his advantage and committed murder. A copycat crime."

Debbie removed a handkerchief from her pocket and dabbed the corners of eyes. "What does that mean?"

"It means someone saw what you girls were doing and copied it to cover up his crimes."

Debbie gasped. "Are you saying it's our fault Ezekiel was killed?"

I almost said yes, but that answer wasn't completely true. It was only part of the issue. The girls only gave the killer the idea of how to cover up the crime—the plan to murder must have already been in place.

"Do you realize that a killer used your antics to his advantage? And he may get away with murder because the police have wasted so much of their time looking for whoever cut your hair."

Debbie began to cry in earnest, but Leah's jaw was set.

The bell at the front of the store rang, and Chief Rose and her two officers entered. Leah's eyes cut over to me. Before that day, I wouldn't believe a young Amish girl could carry so much hate in her eyes. Leah whispered something to Debbie in Pennsylvania Dutch.

The chief smiled. "Don't talk? That's probably the best advice you could give her."

Leah's eyes grew wide.

"What? You're surprised I know your language? I couldn't manage in this town without it." Chief Rose turned to me. "Where's the third one?"

More retching sounds came from the back of the shop. I pointed a thumb in that direction. "In the back."

Chief Rose nodded to one of her officers. "Make sure she's finished with her tummy issues before you put her in the cruiser. I'm not in the mood to clean the upholstery." She handed Leah a piece of paper. "Here's a warrant, by the way. I imagine we will find a pair of sheep shears somewhere in this building."

Leah clenched her jaw so tightly I was surprised we couldn't hear the grinding of her teeth.

I stepped away as the chief read Leah and Debbie their rights and handcuffed them. Instead of feeling relieved that this ordeal was over, sadness washed through me. I slipped out of the shop.

Timothy stood outside, watching through the window. "You did a good job," he said.

I frowned. "It doesn't feel that way. I feel dirty and sneaky. I don't like it."

"You didn't do anything wrong. You helped the police. Now maybe the district can heal."

"To a point." I pulled my cotton gloves out of my pocket and slipped them on. "The person who killed Ezekiel Young is still out there."

He nodded.

"How do you think the bishop and deacon will react when they learn about the girls?"

"I don't know. My fear is they will come down harder on everyone else. I know that's what Deacon Sutter would want to do."

I nodded and then a thought hit me.

"What is it?"

"Miller's at work. Leah's his cousin."

"Oh."

"What am I going to tell him about all this?"

"The truth."

I bit my lip. I suspected the truth about his cousin was the last thing the programmer wanted to hear.

Chapter Forty-Seven

Even though Chief Rose had spoken to Dean Klink and gotten me a full day off of work, I headed to the office that afternoon. I couldn't stay in my big rented house all by myself and stare at that pencil-drawn X on my living room wall. Becky was at Young's all day, and then would head to the elementary school after work to help the teacher prepare for Tuesday afternoon's art class. Timothy had gone to Young's too, to work on the pavilion. Life went on despite the arrest of the three Amish girls.

Chief Rose called to tell me that she had already heard from CNN. The haircutting story received national attention as the newswire picked it up. The Amish way, foreign to the rest of the country, made today's arrests sensational news. The police chief warned me not to talk to the press, and that was fine with me.

On campus, I stepped into the office, and found Clark at the conference table editing video of the college's fall play on his laptop. "Hey boss, Klink told us that you weren't coming in today. He said you dove into a frozen pond and saved a drowning child."

I rolled my eyes. It came as no surprise that the dean's version of the story was more sensational than the truth. I feared what he would make of the three Amish girls. "That's not quite what happened."

"You didn't save someone?"

"I did, I guess, but it wasn't a child. And I didn't dive into a freezing pond." I told him a shortened version of the story.

"Wow. I'm impressed, but the diving in the pond would have really kicked the story up a notch."

"I'm sure it would. Where's Miller?"

"He left about an hour ago. He got a phone call about some type of family emergency."

I winced. I knew the nature of that emergency. "Did he say anything about it?"

"Nah. You know Miller. You have to use a crowbar to get anything out of him."

The door to the computer services office opened, and Dean Klink entered with Collette Williams close at his heels.

"Chloe!" Dean Klink grinned from ear to ear. "I saw your car in the parking lot and called Collette right away."

Clark hid a smirk behind his laptop screen.

"We need to jump on the good press you've created for the college." Collette smoothed a nonexistent wrinkle from her sleeve.

"Good press?"

"Of course, by pulling that drowning Amish girl from the water, you've gotten media attention. This could get national media attention. I only need to confirm a few facts before I blast the press release to all the outlets."

I held up my hand. "Wait, wait, *wait*. I didn't pull an Amish girl from the water."

Collette's head jerked back. She turned to the dean. "Dean Klink, you said . . ."

The dean licked his lip. "Chloe can tell us what really happened." To Collette, he said, "There still could be a story there."

The dean and the publicist sat at the conference table. Clark didn't move. No chance he was going to miss this show. I didn't see a way out of it either. I sat and told them about yesterday's event at Appleseed Pond. Carefully, I left Abby out of the story. I shivered to think what Collette would do when she learned about my involvement with the Amish haircutting.

Dean Klink smacked his hand on the conference table. "That's still a great story. Excellent stuff. Poetic even."

Collette's face was pinched. "I'm disappointed no Amish were involved. Chloe, the Amish angle is something I planned to talk to you about."

My brow shot up. *The Amish angle?*

Collette scribbled on a small leather-bound notebook. "The Amish are such a curiosity in the news and media right now that I believe the college should take more advantage of our proximity to them. We should advertise our ties and closeness to the Amish culture. It may attract students."

Clark coughed to cover a laugh. "You think American teenagers are going to choose to go to Harshberger because there are Amish nearby?"

Collette pointed the end of her pen at him. "Our best strategy in this tough academic market is to highlight our uniqueness. Our location makes us unique. Harshberger is located in a bucolic countryside. Parents see it as a quiet and safe place to send their children."

Clark only shook his head. "Discounting the fact we've had two murders in town in the last year."

Collette glared at him and turned her pen on me. "Chloe, the dean has told me about the close relationship you have with the Amish."

I didn't like where this was going. "I have Amish friends."

"Perfect. In addition to the one about you saving this guy, I want to write another article about you and your ties with the Amish. The college could receive some national attention on this." She flattened both hands on the tabletop. "Did you hear there was an arrest for the haircutting this morning? Three Amish girls."

I didn't say anything but felt Clark watching me.

She smiled. "Stories like that will bring national attention to Appleseed Creek and to Harshberger."

"National attention!" The dean beamed. "That would do a world of good for the college. It may even have an impact on enrollment. High school seniors are choosing colleges now, so now is the time to strike."

I cleared my throat. "I don't think the fact that there have been crimes within the Amish community will convince parents of college-aged kids to send their children to Harshberger."

Collette tapped her pen on the table. "Perhaps not, but the most important thing is to keep Harshberger in the spotlight. Right now, our closeness with the Amish in Appleseed Creek is the best way to do that. Maybe we can do some kind of outreach to the Amish. I spoke to their mayor about it during the parade." She pursed her lips. "I can't say he was that receptive."

Clark choked back a laugh. "Mayor?"

"I think you mean deacon," I told the marketing director.

Clearly, Collette knew little about the Amish. I was much the same before moving to Appleseed Creek, but then again, I didn't plan to use their culture for my own purposes. "For the most part, the Amish take care of themselves. They will resent any offer of help. Also, the Amish in Appleseed Creek are better off than some of the English residents."

Collette looked unconvinced. She stood. "I need to write up this press release. Chloe, I trust you will do everything you can to promote the college. You need to think about what's best for Harshberger."

I gritted my teeth.

The dean beamed at Collette as they left the office.

Clark shook his head. "Boss, I think you might be in trouble with that lady."

Unfortunately, I thought Clark might be right about that.

I went into my office and tried to concentrate on work for a few hours, but Collette and her plans for the Amish worried me. Finally, I couldn't sit there any longer. I poked my head out of my doorway. "I'm going for a walk."

Clark nodded and focused his attention back on his computer screen.

I headed to the stairwell and climbed to the second floor. I'd only been to this part of the building a handful of times. It housed the biology department, its classrooms, labs, and faculty offices. It was also the location of Dylan Tanner's office. The drone of a lecturer speaking to a class of drowsy undergraduates echoed through the hallway. As the department chair, Dylan had a corner office, and I had to walk through his lab to reach it.

Black, shiny countertops covered the examination counters, and four-legged metal stools surrounded each work station. The lab was empty. A tank of tropical fish sat on a rolling cart, and frogs hopped around an atrium. I grimaced, hoping they weren't headed for dissection.

Dylan's office door was closed, and I sighed with relief. He wasn't here. I didn't know what made me come up and snoop around his space. I tried to shake off my curiosity, but it hung there, like a cloud. Again, I knocked on the door, needing to feel extra sure he wasn't in the office. Nothing.

I turned to go, but at the last second, tried the doorknob. The office door swung open. Although the light was off, books and documents clearly covered every surface. The room felt cramped. I peered through windows to the outside where the sunlight had dimmed and softened to pink. It was almost five.

There was another fish tank in the office, this one housing a single blue and red Siamese fighting fish. The fish circled the tank like a shark. I sidestepped away. The keyboard of Dylan's desktop computer was buried under a pile of glossy catalogs. They didn't look like they were about biology. I crept closer to the desk and peered at one of the magazines.

The one on top was opened to a page about Civil War coins. Each listing included an up close, front and back shot of the coin and its current market value.

With a knot in my stomach, I glanced back at the fish. He swam three tight circles in the tank.

Chapter Forty-Eight

I walked home, dodging runoff from melted snow and piles of brown and gray slush. From the gutters of buildings, enormous icicles dripped under the last few rays of sunlight. City work crews wrapped Christmas garland around the town's lampposts and strung blue-and-white twinkle lights from the young trees. For the town of Appleseed Creek, it was full speed ahead toward Christmas.

I couldn't help but wonder how Ellie and Uri planned to spend the holiday. The first Christmas someone was missing from the dinner table was the worst. I wished I could tell them it became easier with the passage of time, but it doesn't. Not really. The void is always there. This would be my eleventh Christmas without my mother, and I felt her absence as keenly as if it were the first. Although the pain was different now, its sharpness dulled by regret for the time lost.

I wondered what my mother would have thought of Timothy. Would she have liked him? Disliked him? Approved of the match? *Was* it a real match? I knew I cared about him, even loved him, but being with Timothy meant being in Appleseed Creek permanently. That was never a part of my plan.

Dylan's sedan was parked in my driveway when I came up the walk. I took a hesitant step. The biology professor hadn't told me he'd be working on the house today. I certainly wouldn't have okayed it if he had. Between what I'd learned at the historical society on Saturday, and snooping in his office, something didn't feel right about the professor.

Tentatively, I climbed the porch steps. I heard a *thwack, thwack, thwack* followed by the sound of something shattering. I threw open the front door. Directly across from me was a hole in the wall large enough for a small child to climb through.

Muslin tarps covered the living room furniture and a sheen of plaster dust covered the hardwood floor. Dylan wore safety glasses and work gloves and took a sledgehammer to the wall. *Thwack!* He hit the wall again, and plaster crumbled to the ground, sending dust and debris into the air.

"What are you doing?" I cried.

He turned around with his sledgehammer poised as if to strike. I took a step back into the doorway.

"Welcome home, Chloe." He still held up the sledgehammer, his eyes appearing boggled behind the safety glasses.

I pointed at the sledgehammer. "Can you lower that, please?"

"Oh, right, sorry about that." He dropped the hammer to his side.

"What are you doing?" I asked again, trying to keep my voice even, though I could still hear the quaver in it.

He blinked at me. "I found the original plans for this house, and there used to be an archway here that led into a breakfast room by the kitchen. I think it's the place you use as a mudroom now. One of the previous owners must have closed it off years ago. I'm putting it back to the way it was, the way it's supposed to be."

"But . . ." I was at a loss.

"The house is going to be returned to its glory. I thought it would be best to start with all of the structural stuff before I moved on to the smaller details."

"But Becky and I live here," I finally managed. "You can't make holes in walls while we live here."

His eyes narrowed. "Why not? This is my house. I own it."

"I know that. You repeat that in every conversation we have." My bag was heavy on my shoulder, which was still sore from holding onto Brock in the pond. I placed it on the floor.

He gripped the hammer a little more tightly. "It's the truth."

"You didn't tell me that you'd be doing this serious of a demolition. This is not like mending a broken latch."

"I don't know what your problem is. I protected your furniture with tarps." He said this as if he did me favor.

"I can't live like this," I whispered.

"What did you say?" he asked.

"You didn't tell me you were coming this time." I paused. "Dylan, you are going to have to leave."

"To leave? This is my house. You have no right to tell me what to do. I'm tired of people telling me what to do. My wife. Now, you," he spat.

The sledgehammer came up a fraction of an inch, and fear gripped me by the back of the neck. Being alone with Dylan when he was in such a temper was not the best idea I'd ever had.

"You're just like Kara. She thought I couldn't do anything right either."

"Dylan . . ." I began.

"If I want to knock a wall down on my property, I should be allowed to do it."

"Why didn't you tell me this house used to belong to your family?"

He blinked at me. "How?"

I pointed to the wall. "We saw the *X* on the wall and knew you planned to knock it down. The people at the historical society told me the house's history."

His face turned beet red. "You have no right to pry into my personal matters."

"I wasn't prying. I needed to know what you were up to. Becky and I have to live here."

He gripped the sledgehammer. "If I didn't need your rent money, I would kick you out."

"Trust me, I don't mind moving at this point." I didn't tell him Tyler was attempting to release us from the lease. I took a deep breath. "Does the demolition have anything to do with Gerald Tanner's coin collection?"

He took two steps toward me. His jaw clenched, and sweat gathered on his upper lip and forehead.

I jumped back into the open doorway. Heat flowed to the outside, but I didn't care. No way would I block my escape route.

I kept my gaze steady on him, and he was breathless. "Did you find the coins? Give them to me. They're mine. You have no right to them."

I took a smaller step back. "We didn't find them, but that's what you're looking for, isn't it?"

"You're lying," he snarled. "You found the coins and are keeping them for yourself."

I patted my pocket, feeling for my cell phone, never taking my eyes off of him. "I didn't. I don't want the coins."

His gaze darted around the room, his eyes wild. "I know they're here somewhere. My family has spoken of them for as long as I can remember. Gerald hid them in the house during the Depression because he was afraid the family would sell them. Then, the old coot could never find them again."

"You think he hid the coins inside of the wall?"

"Where else could they be? I've looked everywhere."

My chest tightened. How had Dylan been able to look everywhere else for the coins unless he had been in the house many times without Becky's or my knowledge? Another thought came to mind. I lifted my chin, facing him. "Did Curt and Brock know about the coins?"

He scowled at me. "No. Do you think I am stupid enough to tell them? They thought this was a standard remodel job."

Relief, albeit a small amount, flowed through me.

A bead of sweat ran down the side of his face. "Kara, you don't understand that I'm doing this for us, so you will come back."

"I'm not Kara," I whispered.

Dylan blinked a few times and placed his free hand to his forehead.

"Are you all right?" I asked. As long as he held that sledgehammer, I didn't dare move closer to him.

"I . . . I have to go." He dropped the sledgehammer to his side, then stumbled to the front door. I sidestepped out of the way and watched as he tripped down the front steps and into his car. He backed out of the driveway, then swerved his way up the street.

My heart pounding, I shut the door behind him and locked it. I leaned my forehead against the door, listening to the frenetic pace of my own breathing and the thumping of my heart, almost afraid to turn around.

After a moment, I spun around and found myself inspecting the hole. At eye level, I could see all the way through to the mudroom and out the back window.

The framed photograph of my mother had shattered on the floor. It must have fallen while Dylan knocked the hole in the wall. The picture itself was unharmed. I grabbed a broom and dust pan from the mudroom and swept up the shards of glass. As I did,

Gigabyte tiptoed into the room, creeping low to the ground on his haunches, looking for any sign of Dylan and his loud hammer. Seeing none, he straightened—although he looked ready to bolt back into hiding at a moment's notice.

I put the broom away and called Tyler. "I need to be out of this lease like yesterday." I told him about my confrontation with Dylan.

"I'm on it. I should have you out of there by the end of the week. In the meantime, I don't like the sound of Dylan's behavior. He seems erratic. I suggest you and Becky camp somewhere else until you can officially move out of there."

I exhaled. "Maybe I shouldn't have mentioned the coins. It . . . um . . . upset him."

"Probably not. Be careful, Chloe. Dylan doesn't sound stable to me."

"I will." I hung up and called Timothy. I wanted to ask him if Becky and I could bunk at his place for a little while. Gigabyte wouldn't like rooming with Mabel, but it was better than the alternative. The only other option was staying with the Troyers, and I knew that would be more than enough reason for the bishop to shun the entire family.

My call went directly to voice-mail. I left a message. Becky would be at the elementary school by now, so I sent her a text telling her to go to Timothy's after she finished at the elementary school. I got one immediately back that said, "OK."

I went upstairs and quickly packed overnight bags for Becky and me with just the essentials. If we needed anything else, we could get it the next day when Timothy was with us. We would be completely out of the house by the weekend—no matter what.

In the kitchen, I tossed Gigabyte's favorite toys and several cans of cat food into my overnight bag. He followed me into the mudroom, where I pulled his cat carrier off the shelf. He hissed and ran from the room.

"Gig!" I groaned. "Come on, buddy. We have to go."

A cat-sized lump hid under the muslin tarp that covered the couch. Casually, I walked in that direction. The only visible part of him was the dark brown tip of his tail, which twitched. I pounced onto the lump. Gigabyte hissed. Finally, I was able to wrestle him out from under the tarp.

I carried the hissing cat to the mudroom and shoved him inside his cat carrier. "I'm sorry." I sucked on the scratch on my left hand. "But it's not safe here anymore," I mumbled. He yowled in my face. I sighed. Poor Mabel was going to be stuck bunking with a very angry cat tonight.

I carried Gig and the overnight bags to the other side of the room. As I did, something dark on the couch caught my eye. A coat. I set Gig and the bag down and picked it up, feeling for the pockets. Dylan. He had left without putting on a coat. As I moved it to the other end of the sofa, my fingers slipped over a jagged seam.

My fingers turned to ice. I lay the coat on the sofa and spread it out so I could get a good look at it. On the top of the right shoulder was a poorly sewn seam of black thread. Whoever had sewn it wasn't confident with a needle. I tugged on either side of the seam, and the thread gave way with little effort, revealing a hole the size of a man's fist—or the mouth of a horse.

I sat on the couch, staring at the hole. Grandfather Zook's words came back to me. "If you find the coat, you find the killer."

Dylan cut off Grandfather Zook's beard. Did that also mean he killed Ezekiel Young?

A cold sweat broke out on my skin. What if Dylan realized that he forgot his coat? What if he knew I'd be able to put two-and-two together? *He had a key to my house.* I had to get out of there. Once he realized his mistake he would come back for it—and no way could I hide what I knew from him.

Gig yowled from his carrier.

I glanced at my pet. "Gig, we are out of here."

I grabbed my own coat and tucked Dylan's under my arm. I stumbled out through the front door carrying the coats, bags, and Gig, placed everything into the Bug, and called Chief Rose.

"Humphrey, what's up? I read the piece about you saving the world in the press. Nice."

"It was the dean's idea." Before she could go on, I said, "Listen, I know who killed Ezekiel."

She sucked in a sharp breath. "Tell me."

I peered over my shoulder, reassuring myself that I was still alone. Then I told her about the coat.

"I do have a piece of wool from Sparky's mouth as evidence, but I'll want that coat to compare."

"You can have it," I said.

"I'm in Newark for law enforcement training. I'll swing by your house on the way home to get it."

I shook my head. "I'm not staying in the house. I'm going to Timothy's."

"Good thinking." She paused. "I'm leaving now. I'll call your cell when I get close to knowing when I can get the coat. Don't lose it."

"I won't," I promised.

Remembering the promise I had made to Timothy in the hospital, I called his cell again, to tell him we were in danger. It rang three times then went to voice-mail.

He probably couldn't hear it over the tools.

When I reached Timothy's house, it was dark. I knocked on the front door. No answer. Neither Danny nor Timothy was home. I tried the doorknob, but it was locked. I swallowed and glanced around, goose bumps rose on my skin. I called Timothy a third time. Voice-mail.

An idea popped into my head. I'd swing by Young's and collect Timothy's house key. Gig yowled as I turned on the engine and backed out of Timothy's driveway. He wasn't fond of car rides.

The restaurant lot was half full with evening diners. The spaces near the flea market were empty except for, to my relief, Timothy's blue pickup truck parked by the second pavilion.

I shoved Dylan's coat under the passenger seat of my car. It was in the lower forties and I thought Gigabyte would be warm enough in the car while I ran into the pavilion to fetch Timothy's house key. I glanced at my cat, his eyes wide. "I'll be a minute."

He yowled. It would be a long time before he forgave me for all this running around.

I jogged to the second pavilion. "Timothy?" I called out while ducking under the plastic sheeting.

No response. I heard the echo of a power tool running at the end of the pavilion near the meat and dairy counter Timothy had started building before the murder. I shivered. I hadn't been inside the pavilion since finding Ezekiel's body. I followed the noise.

My shoulders relaxed a little when I noticed that the sawhorse that had tripped me during my last visit was gone. Perhaps, Chief Rose had confiscated it for evidence. "Tim—" His name died on my lips. The air compression nail gun lay on the ground, humming in the corner of the pavilion. It was not being used.

My body shuddered. About fifteen feet from the gun, I saw the back of an Amish man, his hands in the air. Another man faced him—Dylan Tanner. He held a handgun, with an extra long barrel, and pointed it at the Amish man's chest.

Chapter Forty-Nine

I spun around. *Phut!* Debris from the ceiling fell onto my head, the largest piece the size of a Matchbox car.

"Don't move!" Dylan's voice cut through the air like a razor. I froze.

He narrowed his eyes. "What are you doing here?"

"I—I was looking for Timothy." I shivered. Dylan's gun didn't have an extra large barrel on the end—that extra length was a silencer.

He curled his lip. "He's not here."

I took a huge step back carefully stepping over an orange electrical cord. "I'll go check the other pavilions, then." *We're not going to mention the gun in your hand? That's fine by me.*

The Amish man turned slightly so that he could see me. It was Uriah Young. His hands were still in the air, away from his body.

"Don't look at her!" Dylan snapped at Uri. He caught me in his sights again. "Where are you going?"

"To find Timothy." I turned to go, and as I did, he seemed to remember the gun in his hand—and the man he held at gunpoint. "Stop! Or I'll shoot him. You're not going anywhere."

Slowly, I pivoted on my heels to face Dylan.

"Dylan, let the girl go," Uri said. "She had nothing to do with this."

"She has *everything* to do with this. Everywhere she goes, she's in my way." Dylan's eyes were bloodshot. *Had he been drinking?*

"How could she possibly be in your way?" Uri's tone was condescending. I wasn't sure if that was the best tactic to use against Dylan. "She's just a girl."

"You shut up," Dylan ordered through clenched teeth. "You've said enough already."

Ignoring the gun was no longer an option. I spoke slowly. "What's going on Dylan?"

A smile that did not reach his eyes curled on his mouth. "I'm finally doing this right. No mess-ups this time."

I didn't like the sound of that. "Mess-ups? What do you mean?" I tried to keep my voice level. My knees knocking together sounded like a *thump, thump, thump* in my head. Or maybe that sound was the pounding of my heart.

"Last time," he paused. "Last time, I made a mistake."

"Everything you do has been a mistake." Uri's voice sounded patronizing.

I spoke up. "No it hasn't."

Uri shrugged. "I guess your wife would know that for sure."

Dylan's lips trembled.

Was I imagining things or was Uri trying to keep Dylan's attention on himself? The phone felt heavy in the inner pocket of my coat. If I could get away, I could call Chief Rose on my cell phone.

As if Dylan read my mind, he pointed to the ground. "Cell phone. Throw your cell phone to me."

My mouth went dry. "I—I don't have it."

He shot the ceiling above my head. More debris fell. A chunk of lumber the size of a brick crashed at my feet.

Where was Timothy? If he couldn't hear the gun, couldn't he hear the roof falling in? What about Ellie? Couldn't anyone at the restaurant hear it?

"Phone. Now!" Dylan yelled.

I reached into the inside pocket of my jacket and pulled out the phone. I hit the speed dial button for Timothy's phone then threw it to Dylan's feet. The device clattered to the cement floor. The back of the smartphone broke off and the glowing screen went black. I lifted my eyes to Dylan. "Chief Rose already knows everything. I called her after you stormed out of my house."

He stamped his foot on the floor like a toddler. "That's my house. My house! Can't you get that through your skull?" His forehead was damp with perspiration. "After I am finished with him, you will show me where you put Gerald's coins." Maybe the college professor was on something stronger than alcohol.

I stepped back. "I don't have them. I never had them."

"Liar!"

I tried to keep my voice steady. "Chief Rose already knows you killed Ezekiel. I found your coat. You left it at the house."

His gun fell a fraction of an inch. "My coat?"

"Yes. The one Grandfather Zook's horse took a bite out of when you cut off his beard. Why did you cut off his beard, Dylan?"

Uri cut in. "To throw off the police."

I wished I could see Uri's face, so that I could signal him to be quiet.

Dylan's eyes darted from Uri to me and back again. "I didn't mean to hurt the old man. He was an easy target—one those girls could have easily gotten to." He licked his lips. "I need to decide what to do now. Everything was fine until you got in my way."

Uri scoffed. "Fine? You have to be joking."

"Shut up!" Dylan's voice echoed through the pavilion.

"What are you going to do, Tanner," Uri said. "Shoot both of us?"

Why don't you give him more ideas, Uri?

Dylan trained the gun on Uri's heart. "You shut your mouth."

"If you kill us, it will be another mistake, but this is the one that will ruin your life."

"What mistake did you make, Dylan?" I tried to keep my voice level.

"I killed the wrong twin. After weeks of planning, I killed the wrong one." Sweat gathered on Dylan's upper lip. "I thought it was you!" His voice quavered. "You ruined my life!"

"You killed my *bruder*." Uri loomed over him as if daring Dylan to shoot.

Does Uri have a death wish?

"Uri," I said. "Leave him alone."

His head snapped around. Instead of fury, I saw sorrow. "He killed my *bruder* when he wanted to kill me. I don't deserve to live when my *bruder* died in my place."

My mouth went dry. "Why did you want to kill Uri, Dylan?"

"Don't you use past tense," he snapped. "Wanting to kill Uriah Young has not died away. No, it's gotten much worse with every passing moment."

That didn't sound good.

"He cost me my savings—and my wife."

"Don't you mean your wife's savings?" Uri said.

I wished I could mind meld with Uri, and say, *You're not helping!* Instead all I could do was shoot him a disapproving look.

Dylan wiped sweat from his eyes with his free hand. "Don't mention my wife."

"It's the truth. She left you because you lost the money she inherited from her father's will."

"I gave the money to *you*. You convinced me to invest in the pavilion, and when the contractor you hired ran away with my money, you took no responsibility for it. You found another investor and hired a new contractor as if nothing happened. You went on with your life when mine was ruined."

"It wasn't my fault," Uri said.

Phut! The gun went off. Uri fell against the plywood side of the half-finished cheese counter and slid to the floor. A streak of blood marked his path.

My heart pounded wildly.

Dylan stared at Uri lying on the floor, as if he couldn't believe what he'd just done.

I knelt by Uri's head. "Uri! Uri!"

His face was ashen. Blood soaked the front of his shirt. I ripped off my coat and pressed it to Uri's chest. *Lord, don't let him die.* I looked up. There was a hole in the plywood. The bullet went clean through.

"Get—get away from him," Dylan stuttered.

I picked up Uri's hand and placed it over the coat. "Press down hard." I barely breathed the words.

"Stand up!"

Slowly, I stood.

Without my coat the cold drafty air of the pavilion bit into my skin.

"I should have shot him in the first place, instead of that ridiculous plan." His voice grew quiet, distant. "My wife told me that all of my plans are horrible. Nothing good comes of them." He raised his eyes to me. "She was right."

I felt Uri's hand on my ankle, and he squeezed it with strength. I didn't dare look down.

Dylan panted. "I said get away from him."

I spoke calmly. "He needs medical attention."

"Get away from him now, or I will shoot you too."

I inched away from Uri. "Dylan, you don't want to do this."

"How do you know what I want? Why do you even pretend to care? I want to find the coins in my house. If I find them and sell them, I will have money, more money than before, and Kara will come back." Sweat dripped off the tip of his nose. "But you won't even let me do that. Everyone is trying to stop me from being successful."

There was no point in arguing with him. We had moved long past arguments.

He ran a free hand through his hair and licked his lips. "Now, what am I going to do? You weren't supposed to be in here." He leveled the gun, so that it pointed directly at my chest. "I will have to shoot you too."

A chill ran from the back of my head all the way to my heels.

He shook his head, slowly. "I didn't want to do that, but you left me no choice."

"That's wrong, Dylan, you have a choice." My lungs constricted. "You always have a choice."

"No, I don't," he said through gritted teeth.

With a cry, Uri leapt from the cement floor and threw himself against Dylan's knees. The gun went off as the pair crashed into the vegetable booth. Wood splintered as they hit the floor in a heap.

Uri groaned and rolled onto his side. Dylan lay there for a few seconds with the wind knocked out of him. Somehow he'd managed to keep hold of the gun. I scanned the room for some type of weapon. The hum of the air compressor grabbed my attention. I picked up the nail gun, but the air compression hose was tangled around Timothy's work bench. I knelt on the floor to loosen it, my fingers numb and moving clumsily to remove the kinks in the hose.

Dylan sat up, gulping air. Uri was no longer any help, his breathing choppy as he held a bloody hand to his upper chest.

I almost had the last kink out of the air hose.

Still holding the gun, Dylan stood on shaky legs. "What are you doing?"

The hose pulled free. I turn the nail gun on him, closed my eyes, and squeezed as hard as I could—just like Timothy had shown me.

The nail hit him in the calf. Dylan cried out in pain. I scrambled to my feet and aimed the nail gun at his right hand, the one holding the automatic weapon, and took a shot. A nail hit him in the hand. He screamed and dropped the gun on the floor—and I kicked it as hard as I could. It skittered across the cement floor.

"Police!" Chief Rose and her officers barged into the pavilion through the plastic sheeting.

"She shot me!" Dylan squealed. Blood poured out of the wound in the back of his hand.

Chief Rose examined his wound and arched an eyebrow at me. "A nail gun?"

I blew out a harsh breath. "It was the only thing I could find."

Chapter Fifty

C hloe?" Timothy shouted to me from about twenty feet away. One of Chief Rose's officers held him back.

"You'll be able to see her in a minute," the officer said. "The chief is interviewing her right now."

I called out to him, my voice flooded with relief. "Timothy!"

He wrestled free from the officer and reached me in three long strides, wrapping me in a hug so hard that my sore shoulder cracked. Pain shot down the length of my arm, but I didn't care.

I looked up into his face, still holding onto him. "Where were you?"

He flinched at my accusatory tone, and I wished I could grab the words out of space and shove them back into my mouth.

He frowned and held me tighter. "I was with Ellie. She wanted to walk to the cemetery to visit Ezekiel's grave. The Amish cemetery is on the back corner of the property, and I didn't want her to walk alone. She had come into the pavilion to ask Uri to go with her, but he wasn't here." His blue eyes searched my face. "Are you all right?"

"I'm fine. Dylan and Uri are hurt."

He scanned the room and stopped, transfixed by the blood-stained wall. He swallowed hard. "Where are they?"

"They're both alive and on the way to the hospital. Uri has a gunshot wound to the shoulder and . . .

"And Dylan?"

I bit my lip. "I shot him with your nail gun."

Timothy's mouth fell open.

"In the leg and hand. The construction lesson you gave me came in handy."

He crushed me to him in another hug.

Epilogue

Becky looped back into the living room of our new home. "Did you see the kitchen? Stainless steel appliances like in a professional kitchen. A six-burner range. Think of all the great food we can cook!"

I grinned at her. "We? Don't you mean *you*?"

"Right, me! It's going to be amazing. I can't wait to invite everyone over. I'm thinking I'll make tacos, a real authentic Mexican meal. My family's never had Mexican food. They're missing out."

"It sounds great." I didn't want to dampen her enthusiasm, but I doubted that the Troyer family would ever come to our new home. That would be certain shunning for them.

She twirled about the room. "We should host a Christmas party too. Wouldn't that be fun? I've always wanted to go to an *Englischer* party."

"What do you think an English party is?"

"From what I've seen on television, there's lots of food, laughter, and music."

"We'll see. I'll need to check with the Quills. This is their house, and we will only be here for a short time."

"It will be great. You'll see." She waltzed around the room. "Can we have a Christmas tree?"

I smiled. "Of course. We will definitely have a Christmas tree."

She grinned. "My first one!"

Timothy grunted as he carried Becky's trunk into the house. "What do you have in here? Horseshoes?"

"It's my hope chest, *bruder*."

"Oh." He set it inside the door. "Where does it go?"

"My room," she said. "On the second floor."

Timothy groaned as he lifted the chest.

There was a tap on the frame of the front door. *"G-Gude Mariye,"* a deep voice ventured through the open door.

Timothy nearly dropped Becky's hope chest.

"Timothy, be careful," his sister cried.

With care, he set the trunk on the carpeted floor.

"Bishop Hooley?" I asked.

"M-may I come in?"

"Yes, of course." I gestured to the Quills' sofa.

The bishop stood tall and looked more like the leader he was chosen to be.

"I have already been to your family farm and told your parents that I was wrong to put those restraints on them. They do not have to worry about being shunned from the community. After what h-has happened with the haircutting and attack on my d-daughter, I see how holding too tightly to something can be worse than loosening one's grip."

A smile spread on Becky's face. "So we can visit home again?"

He nodded. "Y-yes, with no fear of me."

Timothy's reaction was much more solemn. "Thank you, bishop."

"How is Sadie?" I asked tentatively.

"She is much better now. Now that she knows who attacked her. She is less timid, less afraid to venture out. S-she told me of her engagement to Ezekiel Young." Tears gathered in the corners of the bishop's eyes. "I h-hope she can heal from that wound too. The man who killed Ezekiel should be punished."

I bit my lip. After his arrest, Dylan went off the deep end, thinking every woman he saw was his estranged wife. Chief Rose said he had a good shot at an insanity plea, but I didn't share this with the bishop. Eventually, both the English and Amish papers would cover the trial. Gerald Tanner's coins were never found.

"And Leah and the other girls?" Becky asked.

The bishop's eyes were sad. "Sadie has forgiven them and chosen not to press charges. However, the chief of police told me if the judge decides to call the act a religious hate crime, Sadie's forgiveness will not matter to the c-court. For right now, the girls are free and home with their families."

Becky fingered her long braid. She'd yet to cut her hair.

"When you are my age, it is easy to forget how it felt to be y-young, to be in *rumspringa*." The bishop laced his fingers together in front of himself as if in prayer. "Even leaders in the ch-church do not have all the answers. *Gott* shows me the way if I am diligent in my obedience to Him."

"He does the same for all of us," Timothy said.

The bishop's eyes were hooded. "Deacon Sutter's unhappy with my change of heart, and I fear he may agitate for a time about the changes in the district."

An angry deacon was never a good thing.

The bishop moved toward the open door. "I have told you what I needed to say. Now, I must go." He tipped his black felt hat and closed the door behind himself.

"Did I imagine that? Or did Bishop Hooley apologize to us?" Becky asked.

"He apologized," I whispered.

"A Mexican-themed Christmas party might really happen, and we can invite the whole family. I'm going to work on the menu." She jumped off of the couch and ran to the kitchen.

"I thought you were going to help me unload the pickup," Timothy called after her.

"Later. Christmas is only two weeks away. I haven't much time," she called from the kitchen.

The doorbell rang.

I shook my head. "Another visitor already?"

I opened the door. Thomas grinned up at me. "Chloe, we have come to take you on a sleigh ride." Beyond Thomas, Grandfather Zook and the other Troyer children waved from a large, open-air black sleigh.

The Quills' home was in the country, four miles from Appleseed Creek. Our nearest neighbor was a half mile away. Because of the house's remoteness, we were one of the last roads for the county to plow. Timothy's truck tires and the bishop's buggy wheels were the only tracks to mar the freshly fallen snow.

Sparky stamped the snow-covered country road, and the bells on his harness rang. Ruth grinned from the front seat of the sleigh. A brown-haired girl about her age, Anna Lambright, sat between Ruth and Grandfather Zook. Ruth, it seemed, had been reunited with her best friend.

Timothy stood behind me in the doorway. "Ready to go on a real Amish sleigh ride?" he whispered in my ear.

"Yes." I smiled up at him.

More than ready.

Dear Reader Letter

Dear Reader,

The idea for *A Plain Scandal* came to me while I was in the middle of writing *A Plain Death*, the first novel in the Appleseed Creek Mystery Series. This was during the fall of 2011. During that time, a group of Ohio Amish were in the local and national news. A half dozen men in a breakaway Amish group in Holmes County, which is right next to Knox County where my series is set, were arrested for cutting off the hair of Amish women and the beards of Amish men in their old district. They did this because they had a disagreement over doctrine and district rules. The men were charged with committing a religiously-motivated hate crime, a federal offense.

Having lived in Ohio my entire life, I can safely say the Amish are seldom in the news even at a local level, and Amish on Amish crime like this is rare. I'm not saying there is no crime in the Amish communities because there most certainly is, but little of it is known outside of the culture. The Amish guard their privacy and prefer to handle any disciplinary actions themselves. The fact the Amish harmed in this case reached out to the local police in Holmes County for help made this story different.

The true story is heartbreaking, and I feel for all the victims involved. However, as a mystery author, I couldn't help but think of how this story could play out in a novel and fit well into the story arch I have planned for the entire series. From that realization, the beginning on *A Plain Scandal* was born.

Of course, I am a cozy mystery author, so although the true story inspiring the novel is dark, this mystery is light and humorous.

I hope this story teaches you something new about the Amish culture. May the characters make you smile, the mystery raise your suspicions, and the romance touch your heart.

Blessings and Happy Reading!

Amanda Flower

Discussion Questions

1. What was your favorite part of the novel? Why?

2. Which character did you identify with the most? Why?

3. The Amish in the novel celebrate Thanksgiving. How is their celebration similar to yours? How is it different?

4. There is an Amish wedding during the novel. How are Amish wedding customs different from yours?

5. What did you think of the author's description of late fall, early winter in the novel?

6. Who is your favorite character and why?

7. Why is the cutting of Amish women's hair and Amish men's beard so offensive to the Amish?

8. The novel includes descriptions of many Amish-owned shops in Appleseed Creek. Which would you like to visit most?

9. Consider the position Becky and Timothy's father is in between the bishop and his children who have left the Amish way. Do you understand his struggle?

10. Chloe is estranged from her father. What do you think about that relationship?

11. Of the antagonists in the novel, which did you dislike the most? Why?

12. What do you know about Amish shunning?

13. Before the end of the novel, who did you think the murderer was? Were you right?

14. What did you think about the conclusion of the mystery? What about it surprised you?

15. If you had the opportunity to visit Ohio's Amish Country, what activity would you most like to do?

In Appleseed Creek, the heart of Ohio's Amish Country, life is not as serene as it seems.

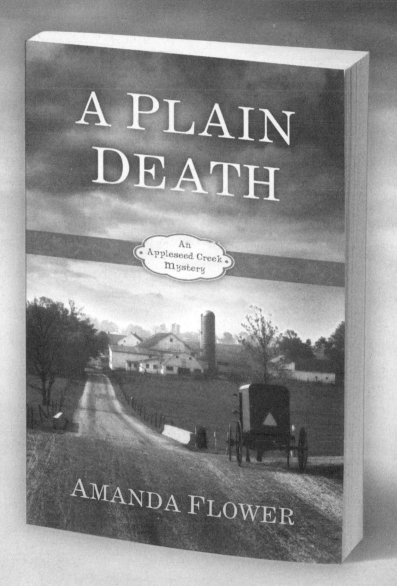

A PLAIN DEATH

An Appleseed Creek Mystery

AMANDA FLOWER

@AFlowerWriter

BHPublishingGroup.com

B&H FICTION